no SECRETS or LIES

no SECRETS or LIES

RACHEL BRANTON

WHITE
STAR
PRESS

This is a work of fiction, and the views expressed herein are the sole responsibility of the author. Likewise, certain characters, places, and incidents are the product of the author's imagination, and any resemblance to actual persons, living or dead, or actual events or locales, is entirely coincidental.

No Secrets or Lies (Lily's House Book 6)

Published by White Star Press
P.O. Box 353
American Fork, Utah 84003

Printed in the United States of America
ISBN: 978-1-948982-03-0
Year of first printing: 2018

Once again for my sister Mary
for always being there.

1

Halla stared at the rows of canned food in her cupboard as she put away the last can of black beans. The neat, orderly rows gave her a sense of security and contentment. She never let herself get too many, though, because there was a difference between preparation and hoarding, and she still, even after so many years, had the urge to stockpile all she could. Just in case. Maybe the urge would never go away. Maybe full recovery was impossible when you went hungry as a child. Maybe it was worse when your parents were responsible.

No. She wouldn't let those years define her. She was a woman now, college-educated, with a successful advice blog that focused on finding one's true self.

"I've done that," she whispered fiercely, staring at the rows of canned goods. "I've found myself."

But no one living in a small three-bedroom apartment with two other women really needed thirty cans of black beans, especially when she had as many cans of refried beans, tomatoes, corn, tuna, chicken, and soup. Her freezer was every bit as packed with tortillas, bread, and strawberry ice cream.

With a sigh, she shut the cupboard and went to the chair that sat in front of her computer in a corner of their living room. She spent much of her day here, so this chair was comfortable. More comfortable, in fact, than her secondhand bed.

As a child, or even in college while earning a bachelor's in journalism and a minor in editing, she'd never expected to make her living as a blogger, particularly as an inspirational blogger. Even when her following had grown to a hundred and fifty thousand by the end of her college years, she'd expected to do something else after graduation. But last year when she'd been offered an online column for a popular news outlet, she found she couldn't give up her own blog. Luckily, the paper's editor was willing to let her share the column and send in only one weekly article, so she'd been able to get a taste of "real" journalism while still posting four times a week on her own site. She now had two hundred and fifty thousand people who received email notifications about her blog, and she was considering adding a few more product reviews so she could quit her part-time news column.

She had thirty new email subscribers since she'd run to the store after a very late lunch. Not bad for a slow Tuesday afternoon. Her gaze ran down the numerous comments on her most recent post about a hiking trip she'd taken but saw nothing requiring immediate attention. Until her eyes snagged on a name, and her heart started beating faster.

Between Oliver Montgomery's comments on her

posts and her comments on his small hiking blog, along with their interactions on social media, she and Oliver had exchanged thousands of communications. It was because of him she'd taken up an interest in hiking—and found that it helped sooth not only her but also her followers. The free hiking gear she tested and occasionally blogged about was a bonus.

Glad you had such a great time, he wrote. *As you said in your post, being out in nature is a great way to center yourself. By the way. I did what you recommended in your Let Go So You Can Hold Tight blog. It worked. Thank you!*

Halla stared at the words. He'd done it. He'd actually talked to his mother, maybe even patched things up with her—and Halla wanted details. He'd posted on her blog only thirty minutes ago. Maybe he was still online. She navigated to Google Hangouts, where they normally connected for private conversation, and while it loaded, she darted a quick look into the small mirror on her desk. With as many video posts as she made these days, it paid to make sure nothing was stuck between her teeth or smeared on her cheek. She ran a hand through her hair. The blond strands were no longer the near buzz cut she'd sported after fleeing Idaho, mostly in defiance of the long hair her parents had forced her to wear, but it was still short and manageable, with enough thickness and a slight wave to sometimes make it look a bit wild like it did right now. She finger-combed it into place, the strands finally long enough to tuck behind her ear. There, she was ready.

Her heart banged against the wall of her chest that much harder. *Only because I'm interested in what happened with him and his family,* she thought. She always cared about her subscribers.

Not the whole truth. She'd be lying if she didn't admit Oliver was special. It wasn't just hiking they had in common. She lived in Phoenix currently, but she'd spent her first fifteen and a half years in Nampa, Idaho, and he had originally hailed from Boise, twenty minutes away, though he now lived in Coeur d'Alene, Idaho, where he worked for the US Forest Service. He knew what it was like growing up where she had, and with only two years separating them, they remembered a lot of the same local events and school rivalries. Enough that it had sparked more than the regular communications between them. She could count on two hands the one-on-one video chats she'd had with subscribers, and only a few of them had become regular friends.

Oliver was also drop-dead gorgeous, which helped, because she was a woman after all. Not gorgeous in a suit and tie, well-groomed kind of way, but in a rugged, outdoorsy way that made her dream of warm nights under an open sky with crickets chirping. Or of beautiful, untouched valleys that stretched as far as the eye could see.

Oliver growing up so close to her hometown did have its drawbacks. He'd still been in his last year of high school when she'd disappeared from Nampa, catching the attention of the national news. Seven months later when her parents had finally picked up her trail in Arizona, he, like all the other residents of Nampa and Boise, had been following events as they'd unfolded. As her father had started fundraising in an effort to locate her and as Halla's foster sister Saffron had fought back, posting the truth of why Halla had run away. Halla had been ready to run again, but the social media outrage had backlashed on her father and saved her.

She'd started her first blog then, talking about running away and finding Lily's house and her foster sisters. Not many of those original blog subscribers were still her followers, and she'd unpublished many of the embarrassingly raw, agonized earlier posts. Oliver had followed her then, he'd confessed to her a few months ago, but he'd been too busy to read blogs during his college years, so he'd let his subscription lapse. Last year, he'd found her *Let Go* blog, had recognized her name, and had annoyingly disagreed with her post. She'd answered back, and they'd been talking almost daily in some form or another ever since.

Now he responded to her video call almost immediately, and Halla couldn't help the warm rush inside her as he appeared on the screen. He had short brown hair and his face, normally covered with a few days' beard growth, was freshly shaven. His blue eyes crinkled at the corners, showing his pleasure at seeing her. His mouth, one she'd dreamed about kissing, was full and wide and smiling.

"Hey, how are you?" he asked, his voice low.

That made her study his background. "You're not at home."

He shook his head. "I'm at my Mom's."

"How'd it go?" A smile tugged on her lips, but she wasn't about to spoil this moment with an I-told-you-so. His happiness was satisfaction enough.

"Go ahead and say it," he told her, apparently reading her mind.

"What?" She blinked at him innocently.

He laughed. "Okay, play it your way, but I readily admit you were right. I wasn't sure if talking with her was going to put a final seal of death on our relationship or if it would fix things, but either way, it couldn't have gotten worse since we had zero relationship to begin with."

"And?" she asked. Oliver had become estranged from his mother when he'd rejected her advice and chosen a forestry career that would keep him in the field, far away from family. From there things had degenerated, growing worse the day he'd been out in the forest, unreachable, when his father had died. She'd never forgiven him.

He leaned forward, lowering his voice further as if to make sure he wasn't being overheard. "I told her I missed her and wanted a relationship. I expressed regret at not being there when my dad died. That's all. She said she would be happy to reconnect. Like you told me, I refrained from saying if she hadn't driven me away, I would have kept in touch and would have been there for my father. I also didn't say that every apology she's ever made me ended with 'but you are wrong and it's your fault.' But at least I didn't have to apologize for something I shouldn't have to apologize for. Though I still feel like she owes me an apology, I let that go because she's never going to change her mind or her view of what happened, and neither am I."

He flashed Halla a smile that did funny things to her stomach. "It feels good," he added. "I have missed her. She can be very loving and giving. She's just been so angry at me, and I've been angry at her. It's good to get past that."

"Exactly. Because it's not about who's right. It's about taking one step closer to each other and trying to find middle ground so you can still have a relationship. You can't replace family." She said this with a hint of guilt, because she'd managed to do exactly that. She'd traded her parents for her foster mother Lily Perez, and for all the foster sisters that came along with her. Of course, Halla's case was different from Oliver's. Far different. She'd done what she had to in order to survive.

"I expect things will come up between us in the future," Oliver added.

"And then you'll just go back to the fact that you regret the years you lost and not being there when your dad died."

He nodded. "Right. No accusations as long as we're both trying because there's no middle ground in accusations." Oliver leaned back in his chair and said a little louder, "Anyway, my sister and brother are excited that maybe we can all finally celebrate the holidays together. Not sure how that'll go over, but we'll see."

"It's barely September. You have a few months to worry about that. How long are you staying in Boise?"

He shrugged. "A few more days at least."

"Better save some vacation time for those holidays you were talking about."

He laughed. "Right."

For a moment, they fell into silence, and though it hadn't usually felt awkward in the past, it did now, and that concerned Halla. Maybe now that the reason they'd initially started talking—or disagreeing rather—was over, they would drift away. It happened often with online relationships.

Panic shot through her at the idea. She who had lived

through an abusive childhood, who had survived on the streets, and who had forged a new life for herself. She who fended off cyber stalkers on a weekly basis. She didn't want to lose him.

Talking to Oliver every day, even if through a public post was . . . well, she looked forward to it, that's all. She didn't have to examine her reasons further.

Had she been fooling herself that Oliver felt something more for her than friendship? And how could he, seeing as they'd never met in person? She'd dated more than a few guys she'd met online, and if they hadn't been lying about who they were or their quirks hadn't driven her mad, they weren't ready to accept a girl who normally wore army boots and camouflage. She could count on one hand how many times she'd worn a dress that wasn't her stand-by church skirt, and each time was when she'd been a bridesmaid for one of her foster sisters. First Zoey, then Bianca, followed by Ruth and Saffron. She and Elsie were the last of the original Lily's House girls, the only ones unmarried. There had been many other foster sisters, of course, and many of those were married now too, but Halla had somehow managed not to get roped into an uncomfortable dress for those events.

Maybe if Oliver knew her in person, they wouldn't get along at all. With him living in Coeur d'Alene and her thirteen hundred miles away in Phoenix, maybe she'd never get a chance to find out.

"Halla?"

She jerked, realizing she'd drifted off. She did that more than she wanted to admit. Her sisters teased her that it was because of her imagination, and they were probably right, but this was one depressing thought she was eager to shake off.

"Yeah?" she said.

"You went away there for a minute."

"Just thinking about it all, how we met. I'm glad it worked out for you with your mom."

"Me too. And I have you to thank."

She shrugged. "You are the one who acted. It's easy for me to urge you to do something when I'm not the one in the hot seat."

"Maybe you should be."

She stared at him, unsure if she'd heard him correctly. "What do you mean?"

"When was the last time you were back in Nampa?"

She spluttered a laugh that was more fake than anything. "Um right. That would have been never—and I don't plan on ever going back. There's nobody I want to see. Nobody I can meet on middle ground."

He nodded. "Still, it might do you good to go. Make peace with the town and your memories. I absolutely agree that your father doesn't deserve the time of day, but he can't hurt you now. And there's still your mother."

An emotion shuddered through Halla, a mix of anger and fear and loss. "She let him chain me to my bed for six months. She was the one who baked my daily bread and brought it to me." Halla kept her voice even as the words left her mouth. This was something she was still called on to talk about periodically, and it no longer hurt her to speak about the past. It was as if she were separate from the memories, from the terrified girl she'd once been. Everyone agreed that the man who'd raised her was insane—he had to be insane—though no one had yet locked him up. "My mother is not a reason to go back. And I have no blood siblings, for which I'm grateful to God every single day."

He nodded again, looking sincere and wise. She wondered if he smelled as good as he looked, and if kissing him in person would be as good as in her dreams.

Stop, she told herself.

He frowned, his forehead creased in concern. "You never talk about it," he said quietly. "At least not to me."

She shrugged. "I don't like to dwell on unhappy memories."

"I remember what you wrote on your blog after he tracked you to Arizona. How awful it was for you. I remember wishing I could punch him out." He hesitated before continuing, "But weren't there any happy memories at all? With your mom? With the town? At school? Do you think you might have blocked out any good? It's understandable, of course, with what happened after, but I've been wondering."

She wanted to tell him to stop poking into her business. She wanted to reach out and sever their connection and forget him entirely. But the idea of not talking to him tomorrow made her heart ache.

Maybe he was right. Maybe her not talking about it unless in a public setting meant she was holding back. Because that's what he was hinting at, throwing her own pseudo psychology back at him. If she thought about it rationally, which she hadn't done much of lately, her current view of what had happened had come through a child's eyes. She, Halla, had been the center of everything.

Her mother was little more than a shadowy figure who had tiptoed around her father as if he'd been the devil himself. Which he very nearly had been.

Halla forced a brittle smile. "I don't think anything good would come of it. If I showed up on their doorstep, he'd probably lock me in my old room and never let me leave." She tried to laugh, but it sounded a little hysterical, even to her own ears.

"I would never want you to go alone, that's for sure." He leaned toward the screen. "Look, Halla, I'm sorry I brought it up. It's just that you're so open about everything except this . . . I feel you shut down whenever the subject comes up. It's like a light switch."

And what does that mean to you? she wanted to ask. *What right do you have to be a part of my secrets?* Instead, she nodded. "Well, thankfully my foster aunt is a shrink, just in case I need one." She laughed it off, this time sounding back to normal.

Oliver lifted his brows quizzically, not cracking a smile, as if a little disappointed in her. Why did he have to be so good looking? He'd probably hate her army boots. Good to believe that so she wouldn't pine over him. Or at least not for long.

"I was hoping that maybe you'd come now," he said, his eyes staring directly into hers, though screens were deceptive and maybe he was checking out her ear for all she knew.

"Why, because you're there?" She said it flippantly, because he couldn't mean that.

"Well, yeah, it would be a chance to meet in person. And Boise is a lot closer to you than Coeur d'Alene."

Her heart was once again drumming that weird, violent rhythm. "And you choose Idaho?" She emphasized with a tiny roll of her eyes. "Not exactly a dream destination. In fact, it's at the top of my least likely to visit list."

Yet even as she said it, she wanted to go. Not to see her mother or to visit the place of her nightmares, of course, but to see him. *Tell me all that mumbo jumbo about my parents was only because you want to see me,* she begged him silently.

"Well, I wouldn't want to make you come all this way just for me," he said with another of his fabulous smiles. "But if you did, we could go hiking."

"As tempting as that is, I have my next news article due on Thursday, and I haven't even started. You'll be gone by then."

"I'll probably stay at least through Saturday. I don't have to be back at work until Monday, so if I leave Sunday morning, that gives me plenty of time." He started to say more but stopped short, his head turning from the computer screen. "Looks like my mother has called in reinforcements. I don't think I'll have the luxury of waiting for the holidays for a family celebration."

"Enjoy it." Halla was both happy and a little envious that his family would be spending time with him.

Oliver called something to whoever had talked to him and then turned back to her. "Look, Halla, think about what I said. About making peace. Maybe I'm not the only one who needs to let go."

This time she didn't censor her thoughts. "I let go a long time ago. You're wrong."

He barked a short laugh. "Maybe so. It wouldn't be the

first time I was wrong. Maybe next time we talk you can tell me a happy memory of Idaho."

"Don't hold your breath."

"I'm good at holding my breath. Just ask the skunk I met last week. Let's talk tomorrow, okay? Goodbye, beautiful."

With that, his image disappeared, leaving Halla staring at a blank screen and wondering about the skunk. He hadn't told her about the animal. The past few days they'd talked about his siblings, about her foster sister Saffron's baby daughter, and Halla's upcoming article. Why hadn't he mentioned the stupid skunk?

"You need to get over this obsession with him," Halla told herself out loud.

"Who are you talking to?" Behind her, Elsie was pushing into the apartment, her hands full of grocery bags.

Halla jumped up and ran to help, peering into a bag full of lettuce, avocados, and carrots. "I could have picked these up for you."

"You know I'm picky about my lettuce, and it's on my way home from the café anyway."

"Do the avocados and lettuce mean you're making taco salad?" Halla asked hopefully.

Elsie nodded, her long, dark curls spilling around her gently rounded face. "As long as you have beans."

"As many as you want."

Elsie's face dimpled. "I knew you would. Payden's coming over, by the way. I hope that's okay."

"Sure. As long as you make enough." Elsie's friend was a healthy eater, which was a good thing since Elsie also loved food and her once too-thin figure had filled out significantly in the past few years. Last summer she had joined their foster sister Ruth at her café Eats and Treats, finally rounding out the "Eats" part of the name, since Ruth's specialty was pastries. After a total of three years in business, they were now looking for a larger location.

"I'll make plenty," Elsie said. "Come in with me. We'll talk while I cook."

Halla detached her laptop from the external monitor she normally used and carried it into the kitchen. By the time their third roommate, Kendall Brenwood, came home from the hospital where she worked as a registered nurse, dinner was nearly finished and Halla's article about the dangers of swimming because of chlorine-resistant bugs was well underway.

"Your cooking is music to my ears," Kendall said, falling into a chair at the table and kicking off her black clogs. "I'm starved."

"It looks like you've already been eating." Halla pointed at a large stain scattered down the front of Kendall's blue scrubs.

"It's cake," she explained. "One of my co-workers is leaving. Thankfully."

"That arrogant surgeon?" Elsie asked, running a leaf of lettuce under the water, though Halla had already washed it. "The one who cheats on his wife?"

"Yep, this was his parting gift. If I hadn't agreed to work for Jenny today, I would have been off and missed his leaving altogether." Kendall's blue eyes became dreamy. "But if I'd had today off, I wouldn't have met the new resident who just started. Seriously, I could stare at him all day."

Halla studied the other woman's glowing face. "That good, huh?"

Nodding, Kendall began unwinding her long blond hair from its bun. She wasn't officially a Lily's House foster girl, but she felt like a sister to them. She'd come to the home three years ago at eighteen, after reconnecting with her biological sister, Saffron, who had been the oldest of the original six Lily's House foster girls. Kendall had stayed at Lily's House, helping Lily and going to school, almost a year before moving in with them to take the spot that opened in the apartment when Ruth had finally married her handsome photographer.

In the beginning, Kendall had been quiet and withdrawn because of some difficult life choices, but after she'd finished her nursing degree, things had changed for her. Halla thought she was finally becoming the person she was meant to be, who she would have been if she'd found Lily's House sooner.

And what about me? Halla wondered, staring down at her laptop. *Am I who I should have been?* Maybe not. She didn't dwell on her own personal tragedy, but it had changed her permanently.

"So did you talk to this new resident?" Elsie asked Kendall.

Kendall nodded. "Quite a bit. He only came in for the staff meeting and introductions, but it turns out we'll have several patients together. Looks like I'll be seeing more of him."

"Maybe he'll ask you out." Elsie dropped the last leaf of lettuce into the salad spinner.

"I hope so." Kendall sighed, propping her elbows up on the table and letting her chin drop into her hands. Her eyes danced. "So, is the food ready yet? I'm starving. Did I mention that?"

Elsie laughed. "You did. It's almost ready. Why don't you two set the table while I finish the meat? Set an extra plate for Payden. He'll be here soon."

Halla finished the sentence she was writing and closed her laptop. Another few hours and a few quotes from a doctor she'd contacted yesterday, and she'd wrap it up.

What was Oliver up to now? Shooting baskets in his mother's driveway with his younger brother or playing with his mischievous young niece?

She was halfway to her feet to help set the table when her tumbling thoughts forced her back down, her gaze fixed on her left hand that was still splayed on the lid of her laptop. "Oliver thinks I should go to Idaho."

"Seriously?" Kendall rolled her eyes as she pulled plates from the cupboard. "He wants *you* to come to *him* for your first real meeting? That is *so* lame."

Elsie laughed. "I think it's a wonderful idea. You should totally go. You know, see if there are any sparks there in person."

"From what I've seen, there are plenty of sparks between them." Kendall set the plates down. "Haven't you seen them argue?"

"I've seen them flirt is what." Elsie sprinkled more salt into her pan.

"I wish he'd invited me to visit him," Halla admitted.

"It would have been more flattering than him suggesting I go see my mother."

Elsie's head whipped around, her full lips open in shock. She stared at Halla blankly for several long seconds before she reached out and turned off the gas under her pan. "He said what?" she asked heatedly, coming over to sit at the table next to Halla. Kendall stood frozen nearby, her face sympathetic.

"He seems to think I'm blocking out some of my past, and that maybe I won't be able to move on unless I go visit her."

Elsie wrinkled her nose. "What do *you* think?"

Halla considered. So many emotions raged inside that she couldn't pinpoint only one. But the idea that there were any emotions except apathy toward her mother was a surprise to her. "I think I've been doing great. And . . . I think she allowed the abuse, so why should I care about her?"

"True," Elsie said. "But she didn't run away and leave you there alone like my mother did."

Halla reached out and grabbed Elsie's hand. Halla remembered the day Lily had brought twelve-year-old Elsie home, beaten and scared, hugging a stuffed wolf, one of the few belongings she'd brought with her when she'd run from her father. "I'm sorry."

Elsie shrugged. "Don't be. My mother was fragile, that's all. Every bit a victim as I was. While she was there, she protected me the best she could—until her mind broke. I had it good compared to you and the other girls. Except that last little bit."

"You forgave her."

"It took time." In fact, Elsie had stayed at Lily's House for two years and then split her time between her mother's and Lily's House until she was eighteen and moved in with Halla. "And my mother is another person now."

"You think my mother was a victim?" Halla glanced up to include Kendall in the conversation, but Kendall only shook her head.

"Don't look at me. My mother was the controller in my family. She was never the victim. After she kicked Saffron out and she didn't come crawling back home as expected, my mother was better, but still . . ." Kendall shook her head. ". . . bad."

Halla knew their relationship was far from ideal, but they seemed friendly enough when they were together. "You talk to her now. What changed?"

Kendall sighed and went to the silverware drawer. "She did. Eventually. A tiny bit. It was enough, I guess, now that I'm not dependent on her."

"So could Oliver be right?" Halla asked. "Because he admitted he might be wrong—and he is wrong a lot." She cracked a smile, but her heart wasn't in it.

Elsie leaned back and crossed her legs. "You never talk about her. Or about that time."

"I don't?" Halla experienced a sense of déjà vu that she knew came from her conversation with Oliver.

Kendall shook her head. "No. Well, on your blog sometimes, and at Lily's House fundraisers. But not at home."

"I guess there's not much to say. I haven't seen her in eleven years." Since Halla was fifteen and a half to be exact. "She brought up the bread that last night," she remembered aloud. "It was broken into small pieces, and I wanted to throw it in her face, but I was so hungry. It smelled like butter. The second she left the room, I ate it all."

She'd gobbled it, actually. Then she'd gone back to pulling at the chain on her ankle and was almost paralyzed with shock when it squeezed off. The once-a-day, bread-only diet had ultimately freed her from her six-month imprisonment. Halla took a deep breath and pushed the memories aside. They couldn't hurt her now. She never even thought about it.

Except that wasn't quite true. Sometimes when people argued, she felt herself starting to cringe. To feel sick inside. And she still avoided most types of bread.

But Oliver was wrong. He had to be wrong.

"If Oliver wants to see me," Halla said, "he should come here. Or we should meet somewhere fun." A hiking destination maybe. There had to be somewhere he'd love to go. He'd talked about Hawaii once. Now that sounded fun.

There, it was decided. She was not going to Idaho.

Probably.

H alla grabbed her laptop from the table and set it on the counter next to the wall where it would be out of the way. "Go ahead and finish dinner. I'll get the glasses." She could feel the other two staring at her, but she didn't want to share anymore. She already felt exposed.

Elsie went back to her pan of meat, which turned out to be ready. She was mixing it with the beans when the doorbell rang. "You guys get everything on the table. I'll go open the door." She practically flew from the room.

"You think she's getting serious about Payden?" Kendall asked Halla. "She hasn't been dating anyone else for the past few months, right?"

"I don't think she'll ever be serious about him. Something would have happened by now, if it was going to. She and Payden have been best friends since she was twelve."

"Twelve? Why haven't I heard that story? I know Payden is Lily's husband's cousin, and he introduced them, but is there more?"

"There's more, but you probably haven't heard it because it brings back other memories that aren't so good."

Halla glanced over her shoulder at the kitchen doorway to make sure she wasn't overheard. Elsie didn't keep her past a secret, but Halla didn't want to ruin her sister's dinner. "He stumbled on Lily right after she found Elsie in an alleyway outside the grocery store where he worked. She'd just run away from her father after he'd beaten her pretty badly. Payden was only a teenager himself. He's been in love with Elsie ever since."

"Oh, that sheds a little light on things." Kendall chewed her bottom lip thoughtfully.

"For the longest time, they only saw each other when we'd pick up groceries or when he'd come to Lily's House," Halla added. "Payden is five years older, and I think Elsie got used to thinking of him as a cousin or a brother. Sometimes she'd set him up with her friends. He'd go, but I could tell his heart wasn't in it. Now every time she breaks up with a boyfriend, he sends her flowers, and they go out for a while. As friends, I guess. Then eventually she moves on."

"Ah, right. I remember he sent flowers right before I switched to the day shift and came back to the world of the living."

"That was him." Halla sighed. "Lily and I might be the only people who think he's perfect for her."

"Five years is a big age difference when you're twelve," Kendall said. "But twenty-two is a different story. Maybe her feelings are changing. Maybe if they really are good for each other, we can come up with a way to help her recognize that."

Halla held up crossed fingers and nodded, dropping her hand abruptly when Elsie, with Payden in tow, came into the kitchen. "Hey, Payden," Halla greeted him. "Good to see you."

"You too. Thanks for having me." He was a big man, a good eight inches taller than Elsie and a bit on the heavy side. He had dark hair, blue eyes, and a sexy, well-maintained scruff of beard that made his somewhat rounded face look preppy and very smart. He was probably a bit of a heart breaker at the high school where he taught math.

"As far as I'm concerned," Halla said, "you're always welcome."

Elsie waited until he was seated before she crossed the kitchen to get the chips they liked to keep separate from the taco salad until the last second.

Kendall slipped into the empty spot next to Payden, smiling at him and nodding her head. When he looked away, she mouthed, "Maybe she'll get jealous" to Halla.

But Elsie didn't appear concerned as she sat across the table from him, next to Halla. "I think that's everything."

They'd barely started eating when the doorbell rang and this time Halla went to get it, thinking of her article . . . and, yes, Oliver and his unsettling comments. She opened the door, surprised to see Tara Levine and Rylee Williams, who, at seventeen and eighteen, were the oldest foster girls currently at Lily's House.

She blinked in surprise. "Hey, girls, come in! I guess. What brings you here? Is everything okay?" Technically, they weren't her foster sisters since they'd never lived together, but most of the Lily's House originals spent enough time volunteering that they felt all the girls there were younger sisters.

"Everything's fine," said the shorter girl, Tara, as she

lifted her chin and tossed her dark hair every which way. "But we saw Elsie's post on Instagram about taco salad." She passed Halla and hurried toward the kitchen.

Rylee nodded in agreement. "Lily's gone to pick up a new girl, and Mario put frozen burritos in the microwave." She wrinkled her nose. "So we bailed. Don't worry—we told him where we were going."

With an endearing smile at Halla, Rylee followed Tara into the kitchen, looking more like a blond model than a girl whose mother had never gotten it together long enough to keep her for more than a few months. She'd been at Lily's house two years already, one year less than Tara, and she would be there until she finished her last year of high school. She'd already asked to move in with Halla and Elsie if there was ever an opening at the apartment, but Halla doubted Rylee would leave Lily's House until Tara could go with her. The girls had been inseparable from the moment they met.

Back in the kitchen, the younger girls had already dragged stools over from the small counter and were heaping taco salad onto their plates. Halla returned to eating, but her appetite was gone. She kept thinking about Idaho and Oliver and the hazy face of her mother, remembered more from newspaper articles than from real life. Halla didn't know the color of her eyes. Were they blue like hers? Or green like her father's? And why did she remember him and not her mother? Why couldn't she remember anything of their home life before her imprisonment except sitting at the dinner table and being hushed?

Kendall was now openly flirting with Payden, which

he appeared to enjoy. Elsie still didn't seem to mind. Maybe she'd set the two of them up, now that Kendall had shown an interest.

Halla forced down the rest of her salad before excusing herself. "I'd better finish my article."

"Wait, we were going to watch something," Elsie protested. "You can write it tomorrow."

"Sorry." Halla rinsed her plate and put it in the dishwasher. "I have another post to do tomorrow, so I have to work on this tonight. But I can write in my room if you need the TV."

"Count me out too," Kendall said. "I'm about to drop. I had a long day, and I need my beauty sleep. I have important things to do tomorrow." She raised her eyebrows a couple times, and Halla knew she was referring to the cute resident.

"Or we could go out to a movie," Payden suggested, smiling. "There's a new sci-fi flick at the mall."

"Ooh, I want to go!" Tara said. "Are you paying?"

Payden laughed at the teen's excitement. "Sure. But we'll have to go right away. It's a school night, and you girls need to get home at a decent time."

Rylee and Tara rolled their eyes, but Rylee only said, "I'll tell Mario we're going with you guys. We borrowed his van, though, so we'll meet you there."

"I'll see if I can get tickets online." Payden brought out his phone.

Kendall jumped up from the table, motioning to the teens. "Before you go, can I talk to you two in the other room for a moment?"

Kendall and the younger girls disappeared, while Halla

helped Elsie put away the rest of the salad. It looked like there would be enough for all of them to have it for lunch tomorrow, for which Halla was grateful. Maybe she'd enjoy it more than she had today.

"I left my wallet in the car," Payden said to Elsie. "You ready?"

"Go ahead, I'll be right there." Elsie gave him a bright smile as he left the room. Then she hurried over to Halla's side. "Did you see the way he and Kendall were talking?" she whispered. "I should have gotten them together before now. I think she likes him."

Halla shook her head. "Not like that."

"I could set them up and see. He's such a great guy, and you know that she needs someone great after all she went through."

Halla stifled a sigh. "Set her up then, but remember she has the hots for that new doctor."

"Oh, right." Elsie frowned. "That might be a passing thing."

"We'll see."

"Yeah, I'd better wait."

Did Elsie seem a little relieved? Halla couldn't tell.

"Go ahead. Kendall and I'll clean up. It's only fair since you cooked."

"But your article."

"I'll get it done. Go!"

Elsie nodded and hurried out the door. Halla was washing the pan when Kendall returned to the kitchen, a satisfied smile on her face.

"What did you do?" Halla asked.

Kendall grabbed a dish rag and began wiping down

the table. "Nothing much. I just got the girls to join my secret operation."

"And that is?"

"To get Elsie to see what a great guy Payden is. The girls are going to comment on how much they like him and what a great dad he'll make and so forth. They promised to be subtle."

Halla rolled her eyes. "And you trusted them? They're teens."

"Who cares if they're subtle. I don't. If she doesn't like him, she shouldn't be stringing him along."

"They're friends. He knows that by now. Besides, talking about leading someone on, Elsie definitely noticed you flirting. She wants to set you up with him now, so your plan might have backfired."

Kendall's grin faded. "I didn't think of that."

"Don't worry. I bought you some time."

"Well, I would go out with Payden if she set me up. He's cute. But it kind of destroys things for me knowing how much he likes her."

"And besides, he's not your dreamy resident."

"Dr. Gorgeous, I'm calling him." Kendall gave a sigh. "He's pretty impressive—and not because he's a doctor. For the most part I've disliked any doctor I've dated in the past two years. But this guy is . . . I don't know . . . nice. Like maybe he wouldn't judge my past. You know."

"I do know." Halla put the pan on a dish towel to dry, pausing a moment to reflect before retrieving her laptop from the counter. "Well, I guess it's back to work."

"You're so lucky to work from home."

"Yeah, but it makes meeting men a bit harder."

"Oliver's nice. I mean, except for the whole weird Idaho invite."

Halla forced a laugh. "Yeah, tell me about it."

"He'll come around." Kendall yawned widely, belatedly attempting to cover her mouth. "Good luck with your article."

"Thanks." Halla considered going into the other room and her more comfortable chair, but the kitchen had something more important: strawberry ice cream. She opened her laptop to bring it to life, then headed for the freezer.

Two bowls of ice cream and a completed article later, Halla sat staring at her screensaver. She felt out-of-sorts, as if the room was too hot but her feet too cold. Her camouflage pants too loose and her tank top too tight. Her hair felt plastered to her head, and she was pretty sure her entire article was the worst drivel she'd ever written. Who was ever going to believe or care that chlorine in pools might not be doing its job?

She wanted more ice cream.

Her laptop screen went dead, a sign that it was definitely time to quit. It did that more often than not these days when it ran out of battery, without even flashing a warning. Fortunately, she was in the habit of saving after every sentence, if not earlier, and her program saved automatically every minute. But a new computer was definitely in her future.

Pushing the laptop farther away, she closed her eyes, folded her arms atop the table, and laid her head on her arms. Oliver didn't know what he was talking about. How well did he know her anyway? Sure, they talked every day, but it wasn't as if he really knew her. She might have permitted him into her life, sharing her triumphs and even at times her upsets, but that didn't mean he knew more than she let him see.

Which might have been his point. Why hadn't she let go with him?

Let go. The partial title of her article took away her breath. She squeezed her eyes shut tight, and a tear squeezed out.

The world fell away.

And she was back in that small room on the second floor, a shackle around her ankle with the chain that attached her to the bed. Her mother came with the bread, once again torn into tiny pieces instead of the small round loaf she'd previously brought. Halla didn't look at her mother or touch the paper plate as she set it on the bed. Her mother had learned not to bring anything that might break. It took all of Halla's effort to hold back until the door closed. Then she crammed the pieces into her mouth, gulping and swallowing too fast. She choked and nearly vomited.

She held a hand against her mouth. No! She couldn't let it come up or she'd be hungry all night and the next day. She forced herself to lie down on the carpet, breathing slowly. When the urge to vomit passed, she pulled herself to a seated position and began tugging against the chain, straining to force the shackle over her heel. It was no use, though, no matter how much weight she lost. After six months, all she had to show for her efforts was a bloody scar on the top of her foot. But she couldn't give up. Blood leaked between her fingers as she pushed harder.

Then, seemingly all at once, her foot slipped free. She

stared at the shackle and then at her bleeding foot for a few seconds, her heart beating erratically. What to do? Her brain said to wait until dark, but her fear screamed "Go!" Because sometimes he came to check on her before bed, and her mother always did. Even if she climbed under the covers, they might think to look at the chain.

In the next second, she was yanking the window open, climbing outside into the cold November air, and stumbling partially down the gable that covered the porch. Until she tripped and rolled the rest of the way, falling . . . falling. She didn't care. It was better than staying in that room. Falling was her choice, at least. She didn't mind dying.

She slammed into the ground, and for endless long seconds she couldn't breathe. Agony shot through her arm. Agony which told her that by some miracle she was still alive. She bit her lip hard to keep from crying out.

She listened for footsteps, ears aching with the effort. There was nothing. Nothing except the blare of the television coming from her own house, where her father was probably eating his rare steak and sautéed potatoes, both cooked exactly the way he liked them.

Mindlessly, she hugged her injured arm to her chest, forcing herself to her bare feet.

She ran.

Halla jerked awake, gasping a little as the dream receded. No, not a dream but a memory. Her face was slick with tears. What was it she'd done that made her father so angry? That had bothered her over the years. She remembered the refusal to eat broccoli and the resulting two-week broccoli-only diet. She remembered being kept home from school for a month after a boy had called.

She remembered running to their pastor in tears, and her father smoothing it all over with a large donation. She remembered him cutting up and throwing out most of her clothes when she'd borrowed a bright pink shirt from a friend. There was more she recalled, but nothing of that last punishment, the reason for the chain and the months of horror.

"No reason," she whispered. There couldn't be any she would accept. And what about her mother? Why had the bread come in pieces that entire week?

Regardless, she knew there had to be answers. She needed answers. Her child memories were no longer enough.

She almost hated Oliver for it. Almost.

I'm going, she thought.

An ache formed in her gut. Whatever she discovered in Nampa, there would be no going back.

E lsie looked around the crowded hallway at the theater. "Where did the girls go?" It was open seating and if they didn't hurry, they wouldn't get decent seats.

Payden shrugged. "I don't know. I handed them the drinks and popcorn and they disappeared. Let's find a seat and you can text them."

He moved deftly around a knot of people, balancing the popcorn they were going to share as well as his drink. Elsie followed him. The movie was popular, that much was obvious, and she was excited to see it. She and Payden always went together to the new sci-fi films. Even when they were dating other people.

Should she set him up with Kendall? Halla hadn't thought so, but Elsie liked Kendall and wouldn't want her to settle for some stuck-up doctor. Kendall had grown up in a high-class family, and one set of her clothes when she'd lived with her mother had cost more than three or four of Payden's outfits, but the two had seemed flirty enough over dinner.

Payden's warm hand touched her elbow. "Hey, don't

worry. They're teens. They probably stopped to talk to some friends."

"Oh, yeah. It's not them."

"What, then?"

"Nothing, really. I was thinking of Kendall. She's nice, right?"

He held open the door leading to the dim theater. "Oh, yeah. I've only seen her briefly a couple times since she moved in, but she's really nice."

"She used to work the nightshift, so she hasn't been around a lot." That and Elsie and Payden hadn't seen each other except for a movie or two while Elsie was dating her last boyfriend. They'd kept in touch with texts, of course.

The theater still had a few low lights on, which indicated Elsie had time to find the girls. She sent out a group text to them.

Tara's reply came back immediately: *You guys are so cute together! You don't need extra people. Besides, we both want to sit way up in the back. Cuddle up with your hunky math guru and enjoy!*

Elsie blinked at the text, her face flushing. What was Tara thinking? She and Payden were only friends. They'd been friends for ten and a half years, and that was that. Two years ago, he had indicated that he was interested in being more than friends, but she'd been too young to even consider it. Besides, she didn't feel that way about him. He was kind. He was handsome. He was special. He was a good friend. But he wasn't for her.

"How about here?" Payden asked, pointing to a row of seats that would put their faces parallel to the middle of the screen. It was her favorite section. She nodded, but she could still see concern on his face at her distraction and wasn't surprised when he added, "You still worried about the girls?"

Elsie smiled. "Oh, no. The girls want to sit in the nosebleed section, so I guess we're on our own."

His laughter came easily. "Probably good for us. They like to talk."

"Good point."

He let her enter the row first and she passed a few people to reach two free middle seats. If the girls had been with them, they would have had to sit closer to the end to find four spots together, and while she was a tiny bit irritated at their lack of appreciation and Tara's inappropriate comment, a part of her was glad. These seats would give them both a perfect angle to view the film.

Settling in the plush seat, she typed, *Payden and I are just friends, but go ahead and enjoy your nosebleeds!*

Rylee's text came next: *Well, you should rethink that friend thing because some kids at his school say all the single female teachers are in love with him. They bring him food and find excuses to go down his hall. He might have a bit of a baby face, but that scruff makes him super handsome. Yum!*

Yum?

Payden and I are OLD friends, she typed. *It's not like that.*

For you, maybe, Tara countered.

Yeah, Rylee agreed. *Everyone knows guys aren't like we are. If they're always around and don't have a girlfriend, they're into you. He's cute. What's not to like?*

That last boyfriend of yours was too thin, Tara added. *You and math genius look hot together. Smart is sooooo sexy!*

Then from Rylee again: *You can't tell us you haven't noticed those incredible brown eyes, can you?*

They're blue! Elsie texted back, frustration making her fingers slow.

Oh, so you have noticed, Tara wrote.

"Problem?" Payden leaned closer to her, and she caught a whiff of his aftershave. Since when had he started wearing aftershave?

She turned the phone over in her lap, so he couldn't see the texts. They were embarrassing enough without sharing them, though he'd probably get a kick out of the girls' comments. So would she normally, but the memory of how Payden sent her flowers whenever she was down made Rylee's comment hit home. Could Payden still want more from her than friendship?

Payden smiled and passed the popcorn. "Did you see the reviews on the movie?"

"Reviews?" she asked a bit stupidly. He did have nice eyes. Dark and large. Intelligent. They were the eyes of a kind man.

"Yeah, people seem to either love or hate it."

Elsie laughed. "Good. Because there is nothing I hate more than a lukewarm movie. We'll probably love it. But if we hate it, we'll have an even better time making fun of it."

The lights lowered, a few sections at a time until the theater was dark. Trailers for other movies began. Elsie turned her phone on vibrate and slipped it into her pocket.

"Well? Is it working?" Tara lifted her head to peer over the heads separating them from Elsie and Payden. Despite what she'd told Elsie, they weren't clear at the top of the theater. They had perfect seats close to the middle and only two rows behind Elsie and Payden.

"Um, maybe?" Rylee craned her neck sideways. "We could move down to the end of the row. We'd see them better."

"Let's not get too carried away." Tara grinned. "Besides, what else can we do? The movie is starting."

"What if Kendall is wrong? What if they really are just friends? And all our encouragement is only confusing things."

Tara shook her head. "No way. I think she's right. Remember what I overheard Lily and Mario saying when Elsie broke up with her boyfriend?"

"That Payden had been waiting a long time for Elsie and maybe it was finally time for them to get together. I remember."

"Before that, I thought he came around because he was Mario's cousin."

"So did I."

"Hey, look!" Tara gasped. "He's putting his arm around her. He's whispering something in her ear."

Rylee twirled a lock of blond hair. "Something romantic maybe?"

Tara could imagine what. Something like, "I can't live without you." Or maybe, "Every day without you in my life is like a day without air." Whatever it was, Elsie whispered something back.

"Maybe we've done it," Rylee said. "Maybe that could be a good job for us in the future—matchmaking."

Tara giggled and was shushed by someone behind her. She clamped her mouth shut, feeling young and silly.

All through the movie, Tara watched Payden and Elsie's heads together. Their closeness was so distracting that she had trouble concentrating on the film. And it was a wonderful film. With damsels in distress, heroic rescues, cool spaceships, and the fate of the world hanging in the balance. Several times, Rylee reached over to squeeze her arm with excitement.

After the film rolled the last credits, Tara jumped up and hurried down to the row where Elsie and Payden were still talking. Tara elbowed Rylee as people bumped past them. "That's true love if I ever saw it," she said. "What do you suppose is so exciting that they don't even notice the film is over?"

"I don't know, but we should definitely find out." Rylee gave a little laugh. They waited until the last people left the row and hurried over to where Elsie and Payden were laughing.

"Looks like you enjoyed the film," Tara said.

Elsie glanced at Payden, her lips twitching. "It was . . ." They both burst out laughing.

"Fabulous!" Rylee finished. "I think I'm in love." She held her hand to her heart.

"With that male chauvinist pilot?" Elsie stared at her in apparent surprise. "You're kidding, right? I don't know what the screenwriter was thinking. The woman has a degree in mechanics, yet *he's* the one who fixes the ship?"

"Right," Payden added. "And he blows up the other spaceships, makes fuel from garbage, and flattens her captors." He and Elsie laughed some more.

"And what's with the little outfit she wears?" Elsie could barely get out the words through her laughter. "He's shivering and she's prancing about practically naked."

Payden made a face. "I was cold just looking at her. And never mind that all her people are going to die because she decides to go back on her word."

That was only the beginning of the critique. Elsie and Payden also made fun of the acting, the dialogue, and special effects. Seeing it from their viewpoint, the film did seem kind of lame. Tara met Rylee's eyes, feeling a little ashamed for having enjoyed it so much.

Rylee shrugged. "I still loved it. But we have to go, so thanks for the movie."

"Yeah." Tara waved and started down the row of seats.

"We'll come with you," Elsie called, her voice still bright with laughter. At least someone was having a good time.

Tara waited until she was sure Elsie couldn't hear before she whispered to Rylee, "Maybe they really are just friends."

Rylee glanced over her shoulder. "Maybe. But if I got along with a hunk like that, I'd marry him in an instant."

Tara considered a moment before shrugging. "Let's text her more things. The worst that can happen is she'll refuse to feed us for a few weeks."

Elsie thanked Payden when he opened the door to his sleek gray Mustang. Her stomach actually hurt from holding in the laughter.

Payden went around and climbed into his seat. He had only to glance at Elsie and they were off laughing again. "So I guess it was us who whispered all through the movie, not the girls," he said.

"A movie like that deserves to be laughed at. Only kids and all their angst could enjoy it."

"Well, they did have that sexual attraction going for them, I'll give them that."

Elsie tried to nod seriously. "What was it he said? I love you more than my space dice?" And they were off laughing again.

"That had to be the best worst movie we've ever seen." Payden finally calmed enough to drive his car from the parking lot.

Back at her apartment building, he walked with her up to her door, and she didn't tell him not to, already knowing he wouldn't listen. He was always a gentleman. Not like her, who sometimes became a little snarky when she didn't get enough sleep.

Before she could help herself, she blurted, "So, you and Kendall. You seemed to get along really well."

Payden's slow blink told her she'd surprised him. "Right, yeah. I told you she seemed nice."

Not exactly the enthusiastic response she'd been hoping for. So maybe it was better to wait like Halla suggested. Yeah, it couldn't hurt to wait.

But who could she set him up with in the meantime? He was twenty-seven already, and she knew he wanted to settle down. He was even looking at buying a house. She'd gone with him to exactly nine different houses to offer a woman's opinion. So far, she hadn't really liked any of them.

They stopped at the apartment door. "Want to come in for a bit?" she asked.

He shook his head. "I have a few tests to grade, and I bet your roommates are asleep."

Kendall, maybe, but not Halla. She was a bit of a night owl these days, often staying up late to finish blogs and scheduling them to post while she was still sleeping the next morning. But Elsie did have to get up early. Ruth was at the café by five every morning and while Elsie didn't have to come in until seven, that still meant an early day. It was only Tuesday, and already she couldn't wait for the weekend when she didn't have to work.

"Okay." She stifled a yawn. "Thanks for suggesting that movie. I had fun."

Payden struck a hero's pose, with his considerable chest out and his hand wiping across his forehead to fling aside an imaginary fluff of hair. "I will save you. Don't worry about the humongous robot bugs on top of the ship!"

"Thank you, my hero! Catch me as I faint!" Elsie giggled and gave him a hug. "See you later." He started away as she opened the door to her dimly lit apartment, turning to wave.

"Oh, wait," he called, thrusting his hand into the front pocket of his jeans. "I forgot. I have an appointment to see another house tomorrow night. Any chance you can come with me? I think this might be the one."

She laughed. "That's what you said the last three times."

"I have to get the hang of this house-buying thing eventually, right?"

"Okay, but I can't get away until four at the earliest."

"The appointment is for five. Should I come here and pick you up?"

"No, I'll meet you. Text me the address." She waved again and shut the door, still smiling.

Elsie reached for the light switch, stopping as she saw Halla on the couch, legs folded under her and her face illuminated by the screen of her laptop. Elsie wasn't surprised to see Halla in the dark with her computer— that was a normal occurrence—but the glistening of tears on Halla's cheeks startled her.

She hurried over. "Hey, what's up?"

Halla punched angrily at her keyboard, not taking her eyes from the screen. "It'll cost a fortune to go to Idaho, and I'm not talking about the plane ticket, which is double the price it would be a month from now. I'm talking about staying at a hotel without bedbugs and eating out and car rental. And I have no idea what date to choose for the return ticket anyway."

There were a lot of statements there, but Elsie decided to pick the most obvious, "You're going to Idaho?" She removed an empty carton of strawberry ice cream from the couch cushion and sat down next to her sister.

Halla looked up at her. "The bread my mother brought was in pieces that last week. I don't know why, and I can't remember the color of her eyes. She had blond hair, I think—or maybe brown—but I don't remember exactly. I want to go back. I want to drive by the high school. I want to talk to my old friends. Maybe even the neighbors."

"And your mom?"

Halla sighed. "I have to know. You see that, right?"

"I do." Elsie scooted closer and leaned her head against Halla's. "What about Oliver?"

"This isn't about him."

"But you're going to tell him, right?"

She shrugged. "It all seems so impossible. I'll blow my entire savings on this trip, just when I finally paid off my college loans and started to get ahead. Part of me is so angry at that. One more crappy legacy from my crappy parents."

"What about driving instead?"

"It's fourteen hours. Maybe I could sleep in my car, if that's not illegal."

"It's not safe, is what."

Halla's nose wrinkled. "It's Idaho."

"It's not safe anywhere." Elsie reached for Halla's laptop. "Look, you go to bed, and I'll text Lily. She's coming home tomorrow, and she'll have some great ideas."

Halla looked relieved, as if she couldn't bear to make one more decision. That she didn't grab for her laptop was even more telling. "Good idea." They both came to their feet.

"You're welcome. And remember what Lily says—to put your pillow over your head and scream and cry because tomorrow the sun will still come up, and after getting it all out, you'll feel like trying again."

Halla hugged her. "I think I'm swearing off men altogether. Look at what they do to me."

"Don't blame Oliver," Elsie said.

Halla ran her fingertips under her eyes, blotting her

tears. "Forget my problems for a minute. Did you and Payden have fun tonight?"

Elsie grinned. "Oh, yeah. It was great. I mean it was bad. Really bad."

Halla lifted her hand. "Don't tell me. I haven't seen it yet."

"Okay, fine." Let her waste her money. "I've been thinking, if Kendall's not a good set up for Payden, what about one of the other foster sisters? I'm thinking maybe Vanessa or Carol."

Halla's head shook back and forth slowly. "Maybe it's time he finds his own dates."

"But he's so great, and he's all alone. I want him to be happy."

"He is great, and he already is happy. Maybe ask him what he wants. I'm betting it's not another setup." With that, Halla turned and headed to her room.

"What he wants," Elsie murmured. "Right. Like he knows." She had to take care of him. In ten more years when she was married with a bunch of babies, she didn't want him to be all alone.

Halla awoke to the smell of bacon and hot chocolate, foods that always made her happy, mostly because they reminded her of Lily's House. She cracked an eye and looked around the room, but nothing in sight would have created that yummy smell. She crawled out of bed, tripping over her discarded pants from the night before but catching herself before she toppled head first into the carpet.

Elsie had been right. She might still have no idea how she was getting to Nampa, but she didn't feel so desperate this morning. With that delicious aroma, something had to go right today. Both her roommates were at work, but all the original fosters had a key, so it could be any of them. Maybe whoever was here would have some ideas for her.

She patted down hair that looked as if it had been through a hurricane, to no avail, and then shuffled out her door, down the hall, through a few feet of living room until she reached the kitchen. There she found Lily Perez in front of the stove, dancing around with the spatula, her earbuds in, and rocking out to whatever music was on her phone. At the moment, her eyes were closed.

Halla laughed and leaned against the doorway where Lily would see her once she surfaced to check the food. She didn't have long to wait. Lily gave a little gasp and pulled out her earbuds.

"Halla! Sorry, I didn't hear you. Hope you don't mind that I let myself in." She dived for the stove without waiting for an answer.

"If any of us minded, we wouldn't have given you a key."

Lily turned the bacon. "Have a seat. The eggs are already finished, and I know how you love bacon, so I made double. Watch the hot chocolate. It was a little too hot five minutes ago."

Halla sat down at the table in front of a Tweetie Bird mug that matched her nightshirt. The girls had given it to her for Christmas a few years ago, along with a newer Tweetie nightshirt, but she still mostly wore this one because it was super soft after years of washing.

Before long, Lily plunked down a plate of eggs covered by six pieces of bacon. It was more food than Halla normally ate in three breakfasts. But some habits were hard to break. Lily had been trying since Halla was sixteen to combat the malnutrition she'd suffered. Ignoring her fork, Halla picked up one of the pieces of bacon, burning her fingers slightly but crunching into it anyway.

Lily smiled in satisfaction. "Had a chat with Elsie this morning. I came over to talk, but you were still sleeping—who sleeps until ten?—and so I thought I'd make you breakfast."

"Thank you." Halla took a tentative sip of the hot chocolate and found it exactly right. She gulped a bit more than she intended, choking slightly. "So, the new girl," she said through a cough. "She's okay?"

"Oh, yeah. She's a little angry. Reminds me of Tara when she first arrived, but she'll fit right in soon enough." Lily fixed Halla with a steady gaze. "But I'm here to talk about you and Idaho."

"I'm assuming Elsie told you all of it?"

Lily shrugged. "All that she knows, I guess. And I have a plan."

Halla set down the half-eaten strip of bacon. Lily was only thirty-two, six years older than herself, and most of the time Halla felt like they were sisters, rather than foster daughter and mother. But that ended where Lily's plans were concerned. Lily was a master planner, and though Halla was organized, she could only aspire to Lily's level of inventiveness and ingenuity.

"Let's hear it," she said. "As long as it doesn't involve a fundraiser."

Lily snorted. "It doesn't. You will take Bianca's truck and my popup camper. And I have a friend in Nampa—Monica—who is going to let you hook up the water and electricity to her house. She was actually willing to kick one of her five kids out of a bed to let you stay at her place, but I know that would make you feel uncomfortable, so this is better. Plus, you can come and go as needed without bugging them, but you'll have the safety of being in a family neighborhood. The camper has a shower and toilet. Tiny, I know, but it's a lot better than that old camper we had when you were still at Lily's House."

"That one didn't have a toilet," Halla said. Not that she'd minded. She and the others had been thrilled to have Mario and Lily take them camping at all.

"Right. This is much better, and all the linens and bedding and dishes are packed inside, so there's nothing to worry about except your clothes and a little food."

"When would I need to have Bianca's truck back?" Bianca was one of the original six fosters, and Halla wasn't surprised at her generosity.

"She doesn't care. She can use her husband's or my van if she needs to transport her pottery. It'll take you thirteen or fourteen hours, depending on your speed, but with two of you driving—"

"Two of us?" Halla blinked. "You shouldn't be leaving the new girl this soon. And Cheri wouldn't be happy." At two months shy of her fourth birthday, Lily's daughter was a handful.

Lily laughed. "Oh, not me. According to Cheri, I've already had my one night a year away from her. No, I meant Elsie. She said she's going with you."

"Elsie has a lot of better things to do than tag along with me." Halla was about to protest further when Lily cut her off.

"I'm glad she volunteered. It's not safe for anyone to travel alone. Besides, remember how you went to California with Saffron when she went to see her mother and Kendall? It's your turn now to put up with someone caring about you, just like Saffron did. It's what family does."

Halla had to laugh. She could do nothing else while Lily was staring at her so fiercely, as if daring her to contradict her words. Then Lily put the final nail in the coffin. "It would make me feel better knowing you're not alone."

Lily had saved her—had saved all of them—and making her worry was the last thing Halla was willing to do. Ever. Lily had given up so much to become their foster mother when she was far younger than Halla was now.

Halla picked up the half piece of bacon and took a bite. "If she's okay with missing work, I'm happy to have her." It was actually a relief not to go alone, now that she thought about it.

"Well, Elsie has to work today and tomorrow, but she said she can bake enough ahead to leave on Friday. So you can leave then."

"Wait, no. I want to go now—or tomorrow at the latest." Before she changed her mind? She didn't want to consider that, but Friday seemed a lifetime away.

Lily touched her hair, attempting to smooth it. "I'm sure you have posts to do before you leave, and if you take time to schedule them for the weekend, you'll have less to worry about. Besides, there's also food to buy, and you'll need to pack clothes." She eyed the Tweetie Bird nightshirt. "You might want to take the new one the girls got for you. If you still lived with me, this one would be in the rag drawer already."

"Okay, okay. I'll wait until Friday. But I'm taking Tweetie—this Tweetie."

Lily laughed and leaned over to kiss her forehead. "Okay. I'll expect updates, and if you need to talk, I'm only a phone call away." She patted the bulge of her phone in her back pants pocket.

"Thanks, Lily," Halla said. "I know you're always there for me, and I appreciate it."

Lily drew her hand one more time across the top of Halla's hair. But it was no use and they both laughed.

When Lily was gone, Halla made her way back to her room for a change of clothes. She needed to shower, and Lily was right about the shopping and posts she needed to prepare. Her anxiety about facing her mother hadn't disappeared, but Lily's presence had given her courage. Lily had always taught them to confront their fears head on, and that's exactly what she was going to do.

Should she tell Oliver about going to Idaho? She had planned on it, but now she wasn't so sure. This wasn't about him or about going to see him, as much as she wanted it to be. This was about her mother and her father. It was even about her old neighbors and her hometown. Fear washed over her once again, but she pushed it back with firmness. There was nothing to fear. She was going to get herself under control, drive to Nampa, and do this thing.

What if going opened doors better left closed?

It didn't matter. This was what she wanted—no, needed—to do, and she wasn't going to think that way now. As for Oliver, she'd keep abreast of his plans, and let him know soon enough.

Halla showered quickly and went to her computer to make a list. A neat, organized list that wouldn't be concerned with feelings.

E lsie worked harder and faster than she had in over a year. She baked bread, whipped up stews and soups, and made meat pies. By the agreement she had with Ruth, she was to take care of the food items while Ruth made all of the desserts and treats, of which they offered a considerable variety. Most people came into the Eats and Treats for pastries and a drink, but more and more came in each day for her soups and sandwiches—and they also had pastries, so the addition of more food items was helping their bottom line.

Besides Elsie's soups and stews, they were thinking about adding something more solid for the dinner period, but before they did that, they would have to hire more help because the café was a hopping place these days, especially at breakfast, lunch, and right after the schools let out. This worked nicely because the girls from Lily's House, or those who had recently left Lily's House, always had a job.

Speaking of which, Elsie was looking forward to Tara and Rylee coming into work. She'd have them package the lunch meat servings so she could spend more time finishing her other food prep.

When Ruth Thomas wandered into the kitchen, Elsie was adding spices to a pot of pumpkin soup that had become quite popular in the last few weeks, even though Halloween was almost two months away. Ruth had a bit of flour on her nose from her afternoon pastry making. Elsie took one look and threw her sister a rag.

Ruth laughed, wiping her dark face and tucking her hair behind her ears. She'd grown out her black locks quite a bit in the past year, and it looked lovely in those kinky ringlets. "I can't tell you how many times I get home and Zane tells me I've got something on my face."

"That's what you get when you're the best pastry-maker in the city, or even the state." Elsie gave her a grin. "Are you really going to be okay with me taking off on Friday?"

"Of course I am. Lily said if I need help, she'll come in, but Bianca already volunteered. I only wish I were the one going with Halla."

Elsie had suspected Ruth would feel that way. She and Halla had been together when Lily found them, weeks after surviving alone on the streets. But ever since Ruth married Zane and he'd become a huge part of her life, Halla had grown closer to Elsie, for which Elsie was glad. As the youngest of the original six, Elsie had been everyone's favorite, but sometimes her age had separated her during their teen years. Though that wasn't so anymore, she loved that she was the one who could support Halla now.

"I'm hoping to be back at least by Tuesday morning,"

Elsie said. "But there's always a chance we'll have to stay longer. I'll leave enough frozen bread dough and sandwich makings, though we'll need more veggies cut. And I've left instructions for Monday's soups."

"That's perfect. If needed, I can make the soups. We'll muddle by. I'm grateful Halla won't be alone."

Elsie's phone buzzed in her pocket. She grabbed it and opened the screen, smiling as she read the text.

"Payden again?" Ruth guessed.

"Yes. He's pretty determined to become a homeowner. I guess that's the next step in his life."

Ruth rolled her eyes. "Seriously? I think the next step in life is for him to get married. Zane and I have been married two years, and we're only beginning to think about a house."

"Well, I've tried setting him up with everybody. I can't really help him anymore."

Ruth stared at her for a few seconds without speaking, then shook her head and left the kitchen. Elsie decided she must have heard customers come into the café. She put down the soup spoon and typed an answer: *Don't worry I'll be there, but don't make any appointments this weekend. I've got to help Halla with some stuff, so I won't be available.*

His text came back quickly. *Wait, what? You're really going to leave me all weekend? I was thinking we could do a Doctor Who marathon. The new ones, I mean. I'm not that much of a fan of the older ones.*

Grinning, Elsie typed back, *No one's that big of a fan. Sorry, not this weekend, but I'll be there at the house at five.* It was going to be a push to get there in time, but she could do it. *Gotta go. I've got two soups on the stove and bread in the oven and I have another batch to mix up before I can meet you.* Besides stocking up for Friday, she still had the regular food to make for the weekend, but she didn't tell him that.

As she washed her hands again before starting in on the next batch of bread, Elsie pondered if there was anyone else she should tell about her pending trip. Maybe her mother. Even though they weren't planning on getting together, they had a good relationship now and her mother sometimes invited her over. She'd recently remarried a man who had three young children and had her hands full taking them places and doing all the activities she hadn't done with Elsie. Not that Elsie minded, at least not too much. It hadn't been her mother's fault Elsie had missed out on so much. She had made peace with her abandonment. Her mother wasn't the person Elsie went to for advice, but their relationship was good, and she liked her young step-siblings.

Halla needs to come to peace with her past too, Elsie thought.

That meant better understanding the role her mother played and coming to terms with whatever she discovered. Elsie had noticed more and more lately that Halla wasn't exactly herself. She dated enough but didn't seem to like any of the men. Only with Oliver could she talk for hours at the computer. Elsie was a little worried about that. Online relationships were great, but they didn't take the place of going out and really getting to know someone. She'd have to make sure that Halla had time to be alone with Oliver while they were in Nampa.

Drying her hands, she brought out her phone again and texted Halla. *Have you told Oliver that you're coming yet?* she wrote. *It would be terrible if he goes back to Coeur d'Alene before we get to Nampa.*

Satisfied that she'd done what she could for Halla's love life, she washed her hands yet again and turned back to her cooking. Now if only she could get this new batch of bread zipped up before she had to leave. She grabbed a bag of yeast.

Elsie gave a little gasp as she drove up to the house where she was supposed to meet Payden. She was ten minutes late, and he was probably already inside because Payden was always on time. It was one of the things she liked about him because he inspired her to keep on track while being kind about it. Today being late wasn't her fault. The bread had taken longer than usual because she'd run out of the right kind of flour and had to make a dash to the store.

The two-story, two-car house was small but very beautiful. The exterior stucco was a honey brown, with steep gables and dark trim. A decorative rock flowerbed lined the curved walkway, a small patch of grass added color, and a big tree gave attractive shade to the house. There wasn't much space on either side between the neighboring houses, but who needed it?

She hurried up the cement walk to the remarkably expansive covered porch, knocking on the door briskly. Two wooden chairs sat on the porch as if in invitation, so when no one came to the door right away, she sat, leaning back in the shade of the tree, closing her eyes and enjoying her first real break of the day. She could hear children playing somewhere, their small voices high and excited. The door opened a minute later, and she jerked upright, her gaze going to Payden's smiling face.

"I see you found the chairs," he said, his eyes sparkling. "They're deceptively comfortable, aren't they?"

She laughed. "Actually, yes."

"I'll have to buy some just like it if they don't stay with the house. Come on in and see the rest." He held a hand out to her. "The kitchen is fairly large. Not like the mini ones you usually find in a house this size."

Elsie took his hand and let him help her up. Directly inside the house was a small entryway with a tiny sitting room on one side where his female realtor sat on a leather couch.

"Hello, Elsie," she said, looking up from the phone in her hand. She wore a dressy navy skirt and a white blouse, coupled with the tallest heels Elsie had ever seen.

Elsie dipped her head. "Hi."

"You two go ahead and look at the house. I'm going to sit here and catch up on a few things. Let me know if you need anything."

Elsie followed Payden into a kitchen that had long countertops of glistening brown granite flaked with bits of gold, green, and black. The sink was stainless steel, and the numerous cupboards reached all the way to the ceiling. Which meant no cleaning on top of them and extra cupboard space. They were painted white, with a bit of a rustic look that Elsie liked immediately. A square table sat in a small alcove next to windows that looked out into the back yard—a yard featuring a patch of bright green grass, high fences that would prevent peeping neighbors and lost balls, and a small cement area with a basketball hoop. Children would have fun here.

"It's light and airy." Not like the dim space at her apartment or the windowless space at the café.

"I knew you'd approve."

Next, he showed her a cozy family room and a mid-sized bathroom. Up the stairs was a master bedroom with a private bathroom and a walk-in closet that she loved. The second floor also held two small bedrooms and an open play area near the stairs. It was obvious the current owners had gone to great lengths to make the house ready to sell because every inch of the house was neat and clean.

"It's larger than it looks from the outside," she said to him in one of the upstairs rooms.

"Yeah, it is."

She stared out the window, down at the yard where Payden's future children would play and felt . . . a little sad.

"What's wrong?" He stepped closer to her, his hand going to her arm. She leaned toward him, feeling safety in his bulk.

"I think it's beautiful."

"You like it then?"

"Yes, a lot. But that shouldn't matter. It's your house after all."

He grinned. "Yeah, but we'll be hanging out here a lot, don't you think?"

The heaviness in her heart lifted. "With a kitchen like that? Probably."

"I can finally teach you how to shoot hoops." He picked a ball up from a basket of toys next to a small bed.

They stood staring at one another for a long moment without speaking. All at once, Elsie became aware of an odd tension between them. Her heart started banging in her chest. Goose bumps spread over her skin. What was all that about? Her gaze jumped to his, only to find he was staring at her, an unreadable expression on his face.

Why did she want more than anything to move even closer? To knock the ball from his hands and to feel his arms around her? To reach her lips up to his? Would it hurt just to have a little, noncommittal fun?

Somehow she stopped herself from moving, from doing anything she'd regret later. This was crazy. Besides, she knew what it was like to kiss him. He'd kissed her once when she was nineteen, and she'd disgruntled him when she'd started laughing. They were friends, she'd reminded him. He'd tried to kiss her again two years ago at her twentieth birthday when he'd suggested they ought to start dating since they were both still unattached. She'd set him up with one of her college roommates to avoid the issue. But maybe she should have really kissed him, gotten it over with so he'd know like she did that they'd never be more than friends.

Yet here she was considering starting something. Wondering what it would be like to really kiss him. To lose herself in his arms.

She shook off the thoughts. Using him now because she was feeling lonely and a little jealous about this wonderful house wasn't something she was willing to do. She didn't believe in friends with benefits.

"I've been thinking," she choked out. "I know the perfect girl to set you up with." Or she would by tomorrow morning, as soon as she called a few of her former foster sisters to see who might be available. Dozens of girls had passed through Lily's House in the past ten years, and Payden would be sympathetic to whatever reasons had sent them there in the first place.

He gave a gentle laugh and stepped back. "Don't worry about that. You've already done your share in that department. You must have set me up at least a dozen times, and it never stuck." He smiled to show that it didn't upset him. "But I've got something else in the works now. Maybe."

"What?" If he'd hit her with the basketball, she wouldn't have been more surprised. "Is it someone from work?" Maybe the new English teacher he'd mentioned. Tara and Rylee had told her all the single teachers at his school had him in their sights, and maybe the English teacher was no different.

Payden faked throwing the ball at her, keeping hold of it at the last moment. "We'll see. Come on, let's go downstairs. I'm going to make an offer."

"Really?"

He tossed the ball back into the toy basket. "I told you I had a good feeling about this one."

"Right."

Downstairs, Elsie took another look at the kitchen, while Payden's agent pulled a contract from her briefcase and began discussing price and earnest money. Elsie tried not to listen. Maybe her thoughts about Payden and kids wasn't far off.

"It's not like he's old," she muttered. He wasn't even thirty yet. By then he might have a kid or two.

Who on earth was he dating? He hadn't hinted at dating anyone. The English teacher was the only woman he'd mentioned recently, and though it hadn't been in a romantic context, Elsie could have missed something. Pulling out her phone, she brought up his high school and looked at the faculty. There the English teacher was, with blond hair shorter than Halla's and a perky nose and not a freckle in sight. Not like Elsie, who still hadn't managed to shed all her childhood freckles. The teacher looked nice, and she was probably smart. Payden deserved to be happy, so Elsie would support him.

"But I'll tell him if I don't like her," she said.

"Don't like who?" Payden asked from the kitchen doorway where he had appeared without Elsie sensing him.

Elsie put away her phone. "Nothing. When will you know if they accept your offer?"

He shrugged. "Maybe tonight."

"Well, don't move in until I get back from Idaho. I'll help you."

He laughed. "I'm pre-approved for a loan, but I think it takes longer than that to close on a house."

He walked her to her car, and things were a little awkward as they said goodbye. She flushed as she remembered her thoughts about kissing him. Crazy thoughts.

"See you later," she said.

"I'll call before you leave. Maybe we can watch something tomorrow night? I'll bring pizza."

"I'm not sure what time I'll get home from work. I still haven't finished the Friday menu, much less the Saturday prep. I also need to pack and get food for the trip." Or make sure Halla picked up the right stuff.

He nodded. "Well, let me know if you need me to help. I'll plan on bringing over pizza either way."

"That would be nice. And let me know what you hear about the house."

"Of course. But I've got a good feeling about it."

The whole conversation was strangely unsatisfying. Stifling a sigh, she returned his wave as she drove away.

6

After Kendall finished checking all her patients, she went back to the nurses' station and there *he* was. Dr. Gorgeous, aka Wylen Gibson, the new resident that made her forget her vow to never date another doctor.

"Hey, Kendall," he said, flashing her a smile. His brown hair was cut a little too short, and his face was narrow, as if he needed a good meal or two, but that smile on his tanned face and the heavy brows over his dark eyes made her heart beat a little faster.

"Hey, doc," she greeted him.

He frowned. "What happened to Wylen? I thought we decided to be friends."

He had asked her to use his first name after he'd been assigned to one of her patients and they'd been stuck hunting down some important test results together for over two hours.

"Right." She gave him a smile of her own. "Hey, Wylen," she corrected.

"How's our lovely Lydia today?" His tone was playful.

Kendall laughed. Lydia Carson was eighty-five and as

wrinkled as a prune, but she had the most upbeat attitude about her pending gall bladder surgery, and she flirted relentlessly with Wylen and anyone else who came into the room. The other doctors seemed to find her irritating, but Wylen flirted right back, and Kendall appreciated his kindness.

"She's ready to get home to her granddaughter and her garden. Oh, and I think she has a gift for you."

Wylen's head went back as he gave a hearty laugh. He was beautiful, even with the scar on his neck that was from thyroid surgery as a teen. He'd told her that was what had made him decide to go into medicine in the first place. The scar gave his otherwise good looks an air of mystery and ruggedness.

Kendall found herself smiling even more. It was something she hadn't done enough of in the past two and a half years.

With a quick glance around him at the nurses who were looking at computers or otherwise occupied, Wylen stepped closer to her. "So," he began in a low whisper that felt like a caress. "What time do you have lunch? I haven't even been to the cafeteria yet. Maybe you could give me the tour."

She glanced at the clock on the wall. "In an hour. Can you meet me here?"

He nodded. "Yep. I'll do my best. Unless someone croaks or something." He was grinning, but his eyes held a hint of seriousness, as if he was already repenting of the joke.

"I think we'll be okay. At least today. See you later." Turning from the counter with her papers in hand, she strode down the hall, trying not to walk unnaturally but so aware of his eyes on her that her heart pounded in her ears.

She turned a corner and paused for a moment, her back against the wall. Only one other man had ever made her feel this flustered, and that meant she was in danger. Serious danger. The last man who'd made her feel this way had nearly destroyed her life, and she'd come too far to let that happen again.

But showing him the cafeteria wasn't a date. It didn't mean anything. Maybe it was better if she didn't let it go beyond that. She didn't believe in love at first sight. Lust, maybe, but in the past that had only brought consequences she hadn't been ready for.

She took a breath and continued down the hallway. She'd checked in on two more patients before her aide, Aria, caught up to her.

"Sorry, another aide and I were helping Dr. Gibson." Her small nose wrinkled. "The patient threw up everywhere and we had to change the bedding."

"Not Mrs. Carson, is it?" Kendall had checked on Lydia Carson moments before she'd talked to Wylen.

"No." Aria smiled, her dark, gently tilted eyes becoming dreamy. "Still, I'd clean up for Dr. Gibson any time. He's amazing."

Kendall laughed, hoping she didn't look that dreamy when she thought about Wylen. "Little old for you, don't you think?"

"Hey, I'm twenty. Only a year younger than you."

"Oh, right." So much had happened in her life that Kendall sometimes forgot she was still so young. She normally felt years older than most of the nurses near her age. Part of that was the way she'd crammed in her education, but most of it was a result of her life events and how they'd permanently changed her.

"Dr. Gibson isn't thirty yet, I don't think," Aria went on. "I heard some of the other nurses talking. They also said he isn't dating anyone."

Great, now everyone was after Dr. Gorgeous. Yet one more reason for Kendall to look the other way. Maybe she should ask Elsie to set her up with Payden after all. If only he weren't so obviously in love with Elsie. Some girls didn't know a good thing when it stared them in the face.

Well, Kendall didn't need any of them. It wasn't as if she wanted to get married right away. She'd learned a thing or two in the past three years.

"Come on, let's get back to work," she told her aide.

Aria nodded and followed her distractedly down the hall.

Lunchtime had ended up being a bust. When Wylen didn't show up at the nurses' station, she asked around and learned that a new patient had been admitted with digestive problems, and he was working with the experienced gastroenterologist assigned to the case. Kendall wasn't unhappy. It was better this way.

Before she could grab her home lunch from the fridge, the charge nurse motioned her over. "Hey, could you go talk to the patient in room 258? I think she's having a panic attack, and needs someone a little less . . . well, you know how Fiona is."

Kendall knew. The older nurse was the picture of efficiency, but her bedside manner was too terse for most patients, especially for the young ones.

"I know you're supposed to be heading out to lunch," the charge nurse added. "But if you could talk to her for a few minutes until the doctors finish looking at her test results, I think it would really help. They did a bunch down in the ER before admitting her."

"Okay. I'll see what I can do." But why she'd been chosen from all the nurses on staff, Kendall hadn't a clue. She started down the hall with the other woman.

Her confusion must have shown in her voice because the charge nurse added, "It's just this patient is very young, and you're the only one besides me with the extra training she needs."

Kendall's mouth went suddenly dry. She knew what that meant. They weren't in the delivery ward, so they didn't see many expectant mothers, especially not ones planning to place their babies for adoption. Kendall had taken the extra classes mostly out of curiosity, but also because she'd wanted to be prepared in case she ever had a patient who might need extra handling.

"Her name is Sage." The charge nurse nodded as if she'd covered everything important and peeled away to another corridor.

Kendall reached the room, taking a deep breath before going inside. Preparing herself.

The woman in the bed wasn't just young—she was a child, really, maybe sixteen or seventeen. Her stomach jutted uncomfortably from her small frame, and her blue eyes in her bloated face looked panicked. Brown bangs matted to her perspiring forehead. An aide patted her shoulder as her breaths came fast and shallow. Her nurse, Fiona, stood nearby, a disapproving expression on her face. She'd probably told the child to relax and had only scared her more. Where were the girl's parents?

Kendall motioned to the aide to leave and smiled at Fiona as the woman's pager went off. "It's the charge nurse," Fiona said, "can you stay here for a bit with Sage? I've taken her vitals. She and the baby are fine, but she needs to calm down. I'll go find her doctor and see if we can give her anything more."

Kendall waited until Fiona left before muttering, "Calm down. Easy for her to say. She's not pregnant."

Sage stared at her for several seconds before smiling slightly.

"Oops, did I say that aloud?" Kendall faked innocence.

"She's judging me," Sage wheezed through her tortured breaths. "They all judge me."

"Not everyone. I don't." Kendall stepped closer to the bed. "When are you due?"

"Three months," Sage panted. "And before you ask, yes, I'm giving her up."

"No, you're not."

"What?" The girl blinked at her.

"You're not giving her up. You're giving her a chance. The best chance." Kendall reached for her hand.

The girl resisted for a minute, then relaxed. Tears started down her cheeks, and she nodded vigorously. "My dad says I'm being selfish and that it's my duty to take care of her, and my mom just cries. They don't understand that it's for her. I love her so much."

Kendall couldn't help the tears escaping her own eyes. "I can see that you do."

She sat there for ten minutes, holding the girl's hand and chatting about nothing important. Sage's breathing gradually slowed to match Kendall's. They started talking about her friends and the baby's father, who she was still dating, and Kendall admired the ultrasound image that someone had given Sage.

Minutes later, a harried-looking woman with the same green eyes and brown hair burst into the room and rushed over to the bed. "Why are you here?" she demanded of Sage. "What happened?" Tension crackled in the air. "Did you fall? Did that boy do something?"

Sage's breath came more rapidly again, and Kendall put a hand on the girl's shoulder. "I'm going out in the hall for a moment to talk to your mother and see if Fiona found your doctor, okay? You sit here and close your eyes for a minute. I'll be right outside the door if you need me."

Sage gave her a look of pure gratitude as Kendall urged the mother from the room.

Outside in the hallway, Kendall said, "Your daughter's stable. But she's having a little trouble breathing, and she's also experiencing some stomach pain that doesn't seem related to the pregnancy, so that's why she's here. They've already taken tests down in the emergency room and the doctors are following up on that. She's been given a mild pain medication that's safe for the baby. The most important thing right now is to help her relax, to breathe slowly. So we want to talk very calmly and quietly around her. That will help a lot. We are monitoring her every minute, and we have oxygen in case she needs it. The doctor will go over the tests with you as soon as he gets here, but maybe before that, you could sit in there with her and watch a little TV, if she wants. No talking about anything stressful, though."

The mother wilted. "I'm sorry. I was just so worried. She's so little to be having a baby, and I—" She broke off and started to cry. Kendall did the only thing she could do: hug her and pat her back until the sobs stopped. She was still patting the mother's back when Wylen showed up with Fiona and two other doctors.

Kendall went inside with them to make sure Sage was still breathing fine. She was. "I'm going to lunch now," she told the girl, "but I'll come back to check on you later."

Ignoring Fiona's icy stare, Kendall exited the room. But not before she saw Wylen smiling at her.

Go away, she told him in her mind.

After being with Sage, Kendall couldn't stay at the hospital another second. She grabbed her lunch from the fridge and drove twenty minutes to the block where Lily's House sat at the end of the street. But she didn't drive all the way to Lily's. Instead, she parked at the beginning of the road across from a house on the corner with a fenced in yard. She didn't often allow herself the luxury of coming here uninvited, but sometimes when she had this desperate feeling, it helped her focus. To remember where she'd come from and how far.

In the back yard of the house, young children were out playing on the swing set and in the sandbox, and Kendall had to focus hard to see which was Teisha. The little girl was younger than the other preschoolers—only two and a half—but she was confident and able. At last, Kendall spotted Teisha in the sandbox, her thin brown hair still wispy as Kendall's blond hair had been well into her fifth year. The child wore an elastic in her hair, a bow clinging precariously to it, cute jean shorts, and a pink top with words Kendall couldn't read. Susan was there, of course; she was never far from Teisha's side. The other children would eventually go home, but Teisha was lucky to have Susan all the time.

Kendall didn't know if Susan ever saw her here on the very few times she'd given into the urge to come without notice, but if so, she hadn't said anything on their official visits. On those days, Kendall used the front door, and she and Susan would walk Teisha to a nearby park, her chubby hands holding each of theirs. They'd play on the swings and inside the little fort, and usually share a treat. Or sometimes they'd walk to Lily's house and visit the horses in the field.

They'd done this weekly since the adoption, except for the first six months when Kendall could only grieve her loss. During those six months, Susan had brought the baby to her at Lily's House monthly as she'd promised in their contract. Not that the contract really mattered to either of them because Kendall had helped out in Susan's preschool, and they'd become close friends before Kendall had chosen her as her baby's adoptive mother.

Teisha's laugh carried to the car, filling Kendall with light. Susan picked her up, sand and all, and whirled her around. This is what Kendall had wanted for her baby. A full-time mommy who wanted a baby more than she wanted anything else. And a daddy who supported her and loved her. Teisha had loving grandparents, cousins galore, and maybe a new little brother soon, if their second adoption worked out.

Kendall had made so many poor decisions, but this wasn't one of them. She'd been fortunate to find Susan and her husband, Jasper, a family who was willing to allow her to share a part in her baby's life. Susan believed that there could never be too many people loving a child, and Kendall was careful never to ask too much. So Teisha knew that Kendall was her birth mommy, and that Susan was her real mommy. She called them Kendamom and Mommy. It worked for both of them.

Susan spied her and waved. Kendall climbed from the car, feeling a little awkward, but Susan was smiling, the highlights in her short brown hair glistening in the sun. Teisha kicked to get down, so Susan set her back into the sandbox in the middle of a group of children and met Kendall at the fence.

"I'm sorry," Kendall said, tears coming to her eyes. "I just needed . . . It's been a rough day. I wanted to see her." But that wasn't quite right. "I wanted to see her happy with you."

Susan reached across the fence and clasped Kendall's arm. "You want to come in for a minute? Or I could bring Teisha over."

Kendall shook her head. "No, she looks happy, and I don't want to interrupt her play. Besides, I have to get back to the hospital." She might not make it back on time if she gave into the temptation to play with Teisha.

"I could have texted you pictures. Saved you the drive." Susan did that all the time, and Kendall should have thought to ask. "And we can move up our next visit,"

Susan added. "If you want. Teisha's learned another letter in the alphabet. She'll be excited to show you. Plus, she's been talking about going to see the horses again."

"I'd like that." Kendall felt a gratitude too large to contain that Susan loved her and was confident enough to maintain their friendship and share her daughter. Kendall might feel more like a big sister on the visits, but that was how it should be.

"Tomorrow night works for us, if you're not busy. That's Thursday, right?" Susan laughed. "Sometimes my weekdays run together a bit."

"I know what you mean. But that works. I'll text you when I leave the hospital."

"Sounds great." Susan glanced at her watch. "I'd better get these kids inside. Their parents will be here soon to pick them up, and we still have a project to finish."

Kendall drove back to the hospital, finishing her sandwich on the way. She hadn't been driving a minute before her phone started buzzing with texts from Susan. Kendall knew they'd be pictures of Teisha, and she smiled.

Halla didn't tell Oliver about her trip. She'd meant to, but they only talked twice before she had to leave, and the first time he'd been heading out the door with his family. When he'd tried to call back, she was shopping, and it wasn't as if she could talk about her decision in front of a bunch of strangers. After she got home it felt weird to call him back about it. But she knew he was planning to stay in Boise until Sunday morning, so there was still time.

Early Friday morning, before anyone should ever be awake, she dropped Elsie off at the café so Elsie could throw together more soup and a chicken salad while Halla traded vehicles with Bianca. Bianca helped her move the suitcases, cooler, and boxes of food into the back of her blue truck, and then Halla headed over to Lily's house, where Lily gave her detailed instructions on how to use the popup camper. When Halla had written copious notes about safety and demonstrated that she knew how to set up the camper—three times, no less—she was finally on her way back to the Eats and Treats to pick up Elsie.

They left Phoenix at ten minutes after six, and Elsie kept Halla laughing as she talked about everything and anything, which kept Halla's mind away from the gravity of what she was doing. Elsie offered to take a turn at the wheel, but Halla knew Elsie's difficulty in parking even her tiny car and refused. They stopped three times for snacks and gas and to use the restroom, which barely added to their total driving time in the end. Bianca's truck didn't seem fazed by the load it pulled.

They reached Nampa at nine, having lost one hour through changing time zones, and both of them were ravenous. "We should stop for dinner before we get to Lily's friend's house," Elsie said as they pulled off the freeway. "Once we set up, I don't think we'll feel like making anything."

"Good idea. Where?"

Elsie shrugged. "You're the one who lived here. Where did you like to go?"

A sinking sensation grew in Halla's chest. "I don't remember going out anyplace."

Elsie was quiet a moment. "It's been a long time. Let's drive around a bit. Maybe something will come to you. Or maybe we'll see something that looks appealing."

The traffic was busy, as Halla would expect for a Friday night. With hands tight on the steering wheel, she tried to focus on both her driving and the businesses lining the street, but nothing looked familiar in the quickly fading light. She drove down 11th Avenue and turned right when most of the other cars did, thinking to stop at the next fast food restaurant they passed.

"Such a small city, isn't it?" Elsie asked. "Compared to Phoenix."

For some reason, that made Halla defensive, and it took effort not to respond. After all, she cared nothing for this town. It had done zero to help her or to punish her father. She'd hoped never to see it again. "Well, I'm sure they have some good restaurants. I mean, something better than the fast food places we've already passed. It's getting late, but it's a Friday night. We should be able to find—" She broke off as her eyes grazed a building a short distance down the road. That was familiar. Something opened up in her chest, something wide and deep and aching.

She slowed, craning her neck and watching traffic to move over. Carefully, she turned into the parking lot.

"Front Burner Burgers?" Elsie asked. "Is it any good?"

"Not sure."

The squat building looked like something that came from a past era. Halla's memory had the building being a bright red and white instead of the dull blue it was now, and there had been a statue of a boy biting into a huge hamburger outside that was missing now, but it was obviously the same building.

"I remember eating here," she said. "I don't know if it was the same restaurant, but it sold hamburgers then too."

Elsie cocked her head as she studied the building. "I think every town has one of these places. They come and go. Changing a few menu items every time they change ownership. Should we go in?"

"I don't know . . . well, yes, let's do go in. I'm curious

to see inside. If we don't like the looks of it, we can leave." Halla pulled on her favorite threadbare sweatshirt. She wasn't exactly cold, but even the air in the truck was a lot cooler than in Arizona. "I'm not sure when I was here or who I came with, but I think maybe some high school friends." That sounded right. She couldn't remember her father bringing the family. He wouldn't have let her come on her own, but he couldn't have known if she'd left the school grounds at lunchtime. She parked the truck as well as she could, taking up two spaces and then some on one edge. "At least they have a lot of parking space."

"They don't seem to be busy." Elsie made a face. "I hope that's not a bad sign."

"Guess we'll find out. If we decide to stay, it certainly won't be the worst place we've ever eaten." Halla meant it to be funny, but Elsie frowned. "Sorry," Halla added quickly. Both of them had spent enough time on the street for that to take on a whole new meaning.

Elsie made a slight dismissive noise. "Ah, never mind me. I'm just annoyed that Payden hasn't texted me to say if he's going to accept the counter offer on the house, or if he'll counter it right back."

Halla paused with her hand on the door handle. "Well, he was nice to bring us pizza last night. And wasn't he in there chopping onions for what seemed like an hour? That's dedication. I'm sure you'll be the first to know what he decides."

"Maybe not." Elsie was frowning now.

"Why? You guys have a fight?"

"No. But he did put anchovies on the pizza. Yuck!" Elsie pushed open her door, ending the conversation, but

Halla knew there was more than anchovies that had upset her sister. Especially when they'd only been on Payden's half of the pizza.

Inside the restaurant, a heavenly aroma wrapped around Halla, making her stomach growl and peeling away the years . . . and suddenly she was standing in this very spot not only with Elsie but with a small knot of friends, whose names she mostly didn't remember. Except for Amy, the only one she'd ever told the truth to about her dad, and Peter, a boy Halla had liked—until he'd tried to call the house.

Halla felt Elsie's hand on her back. "You okay?" she whispered.

The dual vision disappeared. "Yeah. Smells good doesn't it?"

"Like a slice of heaven. Anything that smells this good has to taste good too."

"What are you going to have?"

"What did you have when you came here?"

Halla thought a moment. "A hamburger."

"Let's have that, then."

"It's not going to be the same."

"That's okay. It doesn't have to be exactly like it was back then to trigger memories."

Halla snorted. "If there are any to trigger." But being here had triggered some already.

"I haven't had a hamburger in a year, at least," Elsie admitted.

"Neither have I." Though that was mostly because Elsie cooked for them.

"Hey, look, they have milkshakes. Now that sounds

good." When Halla hesitated, Elsie added, "They have strawberry, your favorite."

"It's not my favorite. And its ice cream, I like, not shakes."

Elsie wrinkled her freckled nose. "Same thing."

"No, it's not."

But Halla did order a strawberry shake because the picture looked good and they didn't have ice cream alone. Her burger she ordered with mustard and ketchup and no weird special sauce. They paid several dollars more than at a chain fast food restaurant, but when the lady at the counter carried over their tray, Halla saw at once that the price was a bargain.

The hamburgers were huge, with two thick, juicy slices of enormous tomatoes, grilled onions, dill pickles that meant business, and lettuce that could have garnered good reviews in a commercial. The beefsteak fries were so plentiful Halla knew she'd never be able to eat them all.

"Amazing," Elsie said, speaking for both of them.

They reached for their burgers and as she took several bites, Halla experienced a weird flashback moment. The memory wasn't clear, but she recalled laughing and eating and the juicy goodness of the hamburgers.

Maybe coming to Idaho wouldn't be as painful as she expected. Maybe she could look up her friends and find out where they were now. It could be good for her memories.

Elsie put down her burger. "He might not tell me first."

"What? Oh, Payden. Why not?"

"Well, on Wednesday when we saw the house, I tried to set him up."

"Again? When are you going to stop that? He's a grown man. He can find his own dates."

"I know, but well . . ." Elsie stared down at her lap.

"Well what?"

"He told me he had it covered. Apparently, he has something 'in the works.' Those were his exact words."

"That could mean a lot of things."

"No, it meant a woman." Elsie reached in her pocket and shoved her phone under Halla's nose. "What if I hate her? What if she objects to us being friends?"

Halla stared at the perky blond woman peering out at her from the screen. "She doesn't look mean. Payden wouldn't pick anyone terrible, right?" Halla hadn't believed Payden would choose anyone except Elsie, but maybe he'd grown tired of always being her second choice.

"I guess." Elsie took back the phone, giving the screen a baleful look before turning it off.

Halla debated on whether or not she should say more about Payden. She reached for her shake instead, popping off the dome lid. The ice cream, pinkened with fresh strawberries, didn't look like a shake at all. It was so thick the mixture would have to be spooned up with one of the long red spoons the cashier had put on their tray. Halla reached for the spoon and took a tentative bite. Flavor burst over her tongue. She vaguely remembered eating a shake like this with a red spoon. More than once. Maybe. But when?

Her world stuttered, blinking between now and the

past. The hand she looked down at wasn't hers, but a child's. And she wasn't alone. Halla's heart pounded. Her breath came too fast, sounding loud in her ears. Nothing else registered. Just the ice cream, the beating of her heart, the small hand. She was afraid of what she'd see—who she'd see—if she looked up. But she had to know. She dragged her gaze upward—only to find Elsie staring back at her.

Halla felt sick. She couldn't eat this ice cream or the rest of her fries, and she certainly couldn't stay a minute longer in the restaurant. "Excuse me. I'll be in the truck when you're finished."

She fled. No walking sedately for her. Instead, there was a full-out sprint to the door and to the truck. Yanking open the door, she lifted herself inside and shut it again, leaning her head against the steering wheel, dragging in breaths and fighting sobs.

Gradually, Halla regained control. Her breathing steadied, and she watched Elsie walking calmly across the parking lot, their shake cups in her hands. She opened the door and climbed inside.

"Okay, that was weird," Elsie said.

"Sorry. It was all too much." Halla felt cold now and rubbed her hands up and down her arms over the material of her sweatshirt.

"You're tired, is all. You should have let me drive while you had the chance." Elsie thumbed behind them at the popup camper. "Because, there's no way I'm pulling that monstrosity in any kind of traffic."

She put Halla's shake in the drink holder. "I tossed the fries, but I knew you'd want this."

Halla murmured an insincere thank-you as she turned

on her phone's GPS. But two minutes later, driving down the street, the cup was in her lap and she was spooning up mouthfuls at every stoplight. The ice cream was delicious. Maybe the best she'd ever had. It must have been that place, not the milkshake, that evoked the memories.

"So what happened?" Elsie asked.

"It was a memory. Several of them. I think I've been there more than once." She assumed one of her friends had suggested the place, but it was far from the school, so maybe something else had been in play. Exactly what, she couldn't begin to guess. "I remembered a couple friends. I'll try to look them up later."

Within minutes they pulled up to the calm cul-de-sac where Lily's friend lived. As Lily had instructed, Halla pulled into the deserted lot next door, rolled over the dirt and weeds, and parked the camper as close to the house as possible. Halla would have rather set up in their driveway, but that would be an inconvenience for the family, and she was fairly certain she could set up well enough in the dirt, even in the fading light.

She'd barely jumped down from the truck when Monica, a petite, olive-skinned beauty with long black hair that curled slightly on the ends, hurried up to meet them. "Hi," she greeted, thrusting her hand out at Halla, her wide mouth stretched in a friendly smile. "I'm Monica. You must be Halla."

"I am. And this is Elsie," she added as Elsie came around the truck and joined them.

"I recognize you both from the Christmas cards."

Halla laughed. "Yeah, Lily likes to get as many of us together as possible. Are you sure we won't be a bother?"

"Of course not. We have all this free space." Monica eyed the camper suspiciously. "But you really should come in to sleep. My boys have a great room with twin beds I'd be happy to have you use. This can't be all that comfortable."

Halla was prepared for the offer. "That's so nice of you, but we don't know how long we'll be, or how late we'll be out. It's been a long time since I've been here and . . ." And what? Talked to Mommy dearest?

Monica gave her a sympathetic look that told Halla she understood why she was in town. Anyone in Nampa who recognized her name probably would. "At least wait until my husband comes home," Monica suggested, "so he can help you set up. He's at a neighbor's. Why don't you come in and chat until he gets home?"

"Oh, but you need to watch this." Halla gave her a grin that might be a little too forced. "It's a snap to put up, or least as long as we still have a little light." That was a stretch because it was almost dark, but Monica didn't protest further.

Halla checked the level of the camper and ended up moving one wheel up on some blocks Lily had provided. From there it was a matter of leveling the front to end with a built-in leveling bar, pulling down the jacks in each of the four corners, pulling out the beds, adjusting the fabric, and using the winch to raise the ceiling. It took time, but none of it was difficult.

"Nice," said Monica, as she accepted the power plug from Halla. "I know right where to plug this."

"Wait, here's the adapter," Halla said. "Apparently this is a thirty amp, and a regular house hookup is twenty."

Monica laughed. "Yeah, I'll just pretend I know what all that means."

Halla grinned at her. "That's what I did when Lily explained."

"But it was really easy to put up." Elsie stood with her hands on her hips, looking pleased. "Let's go inside and see what it's like." Standing on her tiptoes, she pulled her suitcase from the bed of the truck.

"I'll leave you girls to it," Monica said. "If you need anything, please let me know, okay? And I'd love to have you both over for dinner tomorrow night, if you don't have other plans."

"That is so kind of you," Elsie said. "Can we let you know tomorrow? We're just kind of playing it by ear right now. Maybe we can call you before two?"

"Absolutely. Or just show up. I have five kids, so I always make plenty." With another friendly smile that made her dark eyes glow, Monica strode back to her house with the hookups to both the water and the electricity in her hands.

"She's super nice," Elsie said.

"She is. I wonder how she knows Lily."

"They were in college together, I believe." Elsie opened the door to the camper and disappeared inside. A happy squeal followed. "This is so cool. Which bed to you want?"

Halla grabbed her suitcase and followed her inside. "Whichever. Wow, this is certainly cozy."

"Reminds me of that tiny apartment we first shared with Lily before getting the house."

"That wasn't quite this small." Halla laughed as good memories flooded her. They'd all slept crammed into a bedroom on mattresses lined across the floor, and she'd loved it. She'd felt so much safer than under a park bench or at her parents' house—and a lot less lonely.

"I'll take the little bit bigger bed then, if you don't care. I like to spread out. Looks like Lily has bedding for us in these huge zip bags." Elsie dropped her suitcase on the floor and began making her bed.

"I think this is for clothes." Halla pointed to a collapsible cloth shelf that hung down from the ceiling.

"I think I'll leave my clothes in my suitcase on the bed for now. Plenty of room. So that's all yours if you want it."

Settling in didn't take long. Halla put her clothes in the collapsible shelf. She hadn't brought much. A few pairs of pants, a skirt just in case, underclothes, socks and her favorite five tops. The shelf fit all this and her bag of toiletries. She put the two pairs of shoes in the hollow space inside one of the bench seats next to the table, where additional blankets in plastic were also stored. They had a little trouble putting up the shower curtain around the toilet/shower combo, but it gave at least a semblance of privacy. Every bit of the camper was organized, and Lily had gone out of her way to add hooks and plastic holders to make it more comfortable.

These days when Lily took her foster teens camping, Halla knew Lily would stay in the camper with Mario and her two biological children, now three and nine, and a couple of the younger fosters, or perhaps an older girl who was afraid of bugs. The other girls pitched tents, and together with Lily they did most of the cooking outside. It had been a different camper back when Halla had lived at Lily's House, but those times had created memories that she still thought of fondly. She hoped this trip would turn out the same. If not because of her mother, which wasn't likely anyway, then because of Oliver.

Thinking of him, Halla went to grab her laptop from the truck, and while she was there, she parked the vehicle on the street next to the curb instead of in the field near the camper. Briefly, she toyed with the idea of driving by her parents' house, though she didn't look too closely at the thought. First she needed to talk to Oliver.

Inside the popup, she found Elsie tucking the remains of her shake in the freezer section, the cup cut down to make it fit. "You want me to store your shake? Mine's practically melted."

Halla snorted. "What shake? I ate it all."

"I should have known." Elsie laughed and set to arranging the contents of the refrigerator.

As Halla sat on one of the bench seats at the small table and opened her laptop, Elsie asked, "So when do you think you'll see Oliver? He could come over now. I mean it's late and I'm exhausted, which is kind of weird seeing that the only thing I did all day was sit, but I'd be excited to meet him in person."

If Elsie was excited to meet him, Halla was over the moon. But she was also worried because there was a huge chance he might not be anything like she thought. She'd dated enough people after meeting them online to know that much.

"You have every right to be exhausted," Halla told Elsie. "You got up super early to cook all that food and to get the dry ice for the cooler. Plus, you kept me awake the whole trip. Anyway, I'm dead on my feet, so I'd rather him not come over tonight. I want to look my best when we meet for the first time. In fact, I might sleep here on this bench. Getting up seems like too much work."

"You talk to Oliver and I'll make your bed."

Halla came to her feet, albeit a bit more slowly than she intended. "No, I can do it." Making her bed actually sounded better than talking to Oliver. And maybe she'd take a nap first. A nap that lasted all night.

Because what was she going to say? "Hi, and by the way, I know I didn't tell you before, but I'm in Nampa? Please come and see me?" No, not even close.

"I don't mind. Sit down." Elsie peered at her. "Wait a minute. You didn't tell him! Halla Jenkins. I can't believe you. He's the reason you're here."

"No, I'm here to see my mother."

"But he suggested it—and you do want to see him. I *know* you do!"

Halla slumped back into her seat. "Yeah. Pretty pathetic. I just . . . I like him so much, and what if he's . . . ."

"Shorter than you? A hunchback? Has stinky breath?" Elsie puffed out an exasperated sigh. "Seriously, Halla? You've seen him online quite a lot, and any faults he has, it won't be any worse than a guy you don't yet know. If it's meant to be, you'll work out whatever it is."

"But I don't want to lose him." Even saying the words made Halla feel stupid.

Elsie put her hands on her hips. "What on earth are you talking about?"

"We talk all the time. I bounce my ideas off him. What if in person all that electricity is gone? What if he's just . . ."

"An ordinary guy?" Elsie sat across from her and stared at her earnestly. "Look, you have to find out, because right now you compare him to every guy you meet, to their detriment. You need to know what he's like in person so you can decide if he's someone special or if he's going to be a friend."

"You mean like Payden?"

Elsie bit her lip and thought a moment. "Yes, like Payden. And you see how much fun we have. So even if he's not *the one*, you don't have to lose him. And who knows, maybe he's better in person."

Halla rolled her eyes. "I hope not too much better, or he won't like me." She looked down at her camouflage pants, her brown tank top, and the thin sweatshirt she'd put on before going into the restaurant.

Elsie laughed. "Oh, now I see how it is. You're chicken. You had better contact him—or I will."

Halla didn't protest because she knew Elsie had ways of following through. She probably had Oliver's number on speed-dial.

"Go make my bed," Halla retorted. "Or go lie down."

Elsie smirked at her before moving away.

Okay, it was now or never. Halla pulled her laptop closer. Why was her heart banging against her chest again? Was it because she was almost close enough to finally touch him?

8

Halla pulled up Google Hangouts, but before she could click on Oliver's face, a video call came through from Kendall. Halla clicked on it eagerly.

"Hey, Kendall," she said as their roommate's image appeared on the screen. "What's up?"

Elsie came over from the bed. "You're supposed to be calling Oliver," she said in a threatening whisper.

"Kendall called me." Halla let a little irritation seep into her voice but not too much because Elsie only wanted to help. "What am I supposed to do? Ignore her?"

"Oh," Elsie pushed in next to her on the seat.

"I can hear you, you know," Kendall said. "Should I call another time?"

"No," Halla and Elsie chimed together.

Kendall heaved a sigh. "Good, because I need advice. And I didn't want to ask in a text." Setting her elbow on the table in front of her, she let her chin fall onto her hand. "Guess who asked me out today?"

"Dr. Gorgeous!" Halla and Elsie chimed together.

"Yep," Kendall said, "and I told him no."

"You what!" Elsie shrieked. "That makes no sense at all. You've been drooling over him all week."

"Yeah, me and all the single nurses and patients," Kendall muttered. "Anyway, he only asked me because he stood me up for lunch again, and it wasn't even a lunch date—I was only going to show him around the cafeteria. I don't need a pity date."

"Okaaaay," Elsie dragged out the word. "Whatever you say."

"I get it," Halla said. "You really like him. And that scares you."

She'd seen this before in her foster sisters. Once you'd been hurt, it was easy to date a man who wouldn't steal your heart, but if there was any chance you might lose yourself, the choice became harder. In a smaller way, Halla had the same reluctance to meet Oliver, and she'd never had any man break her heart. No, her parents had taken care of that.

After several long seconds of silence, Kendall said, "Well, maybe. But either way, I'm not going out just because he feels bad about not having time to go to the cafeteria. What do I care if he knows the way? If he gets hungry, he can find his own way or ask someone else."

"That's only an excuse," Elsie said. "I mean, he got through medical school, so I'm fairly certain he can find his own way to the cafeteria."

"She's got a point," Halla agreed.

Kendall frowned. "So you think I should have said yes?"

"Duh," Elsie said. Then she pasted on an innocent expression. "I mean, yes. Of course."

Halla shrugged. "I think you have to go with your gut. If you're getting a bad feeling about it, maybe you shouldn't."

Elsie grimaced at her. "Are you talking about you or about her?" To Kendall, she added, "Halla still hasn't told Oliver she was coming, much less that we're here."

"Seriously?" Kendall gaped at Halla. "That's more pathetic than me turning down the man of my dreams because I'm afraid I'll like him too much."

"You still didn't tell us what your gut is saying," Halla insisted.

Kendall's grin didn't quite reach her eyes. "My gut says I'm going to fall head-over-heels in love with Wylan, and he's going to break my heart."

Elsie threw her hands in the air. "Okay, whatever you say, but I think you should give him a chance. I'm going to make Halla's bed now. See you later, Kendall. Love you!" She scooted off the bench.

Kendall leaned close to the screen and said softly, "Look who's talking. What about her ever giving poor Payden a chance?"

Halla lifted her gaze to Elsie, but she apparently hadn't heard Kendall's whisper. "I know. Well, good luck with Dr. Gorgeous."

"You too—with Oliver."

Halla disconnected and before she could change her mind, she clicked on Oliver's face, and then on the video icon. He answered right away. "Hi, beautiful."

Immediately, she did feel beautiful. Strange when two seconds before she'd felt like someone who'd slept too little before driving fourteen hours across three states in a truck, someone who had set up a popup camper not once but four times in the same day. Yet with a single word from Oliver, all that vanished.

"Hi, yourself," she said.

His image was narrow on her computer screen, which meant he was on his phone. "I'm glad you called," he said, "but my battery's about to die. Let me go inside and call you back on my laptop."

"Okay." She caught a glimpse of a basketball and two tow-headed children before the video call disconnected.

He called back within a minute. "Sorry about that."

"I take it you're at your mom's?"

"Yep. I'm still planning on leaving Sunday morning."

She was glad that hadn't changed at least. "What did you do today? Anything fun?"

His blue eyes crinkled in that way she loved. "Yeah, actually. My brother and brother-in-law got off early from work, and we went biking this afternoon. But now they're on baby duty while their wives and my mother go out to yoga or something. We're teaching the kids to play basketball, but since all three of them are five or under, it's not going very well." He didn't appear too unhappy about it.

Halla pulled her knees up to her chest and leaned back, imagining him with the kids. "Sounds like a real party."

His face sobered. "I had no idea everyone would be so glad about Mom and me. It was the right thing to do."

"Speaking of that," she said before he could start

thanking her. "I have some news myself." She released her legs and leaned closer to her computer, too nervous to maintain the casual pose.

"Okay, let's have it, but I hope it's good. You look a little . . ."

Her hands fisted in her lap. "A little what?" She hadn't meant to sound so sharp.

He chuckled. "A little tired is all. I can always tell. Your eyes get that heavy look and—" He broke off and shook his head. "Never mind. Tell me what's going on. But wait, I just noticed something. Is that the side of a tent I see behind you? Are you in a tent trailer?"

"It's Lily's," Halla told him.

He started to speak, but voices drowned out whatever he was trying to say. Halla heard banging, as if someone had pushed a door open too hard. Oliver's gaze strayed from the screen as the voices of children reached her ears.

He started to smile, but then his eyes went wide. "No, Clara. No. Don't throw that!" His image in the screen shook momentarily before turning upside down and disappearing into darkness.

"Oliver?" Halla said in case he could still hear her.

Nothing.

She waited for a moment to see if he'd call her back. Maybe the kids had accidentally shut his laptop and it had gone to sleep.

He didn't call back, so she called him. No answer.

"What happened?" Elsie asked, coming from the bed she'd finished making.

"Not sure. We were weirdly disconnected."

Elsie laughed. "Just your luck."

Halla had to agree.

Elsie took her toothbrush to the sink. "Guess we'll have to get an early start tomorrow instead of figuring out when to meet with him tonight."

"Yeah, right." Leaving her laptop on, Halla arose to dress for bed. She hoped Oliver not calling wasn't a sign that she should turn around and run back to Phoenix. "Oh, that reminds me." She picked up her keys from the table. "There are two keys for the door, so here's one. In case we're separated."

"We'd better be separated." Elsie gave her a saucy grin. "Because I'm sure Oliver won't want to kiss you in front of me—at least not at first."

"That's assuming any kissing will be going on at all," Halla shot back. "I mean, it hasn't with you and Payden all these years. We might be like you two."

Elsie froze, her toothbrush still in her mouth. Slowly, she pulled it out and spat in the sink. "Right."

A little slice of excitement blotted out some of Halla's disappointment over Oliver. "Wait, did you kiss Payden?" How long had she hoped something like this would happen?

"No, I most certainly didn't," huffed Elsie. "You know I don't believe in leading him on."

"So you know how he feels about you?"

Elsie stared. "I'm his friend. End of story." With that, she rinsed her mouth and headed toward her bed.

"Okay, already," Halla murmured under her breath. There was more to that story, though, and she was going to find out what. But not at the moment. Tonight she'd try to sleep and decide what to tell Oliver and how to approach her mother. There would be plenty of time to talk to Elsie once those things were underway.

She changed into her Tweetie nightshirt, paring it with shorts she didn't normally use at home. Camping was different, and the camouflage shorts could pass for daywear if needed.

"You're not cold, are you?" she asked Elsie, who was pulling on sweats.

"No. It's actually warm in here after baking in the sun all day, but it might get chilly at night and you know how I toss off covers."

Halla curled up in her own bed, which was more spacious than she'd expected after Elsie's comment about taking the larger bed. Her eyelids tugged downward as her mouth opened in a huge yawn. It took more effort than it should have to pull the blanket over her bare legs. Not even ten yet—well, eleven in Phoenix—and here she was twenty minutes away from Oliver and she was sleeping instead of going to meet him for the first time? Crazy.

Her phone buzzed with a text, and she grabbed it from under the blanket to see a number she didn't recognize.

Hey, it's Oliver. Sorry about the disconnect. The kids hit my computer with a basketball and it pretty much exploded. My computer guru brother-in-law is looking at it. I'm charging my phone now. It'll be a minute before there's enough juice for a video chat. Do you want to wait, or should we talk tomorrow?

She suspected he'd run right over if she told him where she was, but she wanted to shower before she saw him. *Tomorrow will be okay,* she typed back.

Okay. Tomorrow. Can it be early? We're playing racquet-ball after breakfast.

She wanted to tell him he couldn't play racquetball, but that would mean she'd have to explain why. And what if he chose racquetball over her? *Sure. Early is good.*

Great . . . But you are okay, right?

Yeah. Just been a long day. She wasn't about to say anything personal on whoever's phone he'd borrowed.

Rest up then. I'll call you in the morning. Good night.

Night.

Two seconds after they finished texting, all sleep fled. What was wrong with her? She wanted more than anything to see him, but she wasn't going to tell him she was in town until tomorrow? Was she totally insane? The bed suddenly felt too large.

She sat upright. Maybe there was still time to change her mind. "Elsie?" she asked. No answer. She hadn't really expected one. Elsie could fall asleep faster than anyone she knew.

Halla debated for ten minutes about what to do. Then she practically fell out of bed, grabbed her keys, and crept out of the camper. In the truck, she drove, knowing the way by heart, even though she'd never been to this part of Nampa before.

Eight and a half minutes later, she was driving down her parents' street. The small houses and well-kept flow-erbeds looked eerily the same, as if time had stopped here. Only the trees were taller and fuller. These were the people who'd failed her. The people who must have suspected what was going on at the end of the cul-de-sac but had done nothing to help her.

She hadn't gone to any of them when she'd climbed out of her window and fallen to the ground. Instead, she'd walked most of the night on freezing feet before passing out on a bench by the bus stop, too tired to care that she would probably never wake up. A patrol car had found her there in the wee hours of the morning, and the officer had driven her immediately to a hospital. A doctor put a cast on her arm and treated her for exposure, but she repeatedly refused to respond to any questions about her identity. She'd spent two blessed days in a warm bed, eating and drinking her fill until she was identified and her parents called.

Halla was suddenly cold. Ice cold. She turned the heat up high and inched down the road. Unlike the other houses, her parents' house had no trees in front. There were also probably none in the back yard. No trees to read under or for a child to climb. Trees only brought leaves to clean up, and every fall her father had cursed the neighbors and threw their leaves back over their fences.

The two-story house looked the same as she'd last seen it. From the yellow siding and white trim to the crack in the cement walk and the flowerbeds next to the house. She remembered the flowered couches inside and the scarred table in the kitchen. Would those also be the same? The garage would be full of her father's stuff, of course. His man cave where he often watched games and sometimes had friends over. Her mother and Halla had been forbidden entrance.

What would he do if she went up right now and knocked on the door? He was home because a car sat in the driveway, and he was usually the one who drove.

Her mother would probably be in bed, but he'd likely be reading the newspaper and having a nightcap, either in the garage or in the kitchen. She couldn't remember seeing him without either his newspaper or a drink of some kind, though he'd never been drunk that she remembered. Which made it all worse somehow.

Fury raged through her. She opened the truck door before she knew what she was doing, her bare feet stretching down to the road that still held the slightest hint of warmth from the day. Pebbles on the road bit into the soft flesh of her feet. Her eyes lifted to the window that had once been hers and fear shuddered through her.

"No," she said aloud.

She stared down at her Tweetie nightshirt that hid all but the merest hint of her camouflage shorts. The worn material was clearly visible by the slice of light coming from the open door of the truck. She most certainly wasn't going up to the door like this, and never alone. Never without a witness. Because any man who'd chain his fifteen-year-old daughter to a bed for six months wasn't someone to face by herself. How had her mother stayed with him all these years?

Because her mother was still there. Her flowers still grew in the flowerbeds, the pink miniature roses and white daisies that she'd loved, the ones her father always considered a waste of space.

Halla had turned to climb back inside the truck when a voice startled her. She stifled a gasp, the pounding of her heart easing a little as she realized it was a woman speaking. Not a man. Not her father.

She whirled and saw an older, muscular woman with

short, stiff-looking blond hair that was firmly stuck in a style that belonged to the eighties. "Excuse me?" Halla asked.

"Do you need directions?" The woman sounded friendly enough but cautious. In her wrinkled hands, she held a small plastic garbage bin between them like a weapon. "Are you lost?"

Halla stared at her, glancing at the house next to her parents from where she suspected the lady might have come. Was it the same woman who'd lived here almost eleven years ago? The hair was the same.

The woman smiled, and all doubt faded. Memories flooded over Halla. This woman had made cookies occasionally after school, and she'd often brought a small plate over to Halla and her mother. A kind woman. The only friend she remembered her mother having. A name came to her: Mrs. Moss.

Yet like the rest, she'd failed Halla. When Halla's father had appeared in Phoenix on Halla's trail, the state of Arizona had looked into the matter, and Mrs. Moss had told them things she'd seen. But she hadn't reported the abuse back when it mattered. She hadn't told authorities when a teenager had suddenly stopped going or coming home from school. During her imprisonment, Halla had sometimes peered out her window and had seen her mother talking with Mrs. Moss in the yard. Or even heard them from her room down in her mother's kitchen. But if she'd brought cookies then, Halla didn't know about it.

"I'm fine," Halla said, stepping closer to the truck. "I don't need directions. I know exactly where I am." *And who you are,* she wanted to add. The hate she was feeling probably wasn't healthy.

"Okay, then. Have a nice night." Mrs. Moss retreated to the curb but didn't go inside her house. Instead, she watched Halla intently as she drove away.

Once back at the camper, Halla pulled to the curb, forcing her hands from the steering wheel from which they seemed practically melded. The interior of the cab was stifling hot from the heat that still blasted out at her. What had she expected? That seeing her house would somehow free her? That maybe Oliver would sense what she was doing and come to her rescue? She hated women like that. She'd learned the hard way that the only way she could obtain what she needed was to act.

Pulling out her phone, she began a text to Oliver. She should have done this yesterday. If she had, he might be here with her now.

I'm here in Nampa. That's what I wanted to tell you.

She pushed send. There. She'd acted. Now it was up to him.

9

Oliver stared at the message on his phone, unable to believe his eyes. She was here. In Idaho. Close enough for him to get in the car and go to her.

Of course it was already three o'clock in the morning now, and she'd said to wait. If only he'd checked his phone earlier instead of letting it charge in his room while helping his brother-in-law with his computer, which they'd managed to get working but was now held together with duct tape. He'd have to buy another.

Later though, after he saw Halla.

She was here!

But why was she in a tent trailer or a popup camper—whatever they were calling them these days? She should be in a hotel. The camper meant she must have driven to Nampa. He shook his head, a smile on his face. He should have known. She was a do-it-yourselfer and never seemed afraid of anything.

Except when he'd suggested she visit her mother, which he'd been certain about for all of five minutes until she'd frozen up at the suggestion. He'd regretted the words the minute they'd left his mouth.

He should have invited her to meet him at the Grand Canyon or in Hawaii. Something that wasn't laden with terrible memories of the past. He'd been thinking only of himself, of how it made him feel when she shut down. He should have been thinking more of her. Of romance. Of their relationship.

What did it mean that she'd followed his advice?

No wonder she looked tired. After driving all day, anyone would be exhausted. Did he get points for noticing? Of course, he hadn't said what he was really thinking, which would have been "When you're tired, your eyes get that heavy-lidded look that makes me want to hold you and kiss you and imagine what it feels like to watch you sleep and wake up with you in my arms."

Not exactly something you say to a woman you've never been out with. She'd have probably run for the hills—or Phoenix at the least.

But she was *here!*

He wanted to jump in his car, drive to Nampa, and search every road until he found where her camper was. He kicked himself now for not flying to Phoenix to spend time with her in person. Not only had he made her come all this way, but he'd added the complication of her mother and her hometown when this meeting should be about them and only them.

At the time he'd thought of it, the idea had been sound. Because she didn't talk about her past, and she closed up every time it was mentioned—except for the public recitation she would jump into if forced to talk. Public stuff, with no real emotion or connection, as if she were telling a story of someone she knew and not her own story. That concern had driven him. Because each day he had fallen a little more for her, and before long there would be no going back. He'd wanted to make sure she would be all in with him, holding no secrets.

At the moment, all that seemed selfish. When they'd talked earlier, he'd seen not only the exhaustion but also the sadness in her eyes. She didn't want to do this, but here she was.

He stood up, pacing the room, gripping his phone. No, he wouldn't text her. She'd be sleeping now, and he didn't want to come across like a stalker or overly anxious. He turned off the light and lay down in his bed and told himself to go to sleep.

Yeah. As if.

He grabbed his phone and send a text to his brother, Franklin. *Sorry, I have to cancel racquetball tomorrow, and I might not be at the barbecue too. Something important came up. Really important.*

The answer came back right away, which he hadn't expected. Franklin wasn't exactly a night owl, but he might be up with his eight-month-old son. *No way! I was looking forward to it. Is it work? You aren't leaving early, are you?*

It's that girl I told you about. She's come to Nampa.

The one you've been drooling over for a year? Cool. Ask her to the barbecue.

We'll see.

Oliver didn't know Halla's schedule, or if she'd want

to meet his family. Or if he'd want to share her. But his brother's text reminded him that he was supposed to go home Sunday morning in order to be back at work on Monday. No, he'd email his boss right now and ask for at least another day. He needed time with Halla.

After sending the email, Oliver closed his eyes and tried to count sheep, but all he saw was Halla's face.

10

Kendall didn't mind working on Saturdays. The weekend feeling at the hospital was different, and she saw many people she didn't ordinarily see during her weekday shifts. Plus, having Mondays and Tuesdays off each week gave her uncrowded access to shopping or recreation.

Today the last patient she visited was Sage, who had quickly become her favorite. Last meant she could spend a little more time with her. The charge nurse had given Fiona several other patients, and Fiona was only too happy to be assigned away from the emotional teenager, which meant Kendall was taking care of Sage officially.

Despite their many tests, Wylen and the other doctors had yet to figure out Sage's digestive and breathing issues, but as long as Kendall kept all the visitors calm, Sage was able to control her breathing. The gynecologist had already given the baby the all clear, and that alone had made Sage feel better. Kendall believed what the girl really needed was someone to talk to and support, not medication, but she didn't voice her opinion aloud, except to suggest to Wylen yesterday that he consider recommending a therapist.

Right after that, he'd asked her out—and she'd turned him down flat. Then she'd spent all night trying to convince herself it had been the right choice.

"I sometimes wonder what my baby will be like," Sage said as Kendall checked her vitals. "You know, will she have brown hair like me or black like her dad? Will she love to draw like him or be good at math like me?" Her voice dipped. "I mean, I may never know. I might never get to see any of that."

"You will know some of it," Kendall said. "Most adoptions are open or semi-open these days, and you have a say in what you and the couple choose."

"I know." She heaved a sigh. "But I've heard of so many nightmares, of adoptive couples reneging on letting birth moms see the baby. Or feeling threatened."

Kendall nodded. "Yeah, but there's the flip side to consider that probably explains some of those issues. I've seen birth parents insisting on posting tons of photographs online without permission, sending presents from 'Mommy,' and calling the child by a name they choose instead of the legal name. I mean, that's asking for problems, in my opinion. A lot of problems arise because of things that should have been addressed before the birth."

Sage thought about that a moment. "Right, I guess I was only looking at it from the birth's mother's view. But sometimes I wonder if my dad's right. I mean, I had plans to finish high school, go on a long backpacking trip through Europe. And after that I'd go to college to become an engineer. I want to design and build things. I had it all planned and then . . . this." She rubbed a hand over the bulge of her baby. "But none of it's her fault, and maybe I'm the selfish one, not wanting to give up my dreams."

"How would you support her if you kept her?"

Sage blew out a sigh. "I'd have to go to work. My mom also works, but my dad thinks we could work out a schedule to take care of her. Maybe I could go to night school."

"How does your mom feel about that?"

"My mom's mad at me for not being smarter. She won't say so in front of my dad, but I know she wants me to place the baby because she doesn't want to start over, to be tied down. She also thinks I should be relieved that the pregnancy's almost over. But I'm not. I want to keep her inside forever because then I won't have to say goodbye."

"Yeah. I get that. It's the worse decision ever. I'm sorry."

Sage's eyes moistened as she continued staring up at Kendall. "How will I know if she's okay? Maybe they'll be abusive. Maybe she'll feel abandoned. What right do I have to lay that on her? Logically, I know giving her two adult parents is the right choice, but I worry about these things. And there's so much pressure for me to make everyone happy."

For the past two days, as Sage had poured out her heart about her baby and her boyfriend and her parents, Kendall had debated whether or not to share any of her own story. She was under no obligation to do so, and generally she didn't share Teisha's existence with anyone not close to her, but maybe she had something more to offer this young woman.

"Listen, placing your baby is a decision only you can make. No one else can do it for you. No one else *should* do it for you. You need to listen to your heart and put her first. Believe me, I know how hard that is because two and a half years ago, I was in your position."

Sage's eyes widened. "Really?"

Kendall glanced toward the door and back at Sage. "Would you like to see a picture?"

"You kept her?"

Kendall pulled out her phone and brought up the picture she'd taken Thursday when they had gone to see the horses. "No. I found a wonderful couple, and we have an open adoption. I was lucky because I knew them before I'd decided on adoption, and we became friends. Susan, that's my daughter's mother, runs a preschool, and when her assistant was sick, I filled in, and sometimes I just went there to be with the kids." Kendall held out her phone.

Sage grabbed it eagerly, swiping through the pictures. "She is the cutest thing! She looks like you, but darker."

"Her biological father has dark hair, but she looks like Susan and her husband too. Susan has dark hair and Jasper's blond like me. Both have blue eyes."

"Is that Susan?" Kendall angled the phone for Kendall to see.

"Yep."

"She looks so nice."

"She is. And devoted, both to Teisha and to keeping me in their lives."

"How much do you see her?"

"Well, our agreement says once a month, which turns

out to be quite a lot for most adoptive moms, but it was what we started with. The first six months, though, I could barely look at Teisha without sobbing. I was staying at a place called Lily's House—that's a foster home for teenage girls, though I wasn't there officially because I was already eighteen. Susan would come over and put her in my arms, and finally near the end of the visit, I'd stop crying. Then after about six months, everything was better. I was well into my nursing degree, and it just . . . I don't know. I guess it stopped hurting to see her, and we'd all bonded. Now I see her every week, just about. I even watched her for a few days during their anniversary."

"What's it like when you're with her?" Sage stared greedily at a picture of Teisha laughing as she reached for a horse. Kendall was holding her. "I mean, is it weird? Do you feel like running away with her?"

"Never." Kendall chuckled as she took back the phone. "I would never hurt Teisha by thinking I could take her away. She adores her parents. And being with her is more like, well, having a little sister that you love so much but you know her parents are taking good care of her and love her even more than you do."

"You're so lucky to have that," Sage said, finally relinquishing the phone.

"I know. I was lucky to find Lily's House and that Lily let me stay while I figured out what I wanted to do. My mother was determined that I place my baby for adoption. I told her I'd never do that. But then I started seeing everything Lily did for her two biological kids and all the foster girls, and I knew I wasn't ready. That I wouldn't do it right. Anyway, Lily introduced me to Susan. I think she knew all along that I'd fall in love with them as a family. She knew Susan desperately wanted a baby."

Sage was grinning. "It's like a miracle."

"I think so. And you still have three months to find your own miracle. You can visit with the parents, get a feel for who they are. Even if you don't become as close as Susan and I are, you'll be able to see how things might work out."

"I wish I knew Susan," Sage said. She hesitated a moment before adding, "I guess it's probably better to choose a couple who don't have any kids, right?"

"Oh, I don't know. It might be nice for your baby to have a big brother or sister. My sister and I are super close now. I couldn't imagine not having her."

"I always wanted a big brother." Sage rubbed her stomach again. "What do you think?" she asked the baby.

Kendall smiled wistfully, remembering when she'd talked to Teisha exactly like that. "Well, I'll check back on you later. Your doctor should be in soon."

"I hope it's the cute one."

Kendall laughed. "I think you're in luck. He's the one with the least seniority."

"So the others are probably off golfing?"

"Something like that. But don't worry. I'm sure you'll get the best diagnosis."

"Oh, I'm not worried about that. I've been feeling really good today."

"I'm glad." Kendall started for the door.

"Wait, one more question."

Kendall turned to see that Sage was no longer smiling. "So how do you deal with it?" she asked. "I mean, telling guys. Is it a total turn-off for them? I'm still with my boyfriend, technically, but not really. I don't want to marry him, and I know I have to break up with him. I *want* to break up with him. But I worry that maybe he's the only one who will ever . . . you know, want me for who I am."

Kendall stepped back into the room. "That's a tough question. I've dated quite a bit this last year and a half. I've only told two of them. One wasn't okay with it. The other was. It didn't end up working out between us, but it wasn't because of Teisha. I know the guy I end up choosing will be man enough to accept her. That's just the way it's got to be. Even if it limits my choices a bit."

Sage nodded. "Right."

Kendall was almost out the door again when Sage asked, "Can I see her picture one more time?"

Kendall laughed and brought out her phone. They were still looking through Teisha's pictures when Wylen appeared in the opened doorway, calling out as he came in, "Knock, knock, I have great news."

Kendall slipped the phone into her pocket. "And what's that, doctor?"

"Sage gets to check out. All the tests are negative. We are almost one hundred percent sure that the pains and shortness of breath were caused by anxiety. I've talked to your parents, and they're on their way. I've recommended you all go together to see a therapist for a few sessions to learn ways to lessen your anxiety." Wylen's gaze met Kendall's. "In fact, the woman I'm recommending has a lot of experience working with girls your age. I've chatted with her about you, and she's looking forward to meeting you."

"You called Tessa?" Kendall asked. Tessa Braxton, who happened to be Lily's sister, lived next door to Lily's House and was an active part of helping Lily's girls adjust and recover from the abuse or neglect so many of them had suffered. Tessa had helped Kendall more than she was willing to admit.

"That's right." Wylen took a fold of paper from his pocket and offered it to Sage. "I already gave your parents her information, but here it is for you as well. Please go, okay? I don't want to see you back here. You have enough stress to deal with as it is."

"Thank you," Sage said. "I'll go. Really. I promise."

Just then Sage's IV monitor went off. "Seriously?" Sage muttered. "I swear this thing hates me."

Kendall silenced the monitor and moved to check the line.

Wylen was grinning. "When you're finished," he said to Kendall, "can I talk to you a minute?"

"Sure."

"I'll be out ordering the release papers." With a smile at Sage, he exited the room.

"He is so gorgeous," Sage said. "Isn't he? Come on, you have to notice him, and he likes you too. Do you see the way he looks at you?"

Kendall forced a laugh. "It's strictly professional between us."

"Yeah, right." Sage didn't look convinced. "I know what I see. Anyway, if I ever do decide I want another boyfriend—which I don't right now—he's going to look exactly like Dr. Gorgeous."

Kendall nearly tripped over her own feet. What were

the odds that the girl would use her own secret nickname for Wylen?

"I'll come say goodbye before you leave," she said.

Outside the door, she nearly ran into Wylen. "I thought you were getting her release papers."

"I wanted to make sure to catch you."

"Okay." She started down the hallway, and he kept pace with her. "But first, thank you so much for recommending Tessa. That girl really needs a listening ear."

"I think you're right. I appreciate your recommendation." He came to a stop, his hand going to her arm. "Look, about yesterday when I asked you out, and you said no."

Kendall hoped her smile appeared natural. "You mean when you felt bad for not showing up for lunch again. Don't worry about it. If you're ever able to eat lunch, I'm sure you can find the cafeteria yourself. Or you can tag along with me." Whatever. She wasn't holding her breath, and she didn't need a charity dinner.

He frowned, his eyebrows pulling down in the middle. "That's not why I asked you."

Kendall's stomach began churning. "Oh, yeah?"

"Please go out with me," he asked. "We'll go somewhere nice."

No fair that he asked her right after what Sage had said about him. About them. It was so much better when she was convinced he didn't really like her. Easier to turn him down.

She wanted to say yes. She wanted to scream up and down and shout that she'd love to go out with him. Anytime, anyplace.

That was the problem. She didn't want to like him this much.

"Just one date," he said.

"Okay." The word came out before she could rein it in.

"Tonight? Pick you up at six. Well, better make it seven."

"Fine." She pointed at him. "But if you're late, don't bother coming."

He grinned. "Don't worry. I'll be there." He pointed at the pocket where she'd stored her phone. "Text me the address right now."

Just like that, she had a date with Dr. Gorgeous, the man who was going to break her heart.

She was both excited and scared to death.

11

Something sailed into Halla, and she forced her eyes opened, pushing the pillow off the side of her face. She blinked at the brightness of the light streaming in through the canvas of the popup. It looked like Elsie had taken advantage of a few window openings to let in the morning breeze while it was still cool outside.

"What was that for?"

Elsie faced Halla, one hand on her hip and the other holding a plate of pancakes. "Because your phone is buzzing, and has been for over an hour, I'm betting, because that's when Oliver started texting me."

"Really?" Halla felt for her phone, and Elsie handed it to her.

"You left it on the table."

"Oh. Must have been after I came back last night." She opened the phone. Oliver had texted her ten times.

"Where did you go last night anyway? Was it to see him? I heard you come back in."

"Just driving," Halla said distractedly. Oliver was asking for her address and if he could come see her this morning. "He wants to come." So, she must rate above racquetball after all. That was a good start.

"Then give him the address."

"Right." Halla texted him, and a reply came back immediately.

On my way.

Halla looked up at Elsie, suddenly unable to breathe. "He's coming!"

"You'd better get ready." Elsie waved the plate of pancakes in front of her. "I ate with Monica's family, and we saved you these. I brought syrup and whipped cream too. Nice family, by the way."

"Put them on the table, okay? I need to shower first." Halla popped out of bed and dove toward the cupboard that housed the water heater. It had to be turned on for each use. Zipping the windows closed and grabbing her shampoo ate up another precious minute.

Elsie looked dubiously at the shower curtain. "You sure we got that up right? Monica offered the use of her shower, so I took her up on it. Maybe you should do the same."

"I don't have time to work that out. Boise's only twenty minutes away, and I want to look . . . well, not like something that tossed and turned half the night." No wonder she'd found it hard to wake up and hadn't heard the vibration of her phone.

"Hurry then." Elsie got out one of their own plates and upturned the pancakes on it. "I'll return this to Monica."

Halla shed her clothes and stepped into the square shower basin that was about a foot and a half high. Convenient, she supposed, that the curved basin also housed the toilet, but it felt a little strange to stand in a shower with the toilet nearby looking like a shower seat. "If he comes before I'm ready, you stall him, okay?" She began tucking the shower curtain inside the tub.

Elsie laughed. "Okay, but you have plenty of time. It's not like you do much more with your hair than a little gel."

Did that mean she should do more? Too late for a makeover now.

Halla turned on the water, which thankfully was hot almost immediately. There was nothing more from Elsie, so she must have already left the camper. Halla soaped her hair and body thoroughly. Not much water pressure but enough to do the job.

Wait, where was her conditioner? Had she gotten it when she grabbed the shampoo? Apparently not.

Muttering under her breath, she ducked out of the shower to grab her conditioner and her towel, in the meantime dribbling water all over the floor. Leaving the towel in reach, she ducked back inside and smoothed on the conditioner.

Finally, she turned off the water. Longer than she'd wanted, but less than five minutes, which wasn't bad. That left plenty of time to dry off, throw on the clothes she'd already chosen for this meeting, and maybe even blow dry her hair. It was short enough to only take a few minutes. Mascara would follow, and maybe she'd stroke on a bit of eye shadow and lip gloss.

Voices outside startled her. A man's voice. A familiar man's voice. Her heart sank and soared at the same time.

Oliver! She whirled.

The next moment she was falling backward, grabbing onto the shower curtain as she tumbled over the shower tub walls, bottom first. A little scream left her lips as her head bounced off the cabinet behind her.

"Halla?" That was Elsie.

The door to the camper flew open and Elsie leapt inside, her mouth going wide as she saw Halla sprawled on the floor, wrapped in the shower curtain from knee to neck, her feet still inside the shower, one of them grazing the toilet lid.

Oliver appeared next to her, his eyes instantly taking in the scene. "Are you okay?"

No, no, no! This couldn't be happening. This was not how they were supposed to meet. She had planned to run out of the camper and throw herself into his arms. She was supposed to look great and smell even better. She was supposed to be irresistible.

For a moment, no one spoke as Halla drank him in. Video chatting had not done this rugged man any justice. He towered over Elsie, so he hadn't exaggerated his height. His short brown hair was perfectly arranged, and all that outdoor forestry work had done amazing things for his body. He was sexy and hot and perfect. His gaze sent heat rushing through her.

Why didn't Elsie get him out of here?

Water dripped into Halla's eyes. She could only imagine how graceful she looked with her foot in the toilet and her hair plastered to her head. "Uh, I'm fine," she said, working out one bare arm from under the shower curtain and making sure all her important parts were covered. "Just a little bump on the head. And apparently I owe Lily a new shower curtain."

Oliver and Elsie began to laugh, sending heat rushing over Halla's cheeks. She dragged out her other arm and tried to sit up, clutching the curtain to her neck. "Uh, if it's not too much to ask, can you two give me a little privacy? Huh?"

Oliver looked immediately abashed, but Elsie rolled her eyes. "Okay, but try not to break anything else, okay?" she said. "That includes your head." She motioned to the door and thankfully Oliver preceded Elsie from the camper.

"Great. Just great," Halla muttered. Trust her to make a mess of their first meeting. Stumbling to the door and nearly tripping over the curtain, still wrapped around her wet torso, she locked the camper door. "Now try to get in."

She dried off in record time and dressed, passing over her usual camouflage pants and tank top in favor of khaki shorts and a pink T-shirt. Next, she rubbed the towel over her hair again—no time for the blow dryer—and fluffed it with a dollop of gel. While brushing her teeth, she grabbed her makeup bag and followed with a bit of mascara and a quick brush of pale lipstick that was more gloss than anything. For so many years she'd played down the woman part of her, preferring the tough look and attitude that made her feel in charge, but now, with Oliver here, she wanted to be . . . pretty.

Elsie laughed outside, followed by the deeper rumble of Oliver's chuckle. The sound sent another flush over Halla. Would she ever live down this moment? She wadded up the shower curtain and stuffed it into the shower basin. Then she put the optional cover over the whole ensemble. There, now it looked like a short table or wide seat, with no toilet or shower in sight to mock her.

She was drying off her arms when Elsie knocked on the door. "Hey, you okay in there? You didn't bump your head too hard, did you?"

Halla dumped her makeup into its case and shoved it back on her shelf. "That depends," she called. "Who are you again?" Walking to the door, she opened it.

"Who am I?" Elsie stared up at her with anxious eyes. "You'd better be joking."

"Of course I am." Halla's gaze slid past her, focusing on Oliver. He was staring at her, a silly grin on his face. Probably reliving her disgrace. "How did you get here so fast?"

"Are you kidding? I've been in Nampa for over an hour. I drove over here the minute I woke up. I've been cruising around the city waiting for you to answer my texts. I almost stopped and knocked on two campers I drove by but refrained. Barely."

That made perfect sense, but his eagerness somehow made her feel a little shy. His grin no longer seemed silly but sensual and inviting.

"Sooo, can we come in?" he drawled hesitantly.

She gave a little start. "Oh, yeah, of course. Come in."

"Not me." Elsie was retreating. "I need to ask Monica something. It was nice meeting you, Oliver. Finally." With a smirk at Halla, she left.

Halla waited for the panic to come, but it didn't. She moved aside from the doorway and let Oliver in. His eyes hadn't left hers, and now he leaned forward and hugged her, pulling her up onto her tiptoes with his exuberance.

He chuckled as her breath whooshed from her. "Sorry, you're littler than I expected," he said as he pulled back from the embrace. "I mean, you told me you were one of the shortest of your sisters, but that's hard to gauge on a screen."

"I know what you mean." Every place he'd touched her was on fire. And did his gaze just fall on her lips? His lips looked soft and strong and inviting. If he tried to kiss her, she wouldn't stop him. She'd been playing out this moment for months in her mind.

His eyes met hers once more before he came in for another hug, this time more carefully. His arms felt warm and strong. "So good to finally meet you," he said in her ear. She hoped he couldn't feel the delicious shudder that ran through her.

She wanted to stay like this forever. He smelled so good, something that hinted of the outdoors. "Sorry about the wet hair," she told him.

"Are you kidding?" He laughed as they drew apart again. "It's not every day I get to see a beautiful wet girl dressed in a shower curtain."

Halla groaned. "Can you just forget that, please?"

"No way." His grin was back to being silly again, but she couldn't help grinning herself.

"Okay, well . . . I was about to have pancakes." She motioned to the table. "Do you want some?"

"I stopped and ate right before you called. I'm stuffed. But I'll watch you eat." He made himself comfortable on one of the bench seats.

"Thanks. I'm sure that's such a sacrifice." She settled opposite him when she really wanted to sit next to him and feel his solidness. They were here together. It was almost too much to take in.

"Good thing you're not having any," she added, pouring syrup over the stack. "More for me." There were at least four pancakes, though she could barely take her eyes away from his long enough to count that high.

He laughed again. "If you can eat all those, lunch is on me."

Halla had a sneaking suspicion there were more pancakes than she'd guessed, but she was up to the task. "You forget where I grew up."

His face sobered instantly. "I'm sorry. I know you had things tough with your parents—"

"No, not them." Her breath was gone again, and this time it had nothing to do with him. "I meant Lily's House. I don't ever talk about—"

Silence fell between them. She hadn't meant to admit anything. She hadn't even known herself that it was true. People who knew her in real life would have known she was talking about the foster home.

"I just meant Lily's House," she repeated before taking a huge bite of her pancakes.

The furrow in his brow eased. "Of course you did. Sorry. It's just with you here in Nampa, and all, I thought maybe you . . ." He shrugged, trailing off.

Halla swallowed and stuffed in more pancakes. Things were not going well at all. She waved a fork at him and said around her food in what was probably not a very ladylike manner, "Tell me about your computer."

He relaxed into the seat, which told her he was every bit as worried as she was about the previous direction of the conversation. "Well, we've duct-taped it together and it works, but we can't find parts to fix it, so I'm afraid I'm going to have to buy a new one. Unless my brother-in-law can find a used one of the same model that we can scavenge for parts."

"Sorry." She put more syrup on her pancakes. There were six now that she'd had time to count. They were big, but she was going to win this bet. And that meant spending more time with him. That made her heart sing—and not only because being with him was less time to think about her mother.

"It's okay. My poor little niece started crying. I had to assure her that I still love her and would play basketball with her again. My sister and her husband really can't afford to replace the computer, so I told them I'd been thinking about upgrading anyway."

"That's sweet of you."

"Well, I've wanted to look into something I can connect to the Internet with in the field, so it's an opportunity to see what's out there. I'm guessing I need another device, even with the office's satellite phone we take."

He'd called her a few times using that satellite phone, far out in the wilds of the forest.

"Even then, I'm not sure video-chatting will be easy or fast." He watched as she took another bite of pancake. "At this point, I'm so glad not to have to sneak around to see my siblings that I'll do anything to keep everyone happy. Well, I'm not going to quit my job and move to Boise, which my mom would like, but everything else."

He smiled. "It's good to be back in the family. But my mother is still a little . . . strong willed."

"Good thing I'm not meeting her then." The words came out before Halla thought them through.

"Oh, but I was hoping you'd go to a family barbecue with me tonight." He leaned forward, arms on the table, his hands next to hers where they rested on either side of her plate. "Pretty please? I want to show you off."

She swallowed her pancakes with difficulty. "Um, are you sure about that? I mean, you just got through telling me your mom is strong-willed and then you want to throw me at her? You know I'm going to say something to upset her, don't you?"

"Naw, she's going to love you."

"I'm flattered, really, and I'd love to meet your family, but I'm not sure I'll have time for a barbecue." Halla's stomach was rumbling again now that she hadn't continued to feed it.

"Because of your parents?"

She nodded. "I went there last night, just a drive-by. My dad's car was there, so I couldn't have gone in anyway, but I have to see my mom sometime. The sooner the better. Elsie is supposed to be home Tuesday morning. If I don't see my mother before then, I may have to buy Elsie a plane ticket back to Phoenix."

He grabbed her hands, and her fork cluttered to her plate. "You shouldn't go to your parents' alone."

"I won't. And for the record, I wasn't exactly alone last night either. The nosy neighbor was outside. She saw me."

"When do you plan on going again?"

She shrugged. "My dad likes to fish. I'm hoping that's

where he is today. I thought I'd finish my pancakes and go over." She glanced at her plate pointedly, though she didn't really want him to let go. He released her, but their hands still touched, and she didn't resume eating.

"Okay, so how about this," he said, his blue eyes earnest. "I'll drive you there—I can even wait in my truck, if you want. If he's home, we leave and go do something and come back after lunch. Or I could go in with you if you still want to talk to your mother with him there."

She shook her head. "I don't want to see him at all. I have nothing to say to him that I didn't already say in my statement to family court, which I know my parents received a copy of. That's one relationship I don't want to revisit."

"Understood, and maybe after seeing your mom, you'll feel the same way about her. But at least you'll know, and maybe it'll be like closing a door."

She hated that he was right. She wanted to see her mother, to confront her, to ask her questions, to under-stand how she'd stood by and allowed the abuse. She wanted to stop wondering, even if that meant closing the door forever like she had with her father.

"After that," he continued, "if we still haven't been able to talk to her alone, we could go to dinner—or maybe the barbecue—and try again tomorrow."

Her mother would be at church in the morning, Halla knew that much, but when she'd lived at home, her father had also attended. Would he dare make a scene if Halla tried to talk to her mother alone? He'd always liked putting on a public show of the loving family, so maybe not.

Oliver grimaced, as if worried he was overstepping. "I mean, you could take Elsie instead, but she's not much protection."

"It's not that. Let me think for a minute." Halla picked up her fork, licked a little syrup from the end, and resumed eating. His plan was good, but she hadn't wanted their first moments together to be colored by her family.

She hadn't realized she'd spoken aloud until he said, "First moments? We've been talking almost every few days for a year, lately every day, except when I'm out in the field. This is only one more moment in all of those."

She shook her head. "Not quite." She placed her free hand over his. "I've never been able to do this before." He felt good, more than good.

He turned his hand, enveloping hers. "Good point, but you know what I mean. This isn't going to change how I feel about you."

And how is that? she wanted to ask. But it wasn't a question she'd be able to answer herself right now, and she shouldn't expect him to be able to either.

His thumb moved over the back of her hand, making her heart do funny things. Was this really happening? Could everything be this perfect?

Of course, they hadn't kissed yet, and if she didn't finish these ridiculous pancakes, they'd never get to that part. She'd hoped to do that a lot sooner, and she might have if she hadn't been wearing a shower curtain when he'd first walked in.

"Okay, let's do it your way." She started eating again, more quickly now. He might as well know the real her, and she was never shy about eating. But it was a little awkward with him still holding her hand, so she said, "Would you mind getting me some milk from the fridge? There are glasses in one of the drawers."

"Sure. But with the rate you're devouring those, I'm afraid you'll choke."

"Haha. I have a bet to win, and I take my bets seriously."

"Good."

Halla made short work of the pancakes and milk before heading, with Oliver in tow, to thank Monica for breakfast. Halla escaped listening to an embarrassing recap of the shower event by ducking into Monica's bathroom to relieve her bladder. When she emerged, Monica was insisting on seeing the shower curtain, and Halla let her have it, hoping maybe she would know where to buy a new one for cheap.

"It's actually a lot wider than a normal one," Monica pointed out. "See the seam? I'm guessing Lily sewed two together."

"That I can do," Halla said, although she really meant Elsie could do it. She'd been a whiz at sewing ever since high school.

Between meeting all of Monica's five children and her affable husband, who reminded Halla vaguely of Payden and who towered a good foot and a half over his short wife, thirty minutes passed. They spent another interesting hour listening to how Monica had been one of Lily's roommates back in the beginning when Lily had hidden Saffron, her first runaway girl, in her room at their apartment.

"Well, we'd better get going," Halla finally said. No one would say it if she didn't because at the moment she was the only one with somewhere she had to go. "I have a visit to make."

Elsie sat up straight on the patio chair where they had gathered. "Do you need me to come?"

Halla considered. She was sure Oliver would go with her to her parents' door, since he was driving her to the house, but the idea made her uneasy. If a boy calling the house had caused her father to keep her home from school for an entire month, there was no telling what kind of fit he would go into if he happened to come home while they were there. Never mind that she was an adult who hadn't been under his roof for eleven years. Better to have Oliver wait in his truck and Elsie go with her to the door. Besides, Oliver had already seen her at a disadvantage this morning, and she wanted to retain some dignity.

"I'd like it if you'd come." Halla glanced at Oliver, who nodded in agreement.

"The more the merrier," he said.

Had Halla sounded as grim as he did?

On the way to his truck, she said, "Hey, you're the one who inspired me to do this."

"I know, but I'm wishing I hadn't."

Halla bumped her shoulder lightly into his arm. "I need to do this. You were right. Don't worry. I won't go inside. We can talk on the porch."

Her dad's car wasn't there when they arrived at the house, so Halla and Elsie tramped to the door, following the crack in the sidewalk. When they reached the tiny porch, Halla felt immobilized by a huge weight pressing down on her entire body.

Elsie took her hand and squeezed it briefly. "That bad, huh?"

Halla nodded. "It's weird. Like I'm not myself." She glanced over her shoulder to see that Oliver was out of his truck, his back against the white paint, one foot over the other and his arms folded over his chest. He looked at once both casual and alert. An insane urge to giggle rose to Halla's throat. At least that alleviated the pressure a tiny bit.

Halla rang the bell and then held her breath, cocking her head to hear footsteps. There was nothing. She rang again. Still nothing. She knocked instead.

"It's no use," Elsie said. "No one's home."

"Yeah." The weight suddenly lifted from Halla's body.

"Unless . . ." Elsie tossed her dark hair over one shoulder and looked around, as if checking for eavesdroppers. "I wonder when the last time was anyone saw your mother?"

Halla stared at her blankly as her brain tried to register the significance of the words. Meaning that perhaps her mother had left? Or that she'd died? But that couldn't be, not with her mother's flowers still in the well-kept flowerbeds.

"Let's go. We'll come back later." Whirling, she started down the walk.

Oliver pushed off the truck and met them a few feet from it.

"No one's home," Halla said. "Maybe she's not living here with him anymore, or maybe they both moved." The new owner might like the same flowers her mother had always planted.

Elsie's grimace told her that was not what she'd been suggesting.

"Maybe we should talk to the neighbors." Oliver thumbed toward the house on the left. Mrs. Moss's house. "I'm pretty sure I saw someone looking out the curtain over there a while ago."

Halla shook her head. "Maybe later. Let's go do something else right now." She didn't want to see Mrs. Moss or talk to her.

"It's getting hot. I'm not sure the camper air conditioning will do the job." Elsie said, heading around to the passenger side door.

"There's a mall," Halla said. "Or there used to be. We could try walking around a bit." Until she found her courage.

Oliver opened the door and set his hand on her waist to help her up, sending a jolt of need through her. If the man affected her that way with a simple touch, what would it be like to kiss him? Halla slipped past the steering wheel to the middle of the seat. That was another advantage of having Elsie with her—sitting so close to him.

Oliver wasted no time speeding away, but not before Halla saw the curtain at Mrs. Moss's house move. Why was the woman watching them?

12

Naomi Jenkins stepped back as Tina Moss yanked the curtain from her hand to cover the window. It didn't matter. Even though Naomi could no longer see the young woman, her visage was seared to Naomi's memory. The girl looked the same.

No, that wasn't quite accurate. She was older, more beautiful, and she'd filled in some. Her once-long hair was short and modern.

Reuben would hate it.

But she was still Halla, her baby. She still had the light blond hair that everyone thought came from Reuben's dishwater genes, her face was the same narrow shape, and she was the same height she'd been at fifteen.

Naomi had lived for this day—and also dreaded it. So much lost between them.

"She came back," Naomi whispered.

"I knew it was her when I saw her last night," Tina said, crossing to her green plaid sofa and settling on it. As usual, every hair on her head was in place, styled and sprayed in a way that hadn't changed in the thirty years they'd known each other. Naomi sometimes envied Tina's muscular figure and the way she could pretty much lift anything, though Reuben regularly made fun of her lack of curves by calling her the "boy-woman" or "flat-chested shrew."

Naomi sat at the other end of the couch. Her mind was racing, and she couldn't settle on anything long enough to examine a single thought. For a long time, she simply focused on her breathing. When she was feeling more steady, she'd act. Her long vigil was at an end. In. Out. In. Out.

"You know she's not back for Reuben," Tina said into the quiet.

"No."

"You're going to have to tell her."

The idea frightened Naomi. "Will it make it better or worse?"

Tina gave her a dubious look. "How could it be worse?"

Naomi considered that a moment, the cacophony of competing thoughts receding as she narrowed on the thought. The months after Halla had run away had been unimaginable. Yet even while she'd feared for Halla's life, she'd been proud of Halla's courage. So like that other little girl who'd run away—and yet not like her at all because Halla had come out strong and successful. Not like her mother, who had given up.

My fault, Naomi thought.

Tina was the only one who knew the secret, and only recently when they'd reconnected over craftmaking. Naomi regretted telling her now, though she knew Tina was right.

"On the bright side," Tina said with false cheerfulness, "The craft fair is going well. Really well, actually. People love your new baby quilts, and the bookends all sold. I didn't want to keep so much cash around, so I already did the accounting for what we've sold so far this week, minus your share of the booth fee. There will be more for the weekend, though." She arose and started across the room. "I'll get your money. It's in hundreds like you want it. The change I'll put in with the next payment."

"I'm willing to pay you and your daughter for selling the items too," Naomi said, as she had many times before.

"We're there selling our own stuff anyway." Tina waved the words away. "It's not an issue. And your things attract a lot more business for us." She disappeared so Naomi didn't need to formulate a response.

If Reuben had any idea that while he was at work Naomi made crafts to sell, he'd demand the money or prevent her altogether, so she didn't tell him. She hid her crafts in her linen closet or Halla's old room until she could bring them to Tina.

Naomi waited, her heart still pounding with the excitement of seeing Halla. Tina soon returned with a fold of cash and the fireproof portable safe Naomi had left with her after Halla had run away. The weight of the safe felt comforting in Naomi's hand, as she put it on her lap to take the fold of bills—six hundred dollars. Not bad at all for a week that wasn't an official holiday.

"I'll be with you if you want," Tina offered. "When you talk to her."

Naomi met her earnest brown eyes. "Thank you. You're a good friend." But they really weren't friends anymore.

Not the way they had once been, not in the way friends should be. Give and take, laughing on outings, or sharing news about their children. Reuben had destroyed that too, though she'd gotten bolder in the past few years. No, the women's relationship was more derived from pity on Tina's part and desperation on Naomi's.

Naomi waited until Tina left the room before fishing in her bra to remove the key. Reuben had found it once in her nightstand and had asked her what it was for. She'd shrugged and said it probably went to something they'd thrown away. After that, she'd never made the mistake to leave the key anywhere except in her bra. It wasn't as if they were ever undressed together anymore—they hadn't been since Halla was a small child. Reuben could never bring himself to admit that he needed help in the hormone department, and it had become embarrassing enough for him that he'd finally stopped demanding his husband privileges. Naomi no longer had to endure the long, boring, and sometimes painful episodes in the bedroom, or his recriminations that placed the blame on her. Not that she didn't miss what they'd once had. She'd loved him and their lovemaking in the early days. But that was before he'd taken everything from her. The idea of him touching her now made her want to vomit.

She turned the key, revealing the neat stacks of cash inside. Twelve years of savings, though it was only after Halla had left that she'd earned most of it. Before the crafts, she'd only been able to save twenty dollars a week, stolen from her food budget. Back then, she used to buy extra of something Reuben loved, and then immediately return it for cash. That way there was no trail and nothing for him to harp on. When he told her to buy clothes, she'd sometimes been able to give him copies of receipts for dresses and pants that totaled a hundred dollars or more, when in actuality she'd returned those and bought second-hand items at garage sales.

She'd barely managed to save over a thousand dollars before Halla had run away. Not sufficient to get them far enough away from Reuben. Still, Naomi wished she had run back then, even if they lived on the streets together. Or she wished she'd called the police. It would have been worth anything Reuben could have done to her. Even if they took Halla away. She understood that now.

Three of the hundred-dollar bills finished off another stack of ten thousand dollars, leaving three over to begin another stack. Twelve years of stacks, of planning. Of waiting until Halla returned. There were eleven completed stacks in all now.

Naomi was still taking money from Reuben to pay for her raw materials. She'd even started hawking some of the things in his man cave: a weight set he hadn't used in years, tools he'd never mastered. But she sold only those tools she hadn't already taken to Tina's work shed, where she used them in secret for her crafts. The cut pieces of wood she kept in Halla's old room, which had officially become her sewing room, though she'd kept it exactly the way Halla had left it. Reuben never went in there, but just in case, she was always ready with an excuse for the wood pieces and moved anything finished to Tina's. A wife's place was in the home, he constantly reminded her. Not out with friends or pursuing personal dreams.

I can leave now, she thought.

Fear paralyzed her. If Reuben found out, he'd kill her. She was sure of it. And maybe her fear of him was the real thing stopping her all these years. She'd always told herself she couldn't leave Reuben until she reconnected with Halla. Because going far enough away to prevent Reuben from finding her meant that Halla wouldn't be able to find her either. Halla, her sweet baby.

I failed you. The mocking whisper inside her head taunted, making Naomi feel weak and hopeless. Halla hadn't seemed interested in finding her all these years. What had brought her back now?

Naomi grabbed a stack of cash and rubbed it over her face. With Tina's aversion to cash on hand, she would have blanched at the idea of so much inside the safe. But Tina had no way of knowing how much Naomi put in or took out each time, or what other items she stored inside. It was better that way for both of them. Before going into business with Tina, Naomi had hidden her money inside tampon boxes covered with tampons she hadn't used in over a decade.

The feel of the money calmed her. She could hide. She could leave Reuben, instruct the attorney to send the divorce papers, and disappear forever.

Would Reuben stalk Halla to find Naomi? Dread shuddered down her spine. Maybe not. Halla was courageous, not like her mother, and would call the police. And the man Halla had been with looked strong enough to ward off Reuben. Were they romantically involved or just friends? Naomi hadn't been able to tell.

A new thought made her drop the money back into the safe. What if Halla wanted nothing to do with her?

It would be her right, especially after she knew the whole story.

Naomi dug under the cash for the sturdy, palm-sized jewelry box that held her only other real treasure. She opened it, looking at the gold locket engraved with fancy swirls and the words *I love you*. Her mother had given this to her on her sixteenth birthday. It had been meant to go to her daughter one day and then her granddaughter. Two pictures stared back at Naomi's—hers and her daughter's, both taken when they were teens. Underneath the picture of her daughter was one of Naomi's own mother.

She snapped the jewelry box shut, put it in her pocket, relocked the safe, and went to look for Tina. She found her in the kitchen brewing tea.

"Can I use your truck to take a few things to my storage unit?" There would be time to take a load before Reuben returned from fishing. He'd been staying out well through mid-afternoon most Saturdays.

"Sure." Tina reached for the safe. "Want me to put this away?"

"Actually, I'm going to take it with me this time." Leaving it at the storage unit might not be the safest thing, but she'd hide it among her unfinished crafts or in an old bag of clothes. "And can you help me load my scroll saw and some of my other equipment?"

Tina's mouth opened. "Oh," she said. More a puff of air than a word. "It's time then?"

Naomi nodded. "I think so." When Halla came back, Naomi would tell her everything, and then she would leave. "If she comes again," Naomi added, her heart squeezed by the thought.

"She'll come. I'll call Carl to help load the truck while you go home and see if there's anything else you'll need. We'll help you unload it too."

"Thank you." Naomi pushed back the fear already eating at her confidence.

Tina was right that there were a few items she wanted to make sure to take out of the house, in case she had to leave in a hurry. Mostly her unfinished quilts, her batting and material, and a couple boxes of cut wood. Wherever she ended up, she'd have to start over.

Naomi left Tina's at a run, feeling every one of her sixty-six years. She needed to hurry. If Reuben came home before she did, she'd never be able to explain where she'd been, and if he had any idea of what she planned, he'd never let her leave the house again.

13

The mall was nothing like Halla remembered. Everything seemed to have a coat of old paint on it, and most of the big stores had left. But it got them out of the heat until it was time for lunch.

"So where do you two feel like eating?" Oliver asked.

"I know a place." Halla glanced at Elsie. "If you don't mind."

"You mean that burger place from last night? Sure. It was yummy." Elsie licked her lips for emphasis. "But are you sure you want to go back?"

Meaning because she'd had that weird attack, Halla knew. "Yeah, I'm sure."

"Burgers?" Oliver's brows furrowed. "I was hoping to take you somewhere a little more fancy."

"Oh, that's right. Your family is barbecuing," Halla said. "You won't want to eat hamburgers twice. But this restaurant has other choices."

Oliver chuckled and shook his head. "Actually, we'll be doing steak tonight. I bought them myself yesterday.

And my brother-in-law's cooking is really good. We don't have much time together, though, so I wanted to take you somewhere special now."

Halla smiled. "It is special. It's one of the few places I remember going to when I lived here."

"Then let's go."

At Front Burner Burgers, they all ordered hamburgers, but Elsie decided against a shake and Oliver chose chocolate instead of strawberry. Halla ate her entire strawberry shake first, while Oliver downed his hamburger. Halla kept expecting—maybe even hoping—for a flashback of some kind, but all she felt was contentment. Maybe it was the way Oliver kept looking at her. Or the way his hand or leg would brush hers. At every touch, she craved more.

Oliver finished first and briefly checked his email as he'd done a few times already that morning. This time he let out a triumphant shout. "I've got another day," he said. "I don't have to leave until Monday. I could even leave late afternoon, depending on when you guys take off. I have half the drive you do."

"You asked for another day?" she managed to say past the lump forming in her throat.

He nodded. "Yeah, this morning when I got your text. I have plenty of time accrued, but since we're planning a controlled burn in one of my areas next week and I need to be there, I was worried he wouldn't let me stay. I was going to stay as late as possible on Sunday if he didn't agree, but this is better."

Happiness settled around Halla. Another day with Oliver stretched out like a promise.

The mood was decidedly upbeat as they finished their meal. At least until Elsie asked, "So, what next? Back to your mother's?"

Sudden dread pooled in Halla's stomach. "I don't know. My father will be home from fishing soon, if he's not already." She didn't want to see her mother if it meant seeing him too. She also didn't want to go back to that street. But maybe she didn't have to—at least not today. Maybe today could be for Oliver.

"Tomorrow," Halla said firmly. "I know where they go to church. It might be better there in public. I mean, it's not like we're going to fall into each other's arms and say how much we missed each other. Because I didn't miss her at all."

Elsie frowned, and Halla was aware of Oliver staring at her, but she didn't look over at him, not wanting to see if it was pity or compassion in his eyes. She ran a finger around the lip of her empty shake cup, wishing she had room in her stomach to buy another.

"Won't your father be at the church too?" Elsie began gathering up their burger wrappers.

Halla wasn't sure. "He used to go, but after people said he bribed the priest not to say anything about what he was doing, he might not go now." She could hope for that.

"Either way, approaching your mother in public is a good idea," Oliver said.

Halla dared look at him now. "And waiting until tomorrow frees me up for your barbecue, if you still want to take me."

"Great!" He punched the air with his fist. "Because my brother and sister have sent me twenty texts already asking me what our plans are. I'd told them I wasn't sure I'd be there."

Because he planned to be with her. Their gazes locked with an intensity that seared her. Halla had to look away.

"In the meantime, we could go for a hike," Oliver suggested as he scooted out of the booth.

She whipped her head toward him. "I brought my shoes, but if you think I'm going to wrestle with that shower curtain again before meeting your family, you're dreaming. I'm already crashing their party, and I don't want to be sweaty and disheveled while I'm doing it."

He offered her a hand out of the booth, his eyes glinting with humor. "Oh, yes. There is that. But you're not crashing anything. You have an invite from my sister—it's at her house. Maybe we can hike after dinner. What would you rather do now?"

"Well, I'd like to look up a couple people I used to know. Maybe go see them if they're still in the neighborhood. I'm pretty sure Amy Norton—she's the only girlfriend I remember—will be close because her family owned a lot of land around here and a construction business they all worked at, but I don't know about the guy."

"Guy?" Elsie asked, balancing their two trays, now stacked with garbage.

Halla rescued one of the trays. "Peter Styles, a boy I used to have a crush on."

"Should I be worried?" Oliver's voice was teasing but there was an underlying seriousness in his tone. If Elsie weren't here, would Halla be able to tell him that Peter had been the boy whose innocent phone call to her house had sent her father into a rage?

"I don't think so," she said. "But if he drives a Porsche, I might change my mind."

Oliver laughed harder, lessening her anxiety. "Don't worry. I'll fight for you."

The comment stole her breath away. Made her feel like she was floating. Halla had to tap her foot on the tile to make sure she was still grounded.

Elsie made a face as she dumped her tray. "Count me out on that. I need to call Payden and see if he's heard about his house. I'll stay at the camper, and if it's too hot, I'll go hang out with Monica."

"As long as you come to the barbecue with us," Oliver said, opening the restaurant door for them. "Or meet us, depending on where Halla's friends are and how hard they are to find."

"I'll meet you," Elsie agreed. "I'd rather, if you don't mind. Text me the address."

On the way out to Oliver's truck, Halla said to Elsie, "I know you're supposed to be back in Phoenix by Tuesday at the latest, but it doesn't look like I'm going to accomplish much today."

"What do you mean, not accomplish much?" Elsie whispered, jerking her head in Oliver's direction. "If there were any more sparks jumping between you, this place would be on fire."

Halla felt heat staining her face. "I know. Believe me."

"That's why I'm not going with you to look for your friends and why I'll meet you at the barbecue even though I have to drive Bianca's truck. I want to back you up when you meet his family, but you two need some alone time."

"If you end up having to fly back to Phoenix because

I can't find my mother before then, I'll pay. It's the least I can do."

Elsie shrugged. "We'll see your mom tomorrow. We have all day. If we don't, I'm not leaving you. Ruth will manage without me. She has all the fosters and Lily to help. This is more important."

Halla hugged her. Whatever bad had marked her early life, she wouldn't have found Elsie or any of the fosters if she hadn't needed to run away. She had to remember that. "I love you," she whispered.

Elsie hugged her back even tighter. "I love you too."

After a good hour of Facebook stalking and a few random calls to Amy Norton's family, Halla found her old best friend. She had been a pretty teen and had become a striking woman, one who would be noticed and appreciated in any setting, even if not many would call her beautiful. What surprised Halla was that her last name was now Styles, which was also Halla's old crush's last name. It turned out Amy's husband was named Peter, and the couple lived in Boise. Halla and Oliver headed over.

"I can't believe she married Peter," Halla said as they pulled up to a large, two-story house in an upscale neighborhood.

Oliver chuckled. "Stabbed in the back by your best friend."

"Well, it's not as if I was around."

"Right." He nearly growled the word. "Sorry. Still makes me mad."

"Me too." She started over for the passenger door, but he grabbed her hand, sending jolts of excitement through her body.

"Are you okay if I go in?"

Halla tried to think past the reaction she was having to his touch. "Yes, I'd like you to come in. Amy knew about my dad. Some of it. And I'm sure she's told Peter by now. Well, maybe. If it ever came up. Having you here . . . well, it's like I'm not so pathetic."

His hand left hers and touched her face instead. "You are *so* not pathetic. What happen then happened *to* you, not *because* of you, and it's your parents who are pathetic." His voice was gravelly, as if holding back emotion.

She nodded, giving him a gentle smile. "See? That's why I'm glad you're here."

"Always."

It sounded like a pledge. Like something she should ask him about, but now wasn't the time. Even though his eyes invited her to drown in them.

He pulled away and jumped from the truck, running around to help her down.

"I can get down myself, you know," she told him with a sassy quirk of her lips.

"Oh, I know. It's just an excuse to make sure you're really here."

Her turn to laugh. "I thought there might be more awkwardness between us, especially after the whole shower incident, but there's not."

"I'm glad." The delicious tension was back, and for a moment she thought he might kiss her right there outside her old friends' house. Not exactly what she'd planned, but so far nothing of their meeting had gone as expected. But he gave his head a quick shake, took her hand, and started up the walk.

Amy met them at the door with a toddler on her hip and a huge smile. "It's so good to see you." She gave Halla an awkward half hug, smelling of flowers on a spring day. "I love your hair," Amy gushed. "You're so beautiful. I always knew you would be. And who's this?" Her attention turned to Oliver.

"I'm Oliver Montgomery, a close friend of Halla's," Oliver said before Halla could introduce him.

"Nice to meet you." Amy shook his proffered hand with her French-manicured one. "This little guy is my son, Maddox." The toddler buried his face in his mom's shoulder. "Come on in," Amy said, working her long brown hair out from under her son's face. "I told Peter you were coming. He had to run to the office, but he'll be here in just a moment."

She led the way through their vaulted entry to a family room with a huge TV and a basket of toys, which she dumped onto the tan carpet before setting the child down next to the jumble. "Have a seat." She indicated the couch, and with a sigh, she slumped onto a leather loveseat opposite them and crossed one bare foot over the other. Her toenails were painted a bright red.

Halla scanned the room that looked like an interior designer had been given free reign, from the carefully organized pictures to the vase on the fireplace mantel. The room had been toddler-proofed, though, from the hip down. The room fit Amy perfectly.

"So how have you been?" Amy arched her long neck,

rubbing at the back as if to release tension. "What have you been doing all this time?"

Halla took her eyes from her surroundings. "I'm a reporter and I run a blog. A mix of snarky advice and product reviews and such. It's a lot of work but also a lot of fun."

"Oh, I imagine. It's got to be more interesting than what I do all day. After I had Maddox, I tried to stay at my job, but it didn't work out. Our nanny wasn't very good, and I felt torn in two." She patted her stomach. "So we're having one more, and I'm staying home until they're in school. Then I'll plunge back in."

"Sounds like you have a plan," Halla said.

"Yep. Hopefully. I take it you're not married?"

"Nope."

Oliver took Halla's hand. "Not yet," he added. He winked at Halla, making her stomach heat again. He grinned at her and started rubbing his thumb across the back of her hand.

"Ah, I see how it is," Amy said, seeming happy for them.

Halla didn't respond. Oliver's little display had driven all the questions she'd wanted to ask from her mind. Amy didn't appear to notice as she asked about Halla's life in Phoenix. After that avenue had been exhausted, she chatted about her husband and his job as a site manager at her father's construction firm. She was too polite to ask why Halla had come, but it was apparent after about five minutes that whatever had brought the girls together as teens didn't seem to connect them now.

Oliver caught Halla's gaze and gave her an encouraging nod. Right. She should get on with it.

"So," she began. "I ate at this hamburger restaurant yesterday, and I remembered us being there. I think Peter might have driven us from the high school. It's called Front Burner Burgers now, but I don't remember the name back then. Anyway, that's what made me think to look you up."

"Oh, I remember that place!" Amy looked excited, and her high cheekbones pinkened. "Peter did take us there. Mostly because he liked you. We were only in ninth grade and he was so much older. We thought we were so cool."

"Yeah," Halla said. "I remember how cool we thought we were, leaving school without permission. Especially me. But do you remember why we went there? It's nowhere near the high school."

Amy thought a moment, then shook her head. "I don't know. Maybe Peter does. Maybe it was someplace he knew about."

Halla felt disappointment at that idea, but Amy was probably right. The weird experience she'd had there was likely due more to lack of sleep than to any past memory.

"Oh, wait! I think I have some pictures of us together. I was cleaning last month and stumbled over them. I'll be right back." Amy swooped up her son and hurried from the room. Minutes later she was back with a small box crammed full of photos. It took her a few minutes to find the ones she was looking for.

She sat next to Halla on the couch and handed over a short stack of pictures. Halla thumbed through them, seeing her and Peter and Amy. A few had been taken in the hamburger restaurant, the others at school. Oliver leaned over to look at them. "Your hair. Wow. There's more of it than of you." He wasn't exaggerating. She had been far too thin, and her hair went clear down her back.

"It was kind of long. Gave me headaches."

"Remember how we thinned it out that one time?" Amy said.

"Yeah." Halla's dad had never guessed. She tried to pass the pictures back, but Amy shook her head.

"You keep them. I had everything digitized a few years ago. I have these in a photobook dedicated to my high school years. You can keep these."

"Thanks." The tiny purse Halla carried wouldn't fit the photos, but Amy found an envelope in her box to protect them.

"So weird that Peter and I ended up together," Amy said, leaning over and crowding Halla a bit. She glanced across Halla to Oliver and explained. "My husband had a crush on Halla back then. But after her dad made her stay home from school for a month to get her away from him, things died out a bit. And then when she didn't come back for tenth grade . . ." Amy trailed off, looking embarrassed.

Amy had it all wrong. Peter had still asked Halla out when her dad finally let her return to school, but she had spurned him, unwilling to risk another punishment. She'd briefly thought about confiding in Peter, but what could he do? Somehow she'd avoided him and finished most of the last two months of school. In the end, it made no difference. She'd spent two weeks of May, all summer, and the first two and a half months of tenth grade locked in her room for a sin she didn't remember. Six long months.

"I hope things went well for you after you left," Amy said into the awkwardness. "I wondered where you went— we all did. We thought you were kidnapped. Well, I had some idea that maybe you weren't." She glanced at her son and said in a lower voice, "I even worried that your dad might have . . . done something. I told the police when they questioned me, but they didn't seem to go anywhere with it. I was glad when they found you, and that you didn't have to come back. I hope . . . was it a good place you found?" Amy's regal brow was drawn with concern and her brown eyes showed compassion.

Halla felt a rush of emotion. This was the girl she remembered. The girl who had cared enough to want to know about the bruises, who questioned the reason Halla could never come home with her. Memories flooded back, of Amy protecting her at school from curious students. Of Amy inventing ways for her to stay after school.

"I landed in a wonderful place," Halla assured her. "The best. I have a huge family, one that would even rival yours. But you should know that having your friendship back then, sharing my life with you and having you be there for me, made a difference." Tears formed in her eyes. "A big difference." Just how big, she hadn't realized until this moment.

"Then you're not mad at me for Peter?" Amy wiped a tear under her eye. "Or for not telling someone?"

Halla laughed. "No to both."

"Well, the only reason Peter even noticed me in the

first place was because of our friendship, and he's the best thing in my life besides Maddox, so I owe you too."

After that, the talk dwindled, and Halla decided it was time to excuse themselves.

"Just wait a few more minutes for Peter," Amy implored. "He'll want to see you. Oh, there's the garage now." She popped to her feet

Halla followed suit, casting a meaningful, "Get me out of here look" at Oliver, who nodded—hopefully in understanding.

Peter met them at the door to the living room, where he gave Amy an enthusiastic kiss. He kept a loving hand on her waist as he shook hands with both of them. "Sorry I took so long. It seems everything goes wrong on the weekends."

"I only stopped by to say hi," Halla said. "Amy and I've been catching up."

"Well, I'm glad to see you." He looked past Halla to his son, who was walking unsteadily toward them. "I guess you've met our son? He's barely learned to walk." In three steps, Peter reached the boy, lifted him up, and planted a kiss on his grinning face.

"I sure have. He's a cutie." Halla glanced again at Oliver.

"We have a barbecue with my family we have to get to," Oliver said.

"Oh, you have family here?" Peter asked. Oliver launched into a brief explanation, and then finally they were walking to the door.

On the doorstep, Amy said, "Oh, wait. Peter, Halla was asking about that restaurant you used to drive us to.

Remember that hamburger place? You had just gotten your license, and you took a bunch of us a few times."

"I remember." He looked up at the ceiling in thought. "Um, The Burger Pit. Right?"

Amy snapped her fingers. "Yes. That was it. So why did you choose that place?"

"Wasn't me." Peter shifted his son to his other hip. "Halla wanted to go there. She said she used to go with her mother."

Goose bumps raised on Halla's arms. "Really? I don't remember that. Did I tell you anything more?"

Peter shook his head. "Just that you both ate the ice cream. Strawberry, I believe."

Where did all the air go? Halla couldn't breathe. Strawberry ice cream, he'd said. Memories tumbled over her, but when she tried to examine them, they flitted out of her reach.

Oliver put his arm around her. "Thank so much," he said. "We'd better get on our way."

"Thanks," Halla echoed.

They hurried to the truck, Oliver's hand on her waist, steadying her. As he helped her inside, she saw Amy and Peter waving. They looked good together. Happy.

Oliver drove off before asking, "Did you find what you hoped for?"

She nodded. "I think so." Maybe. Now more than ever she needed to talk to her mother.

14

They still had a few minutes to kill before the barbecue at five, so Oliver drove Halla around to his old haunts in Boise. He showed her the high school, the bleachers where he'd stolen his first kiss from a girl in his French class, the soccer field where he'd had his first volunteer job as a referee, and the theater where he had his first real job.

Gradually the tautness of her body relaxed, and she started asking questions. He figured that was a good sign.

"So about this girl . . . and French class," she said, her nose wrinkling in the most appealing way. "Isn't that a little cliché?"

He laughed, glancing over at her and back to the road. "Maybe. But she was the only reason I even took the class. It's silly now, but it seemed important then. She ended up dumping me for a football player."

Laughing, Halla scratched at a spot on her khaki shorts. "Am I dressed okay? I mean, for the barbecue."

"Perfect, it might be a little cold later tonight, but we'll take off before it gets bad."

"I have to confess that I'm a little worried about your mother. Most mothers don't like the way I typically dress. Of course, I'm not wearing boots or my camo today."

"Which disappoints me a lot, by the way," he said with a grin. He kept his face serious as he added, "Though I would have much preferred you to wear the shower sheet you were sporting this morning."

"Ha ha." She leaned over and slugged his arm. "Anyway, I'll wear my camo pants when we go hiking. If we go hiking. I brought them along with my shoes." She patted a small duffel bag she'd retrieved when they'd gone to the camper to research her friends. It sat on the seat between them, and he'd been tempted more than once to toss it under the seat so maybe she would scoot next to him as she'd done when Elsie had ridden along.

"Oh, we're going hiking. I know of a perfect night hike we can take."

"Sounds great. I don't know how much I'm going to be able to sleep anyway."

"Want to talk about it?" He tried to sound casual, so she wouldn't feel he was pushing. He could see the visit to Amy and Peter had disturbed her.

She chewed on her bottom lip for a moment. "Last night I had a sort of memory flashback, and I remembered eating strawberry ice cream as a child at that restaurant. It was more upsetting than anything else. I didn't see who I was with, but now Peter says it was my mother."

"And?" he prompted after a moment of silence.

"And I love strawberry ice cream. I don't want to give it up because of a stupid memory!"

He would have laughed if her indignance hadn't been

so serious. "Maybe it's one of the good memories. Like the ones with Amy."

It was the right thing to say. "Maybe." Smiling, she settled back and thumbed through her pictures again.

"So these other guys you've dated—do their mothers eventually come around?" he asked. "After they get over the camo, I mean."

She gave him a sincere grin, causing his eyes to stray from the road for far too long.

"Oh, yeah. They usually love me if the guys stick around."

He stopped a little too soon at a yellow traffic light to watch her reaction to his next comment. "I'm surprised one of them didn't snatch you up."

She rolled her eyes. "Well, when you'd prefer to invite a guy's mother over rather than the man himself, there's a problem."

He laughed. "You won't have that problem with my mom, I assure you."

"I don't want to make things bad between you again." Her frown did nothing to mar her beauty, but it did make him want to pull over and kiss it away.

"You won't. It'll be okay. Although she might feel a little threatened." His mother had always been possessive, and when he'd texted her that he was spending time with a girl today, her response hadn't been enthusiastic. Well, he'd cross that bridge when he came to it. "I'm confident you can hold your own. In fact, I'm expecting you to. There will be a lot of nosy questions, I'm sure."

"What kind of questions?" A line of concern appeared between her eyebrows.

"You know. How long we've known each other, etcetera, etcetera." He turned down his sister's street.

Halla didn't talk for a long minute. "They don't know about me, do they?" she asked finally. "About my past."

He guided the truck over to the curb and parked, turning the engine off. He took her hands in his. "No. Of course not. It's none of their business unless you want it to be."

"I've talked about my past a lot." She frowned. "Or about what I thought I knew. How can I have forgotten so much?"

"Trauma, I think," he said. "And did I tell you I was sorry?" He fingered the softness of her hands. "I had no business challenging you to come here. That wasn't my place."

Her mouth parted in a gentle sigh. "Then who would have done it?"

He would have given anything at that moment to lean forward and kiss her—and he would have done so if they didn't already have an audience.

"Thank you," she said, her chin lifting. "We can go now. I'm okay."

He looked past her. "Good. Because we're already here, and it looks like my niece and nephew have found us."

She turned as the kids catapulted from the porch and his sister's grasp to run down the lawn. He jumped out of the truck and met them before they tumbled into the road. "Whoa, there. I have someone I want you to meet."

"A girl, a girl!" shouted the little girl, her short brown hair already matted to her forehead with moisture. The boy joined in the chant.

Oliver pushed them down on the grass, grabbed each of their feet, and pulled them into the air. The kids howled with laughter. "This," he said to Halla as she climbed from the truck, "is Clara. She's five and the ringleader of all things trouble. This other one is Joshua, and he's three, and he's really quite sweet."

"Let me down!" shouted Clara through her giggles. Joshua waved his hands.

"What?" Oliver said. "Huh? Upside down? Halla, do you see any upside down kids?"

"Me! Me!" shouted Joshua.

"Oh, so you are." Oliver laid both kids gently on the grass. "Kids, this is Halla. And you better treat her really nice because she has dozens of sisters. Like a hundred or more. And they're all very protective of her."

Clara's eyes grew wide. "A hundred?" She scowled skeptically at her uncle before shifting her gaze to Halla. "Is that true?" she asked.

"Yep. But I didn't live with them all at once. I grew up in a foster home called Lily's House, and I still help my foster mom with the new girls, so I get to know them all and claim them as sisters. Some stay for only a few months, some stay until they're all grown up. Usually they are at least twelve when they come to Lily's House, but we've had a few younger girls sometimes. And a few that were already adults."

"Wow, that's awesome. I wish I had a hundred sisters!" Clara jumped to her feet and yanked her brother up. "Let's eat!"

Joshua grinned at Halla shyly before running back to the house after his sister, pretending he was an airplane.

Oliver's sister was smiling as they reached the door, her long dark hair fluttering in the evening breeze. "Just when I thought I finally had them calm," she said, shooting Oliver an evil eye. To Halla, she added, "You must be Halla. I'm Crystal, Oliver's sister. I'm so glad to finally meet you. I've heard a lot about you."

Halla shook her hand. "Me too. I recognize you from your picture."

"You're prettier than your picture." Crystal slugged Oliver. "Men don't know good pictures when they see them."

Halla arched a brow at him, and Oliver shrugged. "In my defense, I really don't know which picture I showed her, but I'm sure it was great. You look great in all your pictures." He had at least twenty of them on his phone, but he wasn't owning up to that at the moment. No use inviting more ribbing from Crystal.

"It's okay," Halla said with her usual grin that told him at least she wasn't thinking about her mother anymore.

"We do have one little issue," Crystal said in an under-tone as she gestured for them to enter the house. "Mom's already here, and she invited Reagan."

"What?" The word exploded from his lips, and all at once, he was aware of Halla's eyes riveting on him. He shook his head to reassure her. "It doesn't matter."

Crystal nodded. "I know, but I wanted you to be prepared." She glanced at Halla before adding, "Better fill her in. Come out on the deck when you're ready. And if you decide to take off, I'll understand." With an uncertain grin she disappeared into the kitchen. Seconds later, Oliver heard the patio door shutting.

"Reagan?" asked Halla. "Is she someone I should be worried about?"

It didn't escape him that she used the same words he'd used when asking about her friend Peter. But unlike him, she didn't sound worried.

"Remember that French class and the girl who left me for the football player?"

Halla laughed. "You've got to be kidding."

"Apparently she and my mom ran into each other a few years back. Some planning committee or other. She's divorced now from the football player, and my mom has brought her up in conversation no less than ten times this week."

"Well, this is going to be awkward." Halla was still grinning, so her next words shocked him. "But how do you know if you'll like her if you don't ask her out?"

"I am not going anywhere with her!"

If Halla could ask that, did it mean things weren't going well for him? Maybe he needed to up his game. With all this stuff about her parents, there hadn't been any time to woo her properly. And time was running out.

"Come on," he said, grabbing her hand. "You're my protection. Remember that."

Something sparked in her eyes, but it was nothing compared to the heat that rushed over him at her touch. He was gone. Completely gone. If he didn't kiss her soon, and tell her how he really felt about her, he was going to drive himself insane.

Holding hands, they went out to the deck. The heat of the day was already winding down, but the curtain hanging from one side of the deck roof helped shade them from the angled sun. "Hey, everyone," he called. "We're here!"

For the next few minutes, he was introducing his family: Kevin Reed, Crystal's dark-haired husband who was manning the grill; Oliver's baby brother, Franklin; and Franklin's round-faced wife Malia, who was holding their eight-month-old son, Kamden, in her arms. Malia gushed with friendliness, as always, and Oliver was happy to see that Halla's returning smile was real.

Only his mother hadn't rushed to meet Halla. He let his gaze wander across the deck to where his mother sat in a chair next to Reagan. Both women were watching him, and his mother now beckoned with an imperious wave.

"Come meet my mother," he said, tugging on Halla's hand. His mother was a heavyset woman who had recently developed knee trouble, so he could excuse the lack of manners, but he wanted this part to be over.

"Hi, Mom," he greeted as they reached her.

"Hi, darling." She wore a loose, flowing summer dress with cap sleeves, and her dark hair curled under today, the ends grazing her neck. Her lipstick was a little too bright for his taste.

He leaned over to kiss her cheek. "I want you to meet Halla Jenkins. Halla, this is my mother, Nanette."

Halla pulled her hand from Oliver's and offered it to his mother. "Nice to meet you." Halla's voice was strong, without a hint of nerves.

"Hello," His mother shook Halla's hand briefly before saying to Oliver, "Look who else is here. You remember Reagan, don't you dear?"

Reagan took that cue to jump up and hug Oliver, her perfume wafting over him. She looked better than she had in high school. Her makeup was lighter and her hair more natural instead of sprayed to death. She wore tight jeans and heels that did wonders for her slim figure, and the red top with the V-neck was eye-catching. She was almost as tall as he was.

"Yeah, from high school," he said. "You married that football player. Can't remember his name."

"We divorced last year." Reagan smiled a sexy, come-hither smile he recognized only too well, one that would have sent him scrambling after her in high school. He felt nothing for her now, though. Not even a thread of attraction.

"Oh, sorry to hear that. Well, it's nice to see you." Oliver took Halla's hand again. "This is my friend Halla. She's visiting from Phoenix."

"Girlfriend, you mean," Franklin corrected, coming up behind them, hoping to embarrass him probably, but Oliver was happy enough with the statement, even though his mother's eyes narrowed.

"Oh, you have family here?" Reagan asked.

"In Nampa," Halla said casually. "I don't get back much."

More small talk as they chatted about high school and Reagan's job as a recorder for the city of Boise, and finally Oliver felt they'd completed their quota of politeness. He turned to Halla. "Want to play Frisbee with the kids? They're pretty good." He lowered his voice. "Well, at least Clara is."

"Sure."

He saw Reagan's smile fade as she glanced uncertainly at his mother, who said, "Go ahead and play with them, Reagan. I'm okay watching."

"Okay." Reagan sat and pulled off her heels.

Franklin came up with a pair of Frisbees, and they all spread out. Halla was good, holding her own against Oliver and Franklin, but Reagan soon gave up and played only with the children, which was nice of her, given the circumstances.

At one point he was running for a catch and plowed into Reagan, knocking her to the grass. "I'm so sorry," he said, offering a hand to help her up.

"It's okay." She laughed and dusted her hands on her jeans. "I was in the way."

"Food's ready!" Kevin shouted.

Oliver looked over to see Crystal waving her hands at them, pointing at Elsie, who stood beside her on the deck. He and Reagan began walking across the lawn together.

"Look . . ." She glanced past him to where Halla waited on the grass for them to join her. "I had no idea you were dating someone. Your mother . . . she kind of gave me the wrong idea. But while I'm here, I want to say that I was a real jerk to you in high school, and I feel bad about that."

"Don't give it another thought. And you couldn't help knowing that I was involved with someone."

"You really like her, don't you?"

"Yeah. I do."

"That's good. I'm happy for you. But I think I'm going to find some excuse to leave, if you don't mind."

"I think you should stay," he said. "Really. There's no reason we all can't have a good meal."

"Well, I *am* hungry, so maybe I'll stay for the steak."

He laughed. "You deserve it."

They'd reached Halla, who was watching them. To make sure she had no doubts of his intentions, he grabbed her hand and pulled her to him. "I told Kevin to make your steak well done."

"Good." Her laugh made him feel like he was standing in the sunlight.

Back on the patio, Crystal introduced Elsie, who muttered to Halla, "Sorry I'm late. I was talking to Payden."

"He got the house?" Halla asked.

"Yes," Elsie said with forced brightness. "He countered their counter offer, and they accepted. The house is his."

She didn't appear happy about Payden getting the house, and Oliver had no clue as to why. He cast a questioning look at Halla, who mouthed, "Later."

The nine adults sat easily around the long table on the patio, with Halla between Oliver and Elsie. Crystal's two kids were excited to use their own plastic picnic table, and Malia settled Kamden in a highchair near her. Franklin leaned over to kiss his wife and to give her round backside a little squeeze. She squealed and slapped at him, but he grinned at the protest and settled next to her, placing an arm over the back of her chair.

"I'd give him up, but I love him too much," Malia said, her plump face flushed.

"Well, we women outnumber the men today," Crystal replied. "Just let us know if you need us to put him in his place. I have a little something I can add to his dessert, something that will keep him in the bathroom all night long." She included Halla in her conspiratorial stare, and both Halla and Elsie laughed.

Franklin laughed with them. "Wouldn't be the first time she's tried." He gave his sister a mocking glance before whispering something in his wife's ear.

This is good, Oliver thought. They were all having fun. His family liked Halla, and she liked them. His gaze slid across the table to his mother, who was talking to Reagan. *Well, almost everyone.* His mother wasn't smiling. Was it because he wasn't paying attention to Reagan or because Halla had refused one of her freshly baked rolls? She couldn't know that Halla didn't like bread. Well, there was nothing he could do about that now, but he'd have to talk to his mother about Reagan before they regressed to her trying to force him into a path he had no intention of going down.

As everyone dug in, little Clara left her table and came over to Elsie and Halla. "So are you one of Halla's hundred sisters?" she asked Elsie.

Elsie chuckled. "Yes, I am."

"How old were you?"

"When we became sisters?"

Clara nodded.

"I was twelve. I was the youngest of the original six girls that our foster mother took in. Her name was Lily, and we lived together in a house we called Lily's House, but it was ours too. We all had to work hard to paint and fix it up in the beginning. It was the best house ever. Still is."

"And you?" Clara pointed to Halla. "Were you twelve?"

"No, I was fifteen, almost sixteen," Halla responded.

"Elsie was our baby and the cutest of all of us. She had all kinds of freckles. Before Lily's House, we were in a tiny apartment and we used to climb up on the rooftop to watch the stars."

"Don't give her ideas," Crystal joked, and they all laughed.

"I have only one brother," Clara said solemnly, "but my Mommy is going to have another baby."

Everyone looked at Crystal, who stared back at them sheepishly. "Yeah, um, so I was about to announce that. Surprise! Kevin and I are going to have another baby."

"I hope it's a sister," Clara announced before wandering back to her brother.

Oliver noticed his mother was smiling now at Crystal's news.

As the talk turned to due dates, Reagan suddenly snapped her fingers. "I know you," she said to Halla. "You're the girl who went missing in Nampa, who later showed up in Arizona, and it came out that your dad . . ." Reagan trailed off, her face coloring. "Anyway, I remember that. Sorry, I probably shouldn't have said anything."

Halla's nostrils flared slightly, but her face remained impassive. Too impassive, as if she was stepping into a role that had nothing to do with her personally. "It's okay. It doesn't bother me. Life with my parents wasn't good, so I took matters into my own hands." She glanced at Elsie and added, "Fortunately, as Elsie said, I ended up in a terrific place. With a bunch of great sisters."

"Lucky for all of us." Elsie laid her head briefly on Halla's shoulder, then lifted it and said to Kevin, "Man, I swear this has to be the best steak I've ever tasted. The spices are amazing, and how did you get it so soft? I'm part owner of a café, and mostly I serve soup and sandwiches, but if I could do steak this well, I'd definitely add it to my menu."

Kevin breathed on his nails and buffed them on his shirt in a gesture of pride. "It is pretty good, isn't it?"

He launched into his seasoning method while Oliver gave Elsie a grateful look that she didn't see. Halla did see it, and she shrugged, slipping a hand into his beneath the table. She seemed okay with Reagan's identification, though he purposely hadn't shared any details with his family. He'd wanted to protect her. The idea that someone had hurt her so much still made him furious.

Her touch eased his emotions. This wasn't about him, and he needed to remember that being angry wouldn't help her. He needed to listen and be there if she needed him. Perhaps to deflect interest like Elsie had. Like maybe all the sisters did for each other.

Like his sister did for him with his mother. Not that he'd ever needed it the way the Lily's House girls did. Protecting each other was what family did. They might poke at things among themselves, but they came through with support when it was needed.

The rest of the barbecue passed without incident, and when Reagan excused herself directly after the meal, even before the chocolate cake his sister had made for dessert, no one seemed to mind. No one except his mother, who insisted on walking Reagan to the door.

They ate dessert and chatted for a while after his mother returned to the table, but when his sister brought out her phone to show Halla and Elsie pictures, Oliver began gathering up the plates and carrying them into the kitchen. He'd do his part so he could take Halla somewhere private. He needed to make sure she was okay. He wanted to take her on a hike where they could watch the sunset together. Alone.

His mother followed him inside with a pitcher of water. She looked ready to burst, and Oliver felt a sense of inevitability. He hadn't told her he was planning on staying another day, and now he was thinking it was better he didn't. He could get a hotel in Nampa near Halla instead.

"It was nice seeing Reagan again, wasn't it?" his mother asked.

How to respond? He could play along and hope she let it go, or he could tell her the truth. Franklin had told him repeatedly over the years to pretend to go along with whatever their mother suggested and then go and do whatever he wanted instead, but Oliver didn't like pretense. Besides, his life wasn't in Boise, and Halla wasn't in Boise, so there was only so far he could pretend.

"It was awkward, Mom," he said finally. "For both of us. Why did you invite her?"

"I didn't know you were bringing anyone." She set the pitcher next to the sink where he was rinsing the dishes before putting them in the dishwasher.

"But I told you I wasn't interested in Reagan. I'm seeing Halla." This was probably his fault. He'd told his mother about Halla, but maybe he hadn't communicated how much he cared for her.

She folded her arms over her ample chest. "You barely know this girl."

"I've known her for more than a year."

"Talking on the Internet isn't the same thing as real life. But she isn't for you. You have to see that, Oliver. Not with all that she's been through."

Anger rose in him. He left the remaining dishes in the sink and twisted the water off with an abrupt movement. "That's not her fault."

"Of course not, but it brings extra baggage that you don't need to deal with. It'll affect your lives. Your children's lives."

"And Reagan having an ex-husband wouldn't? We all have baggage, Mom, but the only way Halla's past is going to affect us is that we'll know even more what not to do. Her *real* family, her foster family, is far more influential in her life than her birth parents. They've taught her what's important. She's the most caring, wonderful woman, I've ever met. And she gets me. I love being with her."

He wished he could make her understand how he felt. How Halla understood his love of his job, his need to be out in nature. Their shared love of old movies, obscure bands, and even ice cream. She understood how important his family was to him. Even his infuriating mother.

His mother's chin lifted. "I don't think this girl will make you happy. She'll take you away from here. From all of us."

"No, Mom." He leaned his backside against the sink, hands fisted at his side as he forced his voice to remain calm, though he wanted to rip into her, to hurt her as he was hurt by her words. "This *girl* is the only reason you and I are even standing here talking. And her name's

Halla. Please use it. Halla inspired me to reach out to you because she knows how important family is. I'm here because of her."

His mother tensed, and her voice became prickly. "What are you saying?"

What was it Halla had talked about in her "Let Go" blog? Right, no accusations. Go back to the issue at hand.

He took a deep breath. "I'm saying that I'm glad I'm here, and I'm glad we're a family. I love you, and I want you in my life. I regret the years we've missed out on. I'm sad I wasn't there when Dad died. But I'm never going to live in Boise again, regardless of who I marry. I need to follow my dreams. And if I'm in Coeur d'Alene or end up in Phoenix with Halla, that doesn't mean I won't still be your son and want you in my life."

Unless his mother tried to make him into something he wasn't. Because that had always been the problem. Could she see it now? But he didn't think she was capable of seeing what he saw so clearly.

"We're family," he added, edging away from the accusation he wanted to make. "I love being with you and Crystal and Franklin and their families, but I need to do what makes me happy. What *I* think makes me happy. Please don't let anything get in the way of our relationship."

Tears stood out in his mother's eyes, and she sniffed loudly. "That's all I ever wanted—for you to be happy. I guess I just wanted you to be happy here."

"I know," he said, willing to let her words stand, though he was pretty sure it was her happiness she'd been most concerned about, regardless of what she believed. Maybe to her it was the same thing. He pushed off the sink, opening his arms, and she went into them.

Relief flooded him. He'd passed the biggest hurtle—asserting independence while protecting his relationship with his mother. Maybe they both had learned something since he'd left home.

"Well, I'd better get going," he said, pulling away as his sister, Halla and Elsie in tow, entered the kitchen with more dishes.

"Don't bother helping me clean up," Crystal said. "I hear you're going on a hike tonight. You should go. You're not going to be in town much longer."

There she had to go and remind him that the clock was ticking against him and Halla. Oliver stifled a sigh.

Halla held up the duffel she must have brought in with her, though he hadn't noticed it earlier. "Is there a place I can change?"

"I'll show you." Crystal motioned to Halla.

"I forgot a sweatshirt, though," Halla added. "Will I need one? It's a lot chillier here at night than in Phoenix."

"Probably, but I've got one in my truck."

By the time Oliver dug out his sweatshirt from a bag under his seat, Halla was out of the bathroom, looking stunning in snug camouflage pants and her pink T-shirt. She tried on his sweatshirt, and it drowned her, making her look more adorable than sexy, but he wouldn't say that aloud for a million dollars.

She pulled the sweatshirt off and tied it around her waist. They went outside to say goodbye to everyone, and this time Oliver was happy to see his mother smile at Halla.

He slung an arm around Halla's shoulder. He couldn't wait to get her out of here.

The trailhead of the hike Oliver had chosen for them was only ten minutes away. "It's called Castle Rock Loop," he said as he parked the truck. "It's mostly rock and mountain, with a little wild grass and brush. And flowers in the spring. I would have taken you to a place with more trees, but those are an hour away or more, and I wanted to be up before the sun goes down. This trail is a little less busy than others that are also nearby."

"How far is it?"

"The entire loop is just over two and a half miles. It's an easy hike. We'll get up there in plenty of time to see the sunset. I have flashlights for the way down." He motioned to a small backpack he'd fished from under the seat.

A few other cars were in the parking lot, but their owners were nowhere to be seen as they started up the trail. Five minutes in, a guy on a mountain bike passed them heading down. Halla was happy for a chance to relax. The barbecue had been better than she'd expected, even with Reagan there. She'd felt more embarrassed for the other woman than anything. Maybe Halla could have tried a little more with his mother, but she hadn't seemed interested until the end.

"I told you I don't make a good first impression with mothers," she said.

He frowned. "Your impression was fine. She's just afraid of losing me again."

"Did you have a good talk with her in the kitchen? Crystal looked through the window. She thought it looked serious."

"Which was why she came in, I'm guessing," Oliver responded with a laugh. "It was a good talk actually. I think it'll be okay. You'll like her once you get to know her."

Would Halla get to know her? Halla didn't say the words aloud. The way she felt about Oliver, she wanted to know all his family, even a grouchy mother. But how could she be sure her feelings were returned? He hadn't even kissed her yet. There had been a few times he'd looked close, but nothing had ended up happening. Maybe she should be the one to breach the space between them.

"So why doesn't Elsie seem happy about her friend's house?" Oliver asked into the silence that had fallen between them.

Halla waved a flying insect away. "I think she's afraid of losing him. He might be planning to date another woman. Seriously date, I mean. At least that's what she thinks."

"Wait, this is the guy you told me is in love with Elsie? The one she keeps setting up with other people?"

Halla chuckled. "Right. Payden."

"Well, she can't expect him to wait around forever,"

Oliver said in sympathy. "Especially if she doesn't feel the same way."

"That's just it. I think she does. Or could. But I think she's so used to being friends that she doesn't see anything else."

"He's the guy who worked for the grocery store, isn't he?"

Halla hadn't realized she'd told him that story. "Yes. Lily found Elsie in an alley outside the store. She'd been beaten pretty badly, and Payden, who worked at the store, came out and stumbled across them. When he learned about Lily taking in girls, he started saving the expired groceries to give to Lily instead of tossing them into the garbage. He also eventually ended up introducing his cousin to Lily. Once they married, Payden hung out a lot with us. But he and Elsie were always best friends. She was twelve and he was seventeen—a very young seventeen. I mean, I felt older than him. And then when he did grow up, she was still so young, and it would have been weird, you know? It's not like he didn't date other women."

"But he obviously never told her how he felt. I mean, once they were older." Oliver nudged a large rock off the trail.

"Oh, he tried, but she would laugh it off. I think he always knew what he wanted, but she doesn't see him that way."

"Except now he's moving on."

Halla nodded, reaching to secure the sleeves of his sweatshirt more firmly around her waist. "I think something might have happened between them, but she hasn't told me what." She grimaced. "I guess I've been a little self-centered lately."

"With good reason."

"I'll talk to her tomorrow."

In ten more minutes, they'd reached the top, where a family with young children were climbing the rock formations. A beautiful view of Boise stretched out below them.

"Nice," she said, as she accepted a bottle of water from Oliver's backpack. "Very quick." She felt a little disappointed at how quick.

He took her hand. "Let's find a place to watch the sunset." He led her down another trail.

Halla had noticed there were numerous trails, leading off in different directions, and she was eager to explore at least one of them, especially if it meant being alone with Oliver. The trail he'd chosen eventually led to another group of boulders, smaller than the first group and much closer to the ground. Perfect for watching the sunset.

This is more like it, she thought, surveying the deserted area. *Alone at last.* But her heart was thundering in her chest again.

A squirrel or some other critter rustled through the underbrush, which reminded her of the skunk comment he'd made earlier in the week while she was still in Phoenix.

"Hey, you never told me about the skunk you met," she said, settling next to him on the rocks.

He groaned. "Oh, I was hoping you'd forgotten about that. I didn't mean to tell you."

"Spill it. I'm always looking for good blogging topics," she teased. The banging in her heart was easing now. This was comfortable, being with him like this.

He looked out at the sun, the edge of its circle barely beginning to dip below the horizon. "Well, I was out in the woods, talking to some of my group about the importance of controlled burning, and telling them to watch out for skunks because I'd spotted some earlier. I kicked a log for emphasis and apparently it was hollow, and out shot a skunk. A huge skunk. And he comes right for me, and before I can jump away, he sprays me good, and a couple of the guys next to me as well."

"Seriously?" Halla leaned close to him and sniffed. All that met her nose was a hint of aftershave or cologne and the slightest bit of male exertion. "You don't smell like skunk."

He drew away in mock horror. "You really shouldn't be smelling me after I've been hiking."

She rolled her eyes. "It was barely a hike at all. So what happened?"

"You mean the guys laughing and making fun of me for the next forty-eight hours straight?"

A giggle escaped her. "Sorry. No, I meant how did you get rid of the smell. Tomato juice? But you have to admit it's funny. You preaching about watching for skunks and then one spraying you."

"Yeah, yeah, yeah." He waved his hand at her. "I've already heard that from the guys. But tomato juice just masks the smell, and we didn't have any out there anyway. So we finished our job and stank all the way back to the lookout post, where we washed with a mix of hydrogen peroxide, baking soda, and liquid detergent. It's the only thing I know of that really gets it out."

"Peroxide and baking soda? And you just happened to have those on hand?"

"Oh, they're pretty much a staple for me—for all of us. Even more so now." He laughed again, and for a moment, they sat there watching the reds and yellows and purples of the sunset. The sky had never looked so beautiful to Halla.

When his hand reached out to hers, she turned to find him looking at her. "Come closer," he said, his voice low and seductive. "We both know there's something we have to get out of the way."

"It's not a chore." But she scooted closer until the sides of their hips and legs touched.

His chuckle sent goose bumps over her flesh. "Not any kind of chore, that's for sure. But it hasn't been a part of our relationship before."

"It has in my dreams," she admitted, not caring if the comment exposed her.

"Mine too. You have no idea how much."

They both leaned into the kiss, their arms wrapping around each other. Halla felt herself tumbling and soaring at the same time. His taste enveloped her, and passion ignited all her nerves, tingling to the tips of her toes.

He moaned softly against her mouth, leaving her lips briefly to trail kisses from her cheeks to her ears and down to her neck, only to find his way back to her mouth again. Halla knew in that moment that she shouldn't have worried. Kissing him was definitely not like kissing a friend. It was like coming home, full of brilliant fireworks and celebration . . . and certainty. Rightness.

The sun sank below the horizon, eventually taking the glorious colors in the sky with it. Cuddled up to Oliver, Halla barely noticed.

16

Wylen wasn't late for his Saturday night date with Kendall. In fact, he was ten minutes early and Kendall was still getting ready after her quick shower. Since she had no hint about where he planned to take her, she'd pulled on black dress pants and a bright blue, fitted blouse that masked the fact that she didn't have as much going on up top as she'd like to. She spent the most time on her hair because it took far too long to dry the strands that plunged halfway down her back. She set her normally straight hair in large heated rollers to give it extra body. When she did that after washing and drying it, the wave usually stayed in until the next wash.

When the doorbell rang, she dabbed on lipstick, grabbed black high heels, and hopped to the door as she put them on. She took a moment for a quick breath before throwing the door open. That breath was immediately stolen away as she stared at Wylen. He wore blue jeans that weren't ridiculously snug like so many of the younger men these days, and his muscles did wonderful things for his red T-shirt. She suddenly felt overdressed.

"Wow, you look amazing," he said. His stare warmed her, making her glad she'd taken the extra effort with her hair.

She managed a smile. "You do too." And he really did. It was strange seeing him out of his hospital garb—and dangerous because she was just that much more attracted to him. "But where are we going? It looks like I might be overdressed." Unless he was one of those guys who never dressed up, which would be sad because she liked a good night on the town as much as any woman.

"Well . . . you look so great that I am sorry to say it might be better if you change." He rubbed a hand across his chin, which appeared freshly shaven. Which was good because kissing a man with one or two days stubble was painful and scratchy.

The thought made her blink because there was no way she was kissing him on a first date. All the Lily's House girls made at least one non-kissing date a requirement, and though she wasn't technically a foster girl, she'd decided a long time ago that not kissing a man she liked at least for one date was a good idea. But one minute in Wylen's presence, and she was already changing her tune.

He was saying something about a boat, and she had to yank her attention from his smooth skin back to the conversation. "Okay, I'll just be a minute. Jeans and a T-shirt it is. Wait here a moment." She walked back to her room, shutting the door. She had a pair of stretchy Rock Republic jeans with zipper decoration under the front pockets that were both comfortable and somewhat trendy. They were the last pants she'd bought three years ago when she'd lived at home and her mother had insisted she wear the right kind of clothes. Now she saved them for when she wanted to impress. Her dark gray baseball shirt with the red sleeves would be casual enough to match Wylen, and she felt confident in it, though it wasn't something her mother would have ever purchased.

The grin on his face when she emerged and the way he looked her up and down made her glad of her choice. She slung her purse over her shoulder and they were off. He drove a Silver Camry, which wasn't as cool as her red Audi A3, but still nice. Her car was also a remnant from her days at home, and she would have sold it long ago to pay bills if her mother hadn't purchased it in the first place and owned the title. She was grateful to have the car, but there were many days when the money would have been more useful. Stifling a sigh, she pushed the thoughts aside. Her mother had accepted that Kendall was living her own life, but things between them were still stuck at polite tolerance rather than real affection.

"Where are we going exactly?" she asked to distract herself. "You said a boat?"

"Yes, at a lake. We'll have a picnic there. I hope you like deli sandwiches. I didn't have time to make anything." His grin widened. "I didn't want to be late."

"I'll eat anything." That hadn't always been true but living at Lily's House for a year had cured her of a lot of dislikes.

"Good." His eyes left the road and swept over her. "I know I said it before, but you look amazing. If you were to go around with your hair down like that at the hospital, we might have a few more heart attacks on our floor."

Kendall laughed. It didn't feel like a line, not with the

admiring way he kept glancing over at her. "Thank you," she said.

He stopped at the next red light. "So tell me about yourself. What made you go into nursing?"

That was new. Most of the residents or interns she knew only wanted to tell their own story, mostly about how hard med school was or how much they'd partied during breaks, depending on the man.

"My sister once dated a guy who eventually became a doctor, and three years ago when I first started college, our paths crossed and he inspired me. Before that I was studying interior design." She made a face. "Not really my choice. My sister was estranged from our family for quite a few years—not her fault but my mother's—and she helped me see that I had to do what I loved. So I moved here from California and fast-tracked my RN degree. I even went during the summer. Two long and very packed years. I'll be paying on school loans for a good while, but I love it."

He whistled. "Not everyone could make it through the program that quickly."

She shrugged, having left out too much to feel she was being honest. Studying had been the only thing that stopped her from complete despair after placing Teisha.

"You're good at it too," he added. "All my patients say how much they love you."

Kendall chuckled. "Well, so far they say the same about you."

"Maybe we're too young to be jaded yet." He cast her yet another searing look. "How old are you anyway? I'm twenty-seven, by the way."

Kendall already knew that—along with all the other nurses on the floor. "Twenty-one," she said. "And a half."

He laughed. "Wow, really? I thought you were older."

She felt older. Oh, so much older. "I'm mature for my age." Her mouth felt suddenly dry.

"Okay, well, I'll try not to think of myself as robbing the cradle."

"Good. And I'll try not to imagine you with a cane."

He laughed good-naturedly at that, and they lapsed into a companionable silence. Finally, he said, "So, your sister was estranged from the family?"

Kendall nodded. "Yeah, my mother is a very difficult, controlling person, and my father died soon after she kicked my sister out—who didn't deserve it, by the way. Saffron, that's my sister, got into some trouble, but my mother reacted beyond all reason. My sister has always been a hard worker and a great person. She was still in high school at the time and nearly died, but she was found by the woman who now runs Lily's House. Have you heard of it?"

He hadn't, so Kendall took the opportunity to tell him all about Lily and the girls Lily had helped over the past decade. "After Saffron and I reconnected, I stayed at Lily's House myself while I was in my first year of nursing school."

"Now that I think about it. I might have read an article or two about Lily's House at a café in town. They had some framed posters about it for customers to read while they wait in line."

"The Eats and Treats, I'm guessing," Kendall said. "It's

owned by two of Lily's former foster daughters, and one is my roommate."

"Small world. I used to buy pastries all the time when I was in med school in Washington DC, and when I mentioned that, someone at the hospital recommended the place to me."

"That's because I'm always bringing them in. They're the best in town."

"I can second that." A few seconds passed and then he asked, "So what about you? After your sister left and your father died? Was it tough?"

"I had it a little easier because my mother had to work more hours, so I had more freedom. We're okay now, but it's better at a distance. She'll never be the cookie kind of grandmother for my sister's new baby girl."

"She's married, I take it?"

"Yeah, she turned twenty-eight in July. What about your family?" Better to steer him away from the past until she was willing to tell him everything.

He glanced at her and back to the road before replying. "My upbringing was very boring compared to yours, I'm afraid. Not much drama. My parents are doctors in Nevada where I grew up. I also have a brother who's in med school. My parents both worked part-time when we were young, and Josh and I when through a phase of pulling pranks on each other and the neighbors, but it was all fairly innocent."

Kendall couldn't help the laugh that bubbled up inside her. "Sounds wonderful. I'm guessing they'd like you both to marry doctors?"

"At this point, they are sick of waiting, so I think they'd be happy to see us dating anyone who isn't a stripper or lady of the night." He laughed. "I know it might seem funny with them being doctors, but they're really easy going as far as expectations."

Kendall experienced a measure of hope. The man she eventually married didn't need to have parents that approved of her past, but it would be easier.

"Here we are," Wylen said as he turned off the main road.

The lake she'd been noticing on her right for some time now loomed in front of them. As he pulled into a parking place, she noticed several picnickers in a grassy area, lounging at tables or throwing Frisbees. She didn't recognize the place, but that was true about most places in or around Phoenix. She'd been working too hard in the last three years to do much more than survive.

He retrieved a picnic basket and a blanket from the trunk of his car, and the next thing she knew, they'd slathered on sunscreen and were walking down the dock where boats floated beckoningly. A fit, suntanned man with blond hair stood up from a seat on a mid-sized motor boat and tossed Wylen the keys.

"She's all yours," he said, jumping down to the dock.

"This is Logan," Wylen introduce the man to Kendall, "a buddy of mine from med school. He's letting us borrow his boat."

"My dad's, actually," Logan said. "I sort of inherited use of it when he retired from his law firm. He's not interested in boating anymore." Logan shook her hand, his grip firm. "Nice to meet you."

"You too," Kendall said.

"Thanks," Wylen told him.

Logan grinned. "Have fun you two. I'll be back later." To Wylen, he added. "We're still on for tomorrow, right?"

"Of course. Wouldn't miss it."

Logan nodded and strode up the dock.

Kendall wondered briefly what they were doing tomorrow night, but she didn't let herself ask. For all she knew, they were going on a double date. Her spirits fell a tiny bit at the idea, which was silly. She didn't have any claim on Dr. Gorgeous.

Wylen set down the picnic basket and dangled the keys. "You know how to drive a boat?"

"Not a clue. If it were a canoe or a raft, it would be a different story. I attended ten summer camps as a kid, and my sister married an animator who moonlights as a river rafting guide. I'm really good at paddling and rowing and the like."

"Guess I'll drive then," he said with a wink.

They sat together in the midsection where the steering was located, and soon they were cruising away from the shore. He guided the boat down through a thin section of the lake until it opened to a wider, almost deserted section. Killing the engine, he went to the deck at the front and spread out his blanket. Kendall swept up the picnic basket and joined him.

They ate sandwiches, a bag of chips, fresh fruit bowls, and power drinks. "I should have stopped at your room-mate's café," he said, half apologetically.

"It all tastes great."

"I sometimes go swimming here with Logan and his

wife, but I thought maybe a cruise would be better for our first date."

First date? That implied there would be a second. Swimming would have been fun, but maybe a little too intimate in this setting. She still wasn't sure she should even be here.

"This is nice," she assured him.

"So . . ." he said after a comfortable pause. "River rafting, huh? I've been before, but not here in Arizona."

"I go a lot in the summer on my days off. I get the family discount, which means zero. You should really give it a try."

"I definitely will." His enthusiasm made her laugh.

After eating their fill, they took the boat around the lake, looking at interesting rock outcroppings and the sections where fishes swam in the heavy reeds. They avoided the sandy part of the shoreline, where families romped in the evening light.

Soon they were back at their picnic site, where they spread the blanket again on the boat deck and watched the setting sun cast shimmering colors over the water. "This is so peaceful," Kendall murmured. He was close to her, but not close enough.

It's safer this way, she reminded herself.

As if reading her mind, he slid closer. "You got plans tomorrow night?" he asked. "I mean, if you're not doing anything too important after work, I'd love for you to come with me to Logan's tomorrow. He and I and one of his college buddies get together once a month for dinner and games."

Kendall's heart thudded in her chest. He was asking

her out again, and more than anything, she wanted to say yes. She no longer cared about the danger. She'd always known at some point she'd have to take a chance again because someday she wanted to get married and have a family. Someday had always meant far in the future, maybe when Teisha was in middle school. But love didn't seem to wait for anyone.

Love? No, that's not what she meant. It was just a second date. Never mind her thundering heart.

"I'd love to," she said. "And why don't you go river rafting with me? My brother-in-law is crammed with another animation project right now, but his cousin doesn't mind if I tag along with his other guides. As long as they have space in the boat. Since I know what I'm doing, I'm like unpaid help. You're off Monday, right?" Had she just asked him out? Her roommates would be proud of her.

"I'd love to give it a try."

"I'll call and see if they have space."

"Great, it's a date. Two of them."

He moved even closer, watching her face. She didn't turn away. So much for her no-kissing resolve. She'd been out a few times in the past year since she'd finished her nursing degree, and she'd even kissed other men, but it had always stopped there. Not once had she been tempted for anything more, not when she couldn't see a future. Not when she'd promised herself that she would never settle. Was there a future here? She wanted there to be—desperately. If she felt this way already, after only a few days, she'd better be more than careful. He might be a heartbreak in the making.

His lips met hers, warm and tender, but growing more passionate by the second. She loved the feel of him, the way they moved together so perfectly. A storm could have been raging around them, and all she would notice was the feel of his kiss. The way his tongue glided over her lips. She could stay like this forever.

His arm went up, slipping into her hair as he pulled her closer. She sighed with pleasure and his kiss intensified. She'd stop him soon, but for a moment at least, she'd enjoy it.

His phone beeped, and he pulled away. "Saved by the bell," he muttered hoarsely. "That means it's time to go. We need to get the boat back to the dock before it gets too dark."

Logically, she knew they'd been out for hours, but it felt like only moments. "Good thing probably," she said. "Since we both have an early shift tomorrow."

He groaned. "Don't remind me. I can't wait until I don't have to work weekends anymore."

She laughed. "I don't mind them, actually. It's a change of pace."

"I guess." He made his way back to the steering wheel as she folded the blanket. "Come steer this boat for a bit," he called. "You can't come out on it without at least trying."

"Won't Logan care? What if I crash?"

"You won't. It's easier than driving a car. Just stay away from the shore."

"Okay." There weren't any boats near them anyway.

"Besides, Logan owes me. I'm the one who introduced him to his wife."

"I see."

He stayed close as she drove the boat, recounting the story of how Logan's wife had helped him file his taxes in med school and how he'd passed on her information to Logan, who'd married her two months later at their next school break.

Kendall enjoyed his story, but she enjoyed even more the feel of the motor underneath them and how it responded to her slightest touch. She was disappointed when he took over the wheel as they approached the dock. His strong hands flexed as he eased the boat into place, and she had the nearly irresistible urge to run her fingers over his bare arm.

Logan awaited them on the dock. "Need help getting it on your trailer?" Wylen asked.

"No," Logan shook his head. "You have to work in the morning. I get to sleep in."

"Thanks, buddy." The two shook hands. "I owe you."

"Just come tomorrow night and don't forget the drinks."

"I already got them." Wylen put his arm around Kendall. "We'll both be there. Let Julie know to expect one more, okay?"

Logan's grin widened. "Sure thing. Be glad to."

"If we go by the Eats and Treats, we can pick up their extra pastries," Kendall suggested. "They're closed Sundays, so whatever they don't sell my roommate usually brings home or drops off at Lily's House. Elsie's out of town, but her partner will be happy to see us."

"That's a perfect idea," Wylen said.

They bid farewell to Logan and walked to the truck,

side by side, their hands occasionally brushing. Neither mentioned the kiss, but Kendall was thinking about it. Big time.

They picked up a selection of the pastries before Wylen drove her home. Kendall's heart was beating hard by the time they reached her front door. She wished she hadn't told him her roommates were out of town and hoped he wouldn't ask to come in. She hadn't been into casual sex, even before the pregnancy. If he pushed, their relationship would be over before it began.

"Don't look so nervous," he said. "I'm not going to bite you."

Kendall smiled. "I just . . . I don't make a habit of dating people I work with."

"I know." He blew out a breath, his handsome face growing concerned. "Me either. Not since my second year of med school. Not a good ending. But you . . ." He paused, stepping closer but not touching her. "I really like you, Kendall Brenwood."

He kissed her again, causing the world to swirl around her. But this time he seemed more in control, though she could sense the passion burning dangerously beneath his restraint. The kiss was perfect, if too brief, but even its shortness relieved her.

"See you tomorrow," he said.

She waved and watched him go.

She'd barely changed into her pajamas when a text came through on her phone: *I had a wonderful time tonight, Kendall. I'm excited about tomorrow and Monday. I just hope I don't fall off the boat!*

She laughed and texted back. *Oh, you won't be falling*

out, it'll be me pushing you! I had a great time too. Good night.

Wylen looked up from his car to Kendall's apartment building as he tossed his phone onto the passenger seat. He didn't want to leave, but he was glad that he had. Her nervousness had been clear. He was equally nervous, if he admitted it only to himself. Something about her awoke every desire he'd ever experienced and more, but also a protective urge he hadn't expected.

He'd noticed Kendall from the moment he'd spotted her at the hospital. Her friendly manner had compelled him to seek her out, and that was even before he'd discovered she was a competent nurse whose compassion for her patients made his job easy. She was witty, vibrant, desirable, and more fun to be with than anyone he'd dated in a long time. But she was also very young, though how young he hadn't realized before tonight, and knowing that, he didn't want to take advantage of her. She seemed both attracted to him and afraid, as if he made her nervous. As if she couldn't be sure of trusting him.

She was a study of contrasts, competent and sure one moment, vulnerable and secretive the next, especially when talking about her family. That was something else he hadn't expected. At the hospital, he'd assumed her maturity was from the experience of age. Now he understood there was much more to her than anyone could see at first glance.

What had happened between her and her mother?

Why had she ended up living at Lily's House for a year? He'd have thought she'd stay with her sister rather than a stranger.

Though he'd brought the subject up again a few times during their boat cruise, she hadn't elaborated, and at least twice he'd had the distinct impression she was purposefully redirecting their conversation.

Well, he could wait. They had plenty of time to get to know each other. Tomorrow when he took her to meet his two best friends and their wives, Kendall would hold her own, he had no doubt, but the way they all got along would tell him volumes about her. Maybe even about their future. Back in med school, he'd stopped dating at least three women who had been jealous of his relationship with his friends or who'd taken offense at one of these dinners, until he'd stopped inviting anyone.

Until now.

With a contented sigh, he glanced up once again at the lights in the apartment before driving away. He wished he could kiss her one more time, but tomorrow would come soon enough.

Halla tossed in her sleep. She knew she was dreaming, but she couldn't make herself wake.

The gray-haired nurse was checking her IV line. Halla liked this nurse better than the younger night one, who each of the two nights she'd been here had given her intense looks and kept questioning her about who she was. And how long she'd been away from home to be so malnourished?

Halla had refused to answer her—just as she had the psychologist who'd come to see her two days ago when they'd set her arm. She'd simply clenched her fists and looked away.

But this old day nurse had a gentle manner and a kind smile. Halla almost felt she could trust her. If she told the woman it was her parents she'd run away from, would she believe her?

"I have good news," the nurse said, pausing to pat her hand on top of the sheet. "We contacted the school, and they recognized a picture of you."

A moan escaped Halla's throat as the ever-present dread leapt to life again inside her. The nurse patted her again and told her the story. The school had told them how Halla had missed the first two and a half months of tenth grade, but they had no idea she was a missing person. The hospital called her parents, who'd told them she had gone to live with relatives and had run away from them. They'd confirmed that Halla had been missing for six months.

No, Halla wanted to scream. I was right there in my room the entire time! Chained. Would anyone believe her? Tears leaked down her face.

"It's okay, honey," the nurse consoled her. "Most parents forgive quite easily. They'll just be glad you're safe."

But Halla knew she would never be safe. Not with her father. "When are they coming?" she asked. Her voice felt rough with disuse.

The nurse glanced at the clock. "Any time now. I'll try to talk to them before they come in, but I'm sure you have nothing to worry about."

Halla waited until she was out of the room before ripping out her IV, peeking out the door, and then dashing barefooted down the hallway. She held her gown closed, peering around corners and ducking in rooms to hide when she spotted hospital personnel.

She had to get to the elevator.

One of the rooms she ducked into belonged to an old woman whose mouth gaped open in a loud snore. Halla was about to see if the hallway was clear again when she spied a sweater lying over the back of the chair next to the old woman's bed.

Clothes. She'd need clothes or she wouldn't get far. It was cold outside.

Searching, she found more clothes tucked in a cupboard. She pulled them on. The top was too big, but the pants at least stayed up. The sweater helped stave off the chill in her heart. She'd look for better shoes in another room because the old lady's slippers wouldn't get her far. Boots would be best. And she'd need a coat.

After she got out of the hospital, she'd go south and west, maybe as far as California, where it would be warm and she could sleep outside. But she didn't care if she froze as long as she was far away from her parents and that horrible house.

She ran.

The dream faded and Halla's eyes opened. She was breathing hard. The dream had been so realistic, as if it had happened only yesterday instead of eleven years ago.

She pulled herself to a seated position and rubbed her eyes. Morning light angled through the tent part of the camper, but it was still early enough that she had plenty of time to get ready for her parents' church at nine. That is, if they still attended the same Methodist church, which was a concern.

Pushing the worry aside, she came to her feet, brushing her hair back from her eyes. She felt bleary and anxious, not at all how she'd felt last night after kissing Oliver.

Kissing Oliver. That had been amazing.

Good memories flooded over the bad. She hadn't been able to sleep after the date, and even after Elsie had gone to bed, she'd stayed up responding to her followers and checking her phone for texts from Oliver. She'd teased him about the skunk, and he'd invited her to visit him in Coeur d'Alene, to show her the place where it had happened. The invite was an excuse to be with her, she understood. But he didn't need any excuse. She wanted to go.

A sigh escaped her as she slumped down at the table.

Yesterday the extra day he'd managed had seemed like forever; now it felt like far too little. If only she didn't have to worry about the other reason she was here in Idaho and could focus on their relationship.

"Halla?" Elsie's sleepy voice came to her. "It's not even six. What's up?" She pulled herself from her bed at the other end of the camper and stumbled over, rubbing her eyes.

"Guess I'm a little anxious."

"I know it's tough, but I'll be right there with you." She sat down opposite Halla.

"I asked Oliver to come too." She probably wouldn't have been able to stop him if she tried. "I mean, it's a church. It's not like my father can call the police and have him thrown out."

Elsie nodded. "Having him there is a good idea. He's impressive. And I'm really glad we're not going back to the house."

Halla considered a moment. "Besides missing the opportunity to burn the place to the ground, I think you're right."

"Ha ha." Elsie cracked a smile that didn't quite reach her eyes.

"What about you? Why are you up? Did I wake you?"

"No." Elsie covered a yawn. "I keep thinking about Payden, and his house."

"It's a good thing, right?"

The corners of Elsie's mouth turned downward, and her eyes looked sad. "I thought so. I've wanted him to find someone for a long time now, but I guess I don't like change."

"Maybe things won't change." Halla studied her sister's face. The shadows under her eyes were prominent. Something was obviously wrong, and Halla should have pressed her before now for details. "Did something happen between you two?"

Elsie's face now looked positively green. "Maybe."

"You better tell me. You know if you don't, I'm going to tell all the original fosters. We'll get it out of you eventually."

Elsie let her chin sink into her hands. "Okay, fine. I do need some advice, but I'm not even sure anything really did happen."

Halla leaned forward, nodding. "Go on."

"Well, before he told me he didn't need to be set up and that he already had someone in mind, we were standing really close, and I . . . it was like . . . I mean . . . I was tempted."

"Tempted to what?"

"Kiss him!" Elsie's cheeks burned red. "To be close to him and see what happened. See how I felt."

Halla stifled a laugh at the unexpected confession. "And what's wrong with that?"

Elsie gasped. "What do you mean? I can't *use* him like that. I'm not like Saffron was before she met Vaughn, making out with half the world and cutting them off the second they started to become serious. I care about Payden. He's my best friend. I mean, after all of you. Maybe even more than some of the girls now that they're married."

Halla's smile was sympathetic, but she couldn't keep the amusement from her voice. "Elsie, Elsie, Elsie. Don't you see? You *are* like Saffron. Like she is now. With Vaughn. He's the one she chose, the one who helped her break through what happened to her. She loves him and that made the difference. I think it's time you took a look at how you really feel about Payden. Maybe what you've been looking for is right in front of you."

"What?" Elsie's eyes seemed to grow two sizes.

"Why not give him a chance? You're always talking about how fabulous he is and looking for someone great to set him up with. Which is a little silly if you ask me. It's clear to all of us that you love being with him, and you always have fun together. So what's holding you back? Aren't you attracted to him?"

"No," Elsie started to say, but stopped. "Maybe. I don't know. We never . . . when I felt like kissing him, I think it was because of something Tara and Rylee said to me when we went to the movies. It started me thinking."

"Maybe, but Payden has always cared about you."

"I know, but he doesn't care about me *that* way." Elsie bit her fingernail, which was already short. "At least not now. Anyway, I think it might be too late. He's buying a house. He said he had a woman in mind. Maybe he's already moved on."

"When you wanted to kiss him, did you get the feeling he'd push you away?"

Elsie bit another nail. "No. Maybe, but that was before I told him I'd set him up again. Maybe he made the decision that moment. Or maybe she's why he's buying the house." She blew out a long breath and said more forlornly, "I'll lose him. No woman will ever want her husband to have another woman as a best friend."

She had a point. "Of course not. But let's say he does like you more than a friend. I mean, he's asked you out in the past—on a real date. Look at it from his point of view. You can't expect him to wait around forever, right? He's not that pathetic."

Elsie's chin shot up. "He's not pathetic at all."

Halla held up both hands in exasperation. "My point exactly. If you don't give him hope, he has to move on because he's not pathetic, so why don't you at least give it a chance? You love him. And you'll never know if it's romantic love if you don't stop trying to push him away."

Elsie's mouth opened, thoughts rushing across her face—fear, excitement, anticipation. "You think I'm doing that?"

Halla nodded. "I think setting him up with your friends is a pretty big sign of pushing him away. Maybe ask Payden what he feels. What he wants."

"You think I should kiss him?" Elsie sounded both longing and appalled at the idea.

"Why not? The worst thing that could happen is he could tell you he's dating the teacher—and you already think that."

"He didn't take *her* to see the house." But Elsie's voice wasn't quite sure.

Halla laughed and slapped the table. "You know what? I think you have it as bad for him as I do for Oliver. Maybe more."

"How do you know?" Elsie looked about as innocent as a five-year-old at the moment, and Halla couldn't help thinking that look was part of why Payden had held back for so long.

"Because you don't want him to be with anyone else."

"I never saw us as a couple. He's just always there."

Halla reached out and poked her nose. "Maybe that's the problem."

"I'll think about it." Elsie stood and walked back to her bed and began rummaging through her suitcase. "If you let me shower first, I'll make breakfast for us."

"But the shower—" Halla cut off as she saw that someone had rehung the shower curtain. The holes had all been patched and reinforced with a strip of sturdy plastic and metal grommets.

"Monica did it," Elsie said. "We put it back up last night while you were hiking. We also found the air conditioning unit, but we couldn't figure out how to turn it on. We may have to call Lily."

In the end, both of them showered but neither of them made food. Monica came over to invite them for breakfast again at exactly the same time Oliver appeared in suit pants and a blue button-down shirt, carrying drinks and muffins for the three of them. They cut the muffins up for everyone to share at Monica's after the waffles and sausage she served.

They finished in plenty of time for church. "What if my parents don't attend the same church anymore?" Halla said once they were in Oliver's truck, where she waved goodbye to Monica's family as they left for their own church in their van. "I looked it up last night on my computer, and I know it's not the same pastor."

For that she was glad. She didn't blame the man for not believing her as a child—her father was charming in public and everyone had believed him—but she was happy not to have to revisit that part of her childhood. She'd received an apology letter from him shortly after the state had officially placed her with Lily and the court had approved a five-year restraining order on her parents.

"We can always ask the neighbor where they attend now," Oliver said. "If it comes to it."

The First United Methodist Church wasn't the church closest to her parents' house, Halla remembered as they approached the building, but it was the nearest Methodist congregation. Her father hated wasting gas, so maybe she was worrying all for nothing.

Pulling into the parking lot was like walking back in time. But to her surprise, the dread drained away, and she felt excited.

"You okay?" Oliver asked.

Halla dragged her gaze from the off-white exterior of the church. "Yeah, actually. I feel . . . I must have liked coming here."

He pushed the foot break before taking her hand. "So, a good memory?"

"Yeah. I played with kids here." Her voice turned cynical. "I was away from my father. Come to think of it, I used to love school too."

Oliver's grip tightened. He opened his door, and she slid over to come out after him, but he didn't release her hand as he helped her down. Coming around from the other side, Elsie met them in front of the truck. People were arriving, but Halla didn't see her parents.

"Should we go in?" Halla fingered her white skirt uncertainly. It grazed the tips of her sandals and fluttered in the breeze. Fluttered like her heart. "Maybe we should have come after the service."

"Let's go inside," Elsie said. "We'll sit near the back and watch for them to come in."

People nodded at them with friendly smiles as they entered the building. Someone directed them to where they were serving coffee to the early-comers, but they refused a drink, wanting to stake a claim on the back row of the meeting room.

"I don't see anyone I recognize," Halla said.

"It's been eleven years," Elsie reminded her. "And people move all the time."

Oliver excused himself and went to chat with the pastor. When he returned, he was smiling. "The pastor says Naomi and Reuben Jenkins never miss a week."

Halla wilted a little at the mention of her father, even though she should have expected him to accompany her mother. She suspected Naomi Jenkins had never gone anywhere except the grocery store without her husband.

"What did you tell the pastor?" Halla asked Oliver.

"I said I knew their daughter. He looked at me a little strangely, but he gave me the information we needed."

The music began, and people hurried to find their seats. Halla, wedged between Oliver and Elsie as if they were trying to protect her, studied everyone who passed. She saw her father first, looking thin and old and slightly stooped in his Sunday suit. He was smiling and talking to another man. On his other side walked a woman wearing a sedate blouse in a dark purple, a black skirt, and heavy black shoes. Halla's gaze ran to her, fastening on the shoulder-length brown hair, the downcast eyes, the tension in the woman's slim body. It was her mother, Naomi Jenkins. But time had not treated her well. Her face was heavily lined, all corners of her mouth and eyes drooping downward, as if marked by crippling sadness.

Or perhaps an evil heart, Halla thought.

A woman paused to chat with Naomi, and for an instant, she looked up and smiled. A gleam of light cut through the darkness of her visage. With a start, Halla remembered that smile. Directed at her. A smile that had made her glad.

Her parents moved toward the front of the chapel, and Halla became aware that she was clutching Oliver's hand in a way that was surely cutting off his blood supply. She forced herself to ease her grip.

"That's them," she whispered. "The woman in the dark purple blouse. The gaunt man next to her is my father. They're sliding into that pew on the third row."

Oliver and Elsie stared without saying anything. Oliver released her hand to rub the back of her neck, and Halla leaned into him gratefully.

Halla didn't hear the sermon. She stood with the crowd when it was time and sang songs, but she had no recollection of the priest's message. All that mattered was the bent head of the woman, who sat a few inches away from her husband, never touching or whispering to him. Never looking his way. Like two strangers who didn't know each other.

Even as Halla had the thought, her father's arm went around her mother's slender shoulders, beaming at something the pastor said. Naomi let herself be pulled over, but within a few minutes the arm was gone, and there was space again.

Halla remembered sitting next to her mother in this very room. Naomi would slip her treats and rub her small hand. She was never allowed to lay her head on her mother's lap—her father hadn't allowed that, but either he hadn't seen the treats or hadn't cared about them.

Only after Halla had been with the children later, her father nowhere in sight, had the tension drained out of her little body. Her mother had often been there with her, singing and playing.

A surge of longing fell over her. *I want my mother,* she thought.

Naomi felt different. Maybe it was knowing she'd be leaving soon, that she'd never have to sit here with Reuben again. Knowing she would finally act. That she would see Halla at last. Regardless of the hard things Naomi would have to say, she was happy for it to be over.

Yesterday, she'd not only taken her tools and the money to the storage shed, but she'd bought a used Subaru with cash, a car that now waited for her near the storage lot. She'd made sure it had a towing package, and she'd rented a small moving trailer for her belongings.

But what if Halla didn't come soon? What if she'd changed her mind about seeing Naomi?

Before desperation could flood her, Naomi focused on the pastor's words. He was talking about slaying demons. He meant temptation and sins, but she knew who her demon was: Reuben.

She'd wait another week for Halla and then go looking for her. If necessary, Naomi would contact that woman at Lily's House and explain. Halla's foster mother might not be happy to hear from her, but surely she'd pass the message on.

Or maybe that would only provoke Halla to request another restraining order.

Once again despair threatened to overcome Naomi, but she pushed back the blackness, staring up into the pastor's face. *Courage,* she told herself.

When the sermon was over, Naomi arose and followed Reuben to the end of their pew, where he began talking to a few men, blocking her way. Naomi stifled her irritation. It wouldn't be long now before he'd never control her again.

She wasn't surprised to see Pastor Kamet bearing down on her. He was relatively new here, the third pastor they'd had since Halla left, and he'd privately expressed concern about her relationship with Reuben. Despite Reuben's outer show, Pastor Kamet seemed to understand that all wasn't right in their house. So many times, Naomi had been tempted to tell him the truth, to enlist his aid in finding Halla. But Rueben, with that uncanny ability he had to sense when trouble loomed, had begun making sure she didn't have much time to speak to the pastor—exactly as he had with all the rest of her friends.

Pastor Kamet was a studious-looking, brown-haired man with all height and no bulk. With his long legs, he could move fast if he wanted. One of Reuben's friends moved to let the pastor approach Naomi, forcing Reuben away from the end of the pew.

"How are things today?" Pastor Kamet asked her.

Naomi glanced to find Reuben staring at her, though

he should be too far away to hear her quiet response. "I'm good. Thank you."

"Were you able to talk to the man who knew your daughter?"

Naomi froze. "What man?" she wanted to demand. And more important, "Which daughter?"

She said neither, but Pastor Kamet pointed to the back of the chapel. Naomi turned and there she was: Halla. She'd come! Naomi gasped and pushed into the aisle, sensing Reuben's attention but not caring what he might do.

Halla sat in the last pew with the two friends she'd been with the day before outside the house. She was staring back at Naomi.

The pastor spoke again, but Naomi didn't hear his words. She moved rapidly down the aisle. Somehow Halla had remembered this place. Did it bring her any good memories? They had made some here, especially on the days Reuben had stayed home sick.

Halla arose and stood staring across the space and the people separating them. She wore a sky blue top and a long, flowing chiffon skirt in a bright white. Naomi could see her holding the hand of the handsome, solid man next to her.

Naomi came to an abrupt stop at the end of their pew. "Halla," she said, faintly and then again with more effort. "Halla." She wanted to leap pass the man and pull Halla into her arms, but the stunned look in Halla's eyes forbade such intimacy. Naomi knew she hadn't earned it. Her hand lifted, straining as if of its own accord to reach Halla, but she forced it back to her side.

"I'm Oliver Montgomery," Halla's friend said, offering his hand. His grip was warm and strong and gave Naomi courage.

The dark-haired woman on Halla's other side gave her a wave. "I'm Elsie Reynolds. I'm Halla's sister—foster sister—and roommate."

"Nice to meet you," Naomi said, nodding.

A few precious seconds passed in awkward silence before habit made Naomi glance over her shoulder to where Reuben stared in their direction. He'd stopped talking and his eyes were fixed on Halla. He didn't seem to know her. Had Halla changed that much, or was he blind? Because Naomi had known Halla the instant she'd spied her from Tina's house. Only Naomi's shock and fear about the confessions she would have to share had prevented her from screaming in joy and running to her in the street.

"I-I . . . can we talk?" Naomi asked, unable to keep the yearning from her voice.

Halla dipped her head in assent. "Let's go outside."

Halla, still holding Oliver's hand, preceded Naomi from the church. Elsie followed a half pace behind Naomi. Outside, they all stood blinking in the sunlight. Most of the congregation would be staying for Sunday School, but those who passed them, going in or out, stared at them with curiosity. A few greeted Naomi, but she had eyes only for Halla.

"I'm glad you came," Naomi said softly. "I hoped you would."

"I came for answers." The sound of Halla's voice took Naomi back in time, to years before Halla's birth. She sounded so much like Becka. "I want to know what happen. Why you . . ." Halla trailed off, her eyes concerned as tears began dripping down Naomi's cheeks.

"I have answers," Naomi managed to say. "I should have told you them long ago. And I should have protected you better. I'm sorry that I failed you."

Halla's eyes filled with her own tears, and Naomi recognized the expression on her face. It was hope. So many times before that hope had been utterly decimated, but Naomi wouldn't let that happen now. Halla was strong, and Naomi would finally be strong with her.

"Naomi!" came a loud shout. They all gazed at the church to see Reuben striding through the door toward them. "Where are you going? The meetings aren't over. Come back here."

Ignoring him, Naomi turned hurriedly in Halla's direction. "We'll have to leave. He won't let us talk here. Would you be willing to—?" Her voice broke off as Reuben put a hand on her shoulder, hauling her backward.

"Who are you talking—" He broke off, his eyes fixing on Halla. "You," he said with a twist of his lips. "You have no place here. Or have you come crawling back like your mother?" He gave a snort of derision. "You're no better than she was."

Halla stared at him. Naomi was proud to see there was no fear on her face. Apparently, Reuben, with his wrinkled face and hunched shoulders, was no longer the same man who had made her sweet baby cringe in her room as a child.

"I have nothing to say to you," Halla said, shoulders back, her chin high. "I'm not afraid of you, and you can't hurt me. You're just a wasted, mean old man who should be rotting in jail." To Naomi, she added. "Come with me. Let's go somewhere to talk."

"She's not going anywhere," Reuben's fingers dug more deeply into Naomi's shoulder. She'd have marks from it later. "Naomi, go back inside the church. I'll deal with this."

Naomi wrenched away from him, but instead of turning toward the church, she moved closer to Halla. "I'm going with my daughter." She couldn't help the shaking of her voice.

With a growl, Reuben lunged for her, but Oliver stepped between them, intercepting Reuben and pushing him roughly back. "You heard her, Mr. Jenkins," he said. "I think you're the one who should be going back inside the church."

Reuben let out a slew of profanity and tried to push around him, but Oliver grabbed his shirt in the middle of his chest, holding him in place. "Stay away from them," Oliver growled.

Reuben's head popped backward as he stared hatefully up into Oliver's face. "She's my wife, and I'll thank you to remove your hands."

"Not a chance," Oliver returned. "I've been waiting a long time to meet the man who would chain a helpless child to a bed. One more attempt to pass me, and I'll hit you. Hard." Oliver balled the hand that wasn't detaining Reuben, his impressive muscles flexing.

Reuben spluttered, but he didn't try to move. Oliver took out his keys and tossed them to Halla. "Maybe go wait in the truck? I'll keep him here until you're inside."

Halla gestured, and Naomi took a few steps toward her.

"Naomi. Stay," Reuben ordered, as if she were his dog. Which she had been for too long.

She turned. "Or what? You're going to chain *me* to the bed? No, Reuben, I'm done. I only stayed with you so Halla would know where to find me. That's all. You will never see me again." With that, she hurried past Halla and Elsie into the parking lot, pausing to wait for an indication of which direction they were headed.

She felt more than saw Reuben lunging after her, but Oliver hit him, knocking him to the sidewalk. Reuben jumped back up but didn't try again. His shirt was crumpled where Oliver's hand had gripped it, and his lip was bleeding. Bleeding as Naomi's had far too often over her decades with Reuben. Oliver's arms were loose and ready at his side, as if prepared to stop Reuben again, if needed. Behind them, Naomi could see Pastor Kamet coming from the church, along with a few parishioners who must have gone to get him.

At Halla's touch on her arm, Naomi hurried away, glancing over her shoulder every so often. The pastor was talking to Reuben now, who waved his arms wildly as he responded. Halla reached a white truck and opened the door. Oliver must have been keeping an eye on them to see when they reached the truck because he turned and jogged toward them.

Relief poured through Naomi. Nothing was going the way she'd expected, but exactly what she'd expected, she really didn't know. At least she was with Halla and they would soon be far away from Reuben.

By the time Oliver reached the truck, Pastor Kamet was coming after him. Reuben, thankfully, waited on the sidewalk with the other parishioners.

"I'm sorry to cause all this trouble," Naomi told Halla as they waited for the pastor. "I didn't think Reuben would follow me outside."

The slightest of smiles touched Halla's face. "It's okay. It worked out."

Pastor Kamet arrived at the truck. "What's going on here?" he asked Naomi. "Reuben says these people are forcing you to go with them."

Naomi had to give the pastor credit for being brave enough to come after her if that was what he believed. She gave a harsh laugh. "He's lying. This is my daughter. I want to talk to her."

"Your daughter?" Shock filled the pastor's face. "But I thought she was . . . deceased."

"Which daughter?" Naomi wanted to ask for the second time that day. Instead, she said, "I suppose Reuben told you that."

"Yes, when I first arrived. He said not to bring it up. That it upset you."

Reuben was only protecting himself, of course. Never her. But in this case he hadn't been lying, at least not completely. Naomi held out a hand to shake the pastor's. "Thank you for your sermons. But it's time to slay my demon." Her mouth quirked slightly upward at the word demon. "It's been nice knowing you. You have lifted me more times than you'll ever know."

"Well, okay then. If you're sure."

"I've never been more sure about anything in my life."

The pastor nodded at all of them and retreated.

"Reuben will not like that answer," Naomi said, looking at Oliver. "Would you mind terribly taking me with you? Somewhere we can talk. After we finish, I have a place to go. Away from Nampa." Away from Reuben, she meant, but everyone already knew that.

"Gladly," Oliver said. "It's going to be a bit of a squeeze, though, and hopefully we don't get pulled over by the police, but we'll fit."

"We'll have to make sure we're not followed," Naomi added. Because she could still see Reuben fuming on the sidewalk as the pastor walked toward him.

Oliver looked at Halla. "Where should we go?"

The respect in his voice and the admiration in his eyes made Naomi happy for her. Halla had chosen well for herself. Now if only Naomi could make her understand, could maybe find even a small margin of forgiveness in Halla's heart. Not that she deserved it. But she'd change that—starting today.

"We should go to Front Burner Burgers," Halla said. "If they're open today. I think I'd like some ice cream."

Naomi fought with her emotions before she could say, "Strawberry?"

19

Halla sat across the table from her mother. The encounter with her father had been strangely satisfying. Her mother had chosen her. It might be silly after all these years—and certainly far too late—but it gave her hope.

Oliver had been right. Oliver, who looked mighty pleased with himself at the moment. Halla understood why—she'd have liked to punch her father too, but she was happy that at least someone had hit him. He and Elsie were sitting in another booth together, leaving Halla and Naomi alone.

"We used to come here when you were a child," Naomi said. "Back then it was the Burger Pit, or something like that."

"We had ice cream?" Halla put a spoonful of thick strawberry shake into her mouth.

"Always. We'd come when Reuben was working. Just you and me." Naomi's smile fell. "But he found us once. You were about twelve. He didn't like that there were some construction workers here, and he made a big scene, saying they were checking you out, and that I came to meet someone. After that, we came only a few more times, but we were so nervous that he'd show up, we finally stopped. I started buying ice cream at the store."

Her father hadn't liked that either, Halla remembered. He didn't want them to gain weight. But somehow there had still been ice cream when he wasn't home.

"What made him do it?" Halla asked. "I remember Peter calling and him grounding me for a month, even from school. I remember him ruining my clothes when Amy let me wear one of her shirts. But what would make him chain me up?" The words were hard to say, harder than telling strangers it happened.

Naomi buried her spoon inside her shake and pushed the cup aside. "To even begin to understand that, you have to know about Becka."

"Becka?" Halla gripped her red spoon tightly. "I don't know who she is."

"Reuben wouldn't let me tell you."

Reuben, she kept saying. Not your father. Was that intentional?

"Becka was our daughter."

Halla started with the news. "I have a sister?"

"Not exactly." Naomi's eyes closed briefly in pain, and then the words rushed out. "Things were good after Becka was born," she said. "She was beautiful, with light brown hair and big blue eyes. But even as a toddler, she hated Reuben. He was too hard on her. Wouldn't let her do anything. By the time she was sixteen, she'd sneak out of her room at night, and she began secretly dating a boy who was a couple years older. Reuben put a security lock on her window and started searching her belongings every day. When he found a pack of cigarettes in her school bag, she claimed they weren't hers, that it was a joke someone had played on her, but he wouldn't listen. He beat her." Naomi wiped the tears from her face with both hands. "It was so bad, I was scared he'd kill her. The next day, she stole all the money from Reuben's wallet and my purse and ran away with her boyfriend. Reuben was furious. At first he searched for her, and then he disowned her."

Halla felt a surge of admiration that Becka had found the courage to leave. Whether or not she'd been telling the truth about the cigarettes, Becka had been able to get out from under their father's control. Halla wondered how old she'd been when Becka left. She couldn't remember any sister, so maybe she'd been a toddler at the time.

Questions stuck in her throat at the pain in her mother's eyes, but Halla finally forced one out. "Did you ever see her again?"

Naomi nodded, the pain bleeding to her entire face. "She came home a year later with a brand-new baby. A very tiny but healthy baby. But Becka was thin and tired and sick and didn't even argue as Reuben screamed at her for hours. I thought we could finally be a family and help her with the baby. It didn't work out that way, though. After a week, Becka was feeling better, and she decided to contact her boyfriend and tell him about the baby. Apparently, they'd split, and he didn't know, but she still loved him. Reuben tried to stop her from leaving. He didn't want that boy anywhere near Becka or the baby. He threw her against the wall." Naomi gulped for air, as if she couldn't bear to continue. Halla put her hand over Naomi's where it rested on the table.

They sat that way a few minutes until Naomi went on, apparently finding courage in Halla's touch. "One of her eyes was bleeding, he'd hit her so hard. She ran outside to the old car she'd come in, falling a few times, she was so dizzy. But she got away. She yelled that she'd come back for her baby—with the police if she had to. She hit our garbage can on the way out. I don't think on purpose. I think she was still dizzy." Naomi's shoulders shook now. "There was an accident. Not even a block away, she crashed . . . and died."

"No," Halla whispered. What a horrible thing to have endured.

Naomi wasn't finished. "Of course any injury she had before the crash went unnoticed. The police came, and nothing was said about the baby. Becka had given birth at her friend's and never registered her birth, so Reuben figured out how to register the baby as our child." Naomi's eyes fixed on Halla, as if begging her to understand. "I was forty, and I didn't think anyone would believe us, but they did. I didn't get out much except to church, so he made me stay home for a few months, and when we showed up with the baby, no one said anything except to congratulate us."

Halla's thoughts were racing. *Becka dead, her baby being raised by Naomi and Reuben.* Then she knew what Naomi hadn't yet said, at least not in so many words. "Me," she guessed, taking her hand from Naomi's and letting it fall to her lap. "I was the baby."

Naomi nodded. "You were. The best gift of my life."

Halla had barely grown used to the idea of a sister, and now Becka wasn't a sister at all, but her mother. And Naomi, this woman in front of her, was her grandmother. That explained Naomi's age, why she didn't call Reuben her father, and the comments Reuben had made about her mother at the church. But it still didn't explain why Halla had been locked up or why her mother—her grandmother—had brought the bread to her room in pieces that last week.

"Reuben said it was God's way of giving us back what we'd lost," Naomi continued, though Halla wasn't sure she wanted to hear more. But of course, she would have to follow this path to the bitter end. "By then I didn't care about anything except you. I handled him. Got you out of the way when he was in a temper, and it worked. For a while."

"Until it didn't."

"Right." Naomi swiped a hand across her eyes, the fingers coming away wet. "You were a lot like Becka. Smarter, though, because you understood from very early on that you couldn't let Reuben know everything. But it all changed when you were a teen and began wanting to go over to friends' houses and participate in after school clubs. It didn't help that you were beautiful. Reuben started to see danger everywhere, and he made you stay home. I couldn't protect you anymore. And then . . ." Naomi took a deep sigh. "Then one day you said you were going to run away if you couldn't have any kind of a life. That you'd go live with friends. He flew into a rage and told me he'd never let you do what Becka did. He came home with the chain the next day. And he'd lock your door when he wasn't home so I couldn't get in."

"Why didn't you do something?" Halla didn't mean to say the words.

"I thought it would blow over, that he'd have to let you go back to school."

Anger boiled through Halla, anger that had been building from the moment she'd laid eyes on Reuben again. "Blow over? That shouldn't have lasted even a day. You fed me only bread!"

"No! Bread with cheese inside, with pizza sauce, with eggs." Naomi's voice was pleading. "With every filling I could imagine, and when he discovered that and began cutting up the bread to make sure I wasn't cheating, I put milk and butter in the dough. And protein powder that I hid from him under the sink behind the cleaners and the garbage can. I tried."

Halla's hands fisted below the table in an effort to maintain composure. "Not hard enough," she said darkly. "You should have told someone."

"I know, but at the time, I was so afraid they would find out what we'd done and they would take you away. That you'd go to your father's family."

Father's family? But Halla couldn't follow that thought now. "Anything would have been better. I almost died!" Not just from falling off the roof, but from malnutrition. "You should have called the police."

Tears slipped down Naomi's face. "I know. I've told myself that every day for the past eleven years. And it's something I will continue to live with until the day I die.

But I've always loved you. I wish I could have been strong. I kept thinking he'd let you go back to school, and we'd figure something out. I was saving money so we could run away."

Since Halla had escaped, they would never know if Naomi would have let her die. For a blinding instant, Halla hated the woman, hated how she had lied, hated how she hadn't protected Halla or Becka. Fury, outrage, and hurt billowed like a black oily substance in her head, filling all the crevices, overshadowing every other thought.

Naomi's shoulders wilted, as if all her strength had leaked away. As if she knew Halla would never forgive her. "I'm sorry," Naomi said quietly. "I know that nothing I can do will ever make up for what happened." Her chest heaved, but she swallowed any sound from the silent sob.

Halla experienced an urge to run away, to run away and never look back. One thing stopped her: Naomi telling Reuben at the church that the only reason she'd stayed all these years was for Halla. No doubt she'd endured countless abuses for those eleven years, but somewhere along the way, she'd found enough courage to stand up to him. That thought alone penetrated the blackness in Halla's mind.

Halla swallowed hard. "So what now?" Did Naomi think she would come home with Halla? Because despite the teachings Lily had instilled in Halla over the years, she didn't think she could handle that.

"I have a plan, and I've talked to an attorney," Naomi said. "I thought I might find myself a place in Phoenix since that's where you're living. Maybe I can see you sometimes, if you don't mind. I just have to make sure Reuben doesn't know where I am. He'll hurt me."

The fear behind those three words sank into Halla's heart. Naomi thought he'd kill her for leaving him. And why not? He'd almost killed Halla for much less. Her anger and indignance at Naomi slid away, as if making room for pity and concern. "Oh, Mom," she murmured.

Naomi's gaze lifted to her, wet, reddened, and hopeful. "I'll be okay. I'll get a restraining order. But I don't want him to come after you to find me either, so . . ." She reached into her big black purse for a pen and paper. "I have a phone, just not on me right now. It's in the car I bought. It's one of those pay per minute ones for now, but maybe in a week or so, you can call me?" She jotted down the number and pushed it at Halla.

"Okay." Halla put the paper into her pocket without looking at it. She'd decide later whether or not to call.

Naomi took a breath and said, "Now about your father."

Halla's breath rushed out of her. *Her father!* She had a father who wasn't Reuben Jenkins. A sliver of joy cut through her lingering anger. "You know who he is?" She couldn't hide her eagerness.

"His name is Brock Watson. He's forty-five now, I believe. Nineteen when you were born. I've looked for him the past couple years, but his parents are dead, and he didn't have siblings. I finally found an aunt. She told me he moved to Colorado more than a decade earlier, and that he works as a pipefitter. That was two years ago. She didn't have an address. They'd lost touch, and she's since moved to Florida."

Colorado at least narrowed it down. "Does he know about me?"

Naomi frowned. "He came to the funeral. He'd heard Becka was pregnant and asked about the baby. Reuben told him she had still been pregnant when the accident happened."

"So he thinks I'm dead." At least that was better than not caring. But Halla's anger stirred once more. Naomi had cheated her out of knowing her father.

"He was only nineteen," Naomi said. "I thought I could do a better job." Tears started again. "I was wrong."

Unable to reach out to her but equally unable to do nothing, Halla grabbed her shake and started spooning ice cream into her throat. She'd thought this trip would be a way to close a door; instead it had opened two of them. One with her mother—grandmother—and one with her biological father.

"It's a lot to take in," she said after she'd eaten most of her shake and Naomi had wiped away the tears.

"I'm sure it is." Naomi regarded her sadly. "I think maybe if you could drive me to my car now, that would be for the best. We can talk more later, if you'd like."

"Okay." Halla was relieved. She wanted to talk everything over with Oliver and Elsie because right now she teetered between fury and pity.

She waved to Oliver, and he and Elsie hurried over. "We're going to take her to her car now."

Oliver's eyes were full of questions, but he only nodded. "Okay, let's go squish into my truck again. I should have bought a King cab."

"This time you sit on my lap," Elsie said to Halla. "I was sure I was squishing you."

Halla somehow found a grin. "You kind of were."

Oliver put an arm around her, and Halla felt comforted. She had to remember her thoughts of earlier that everything she'd gone through in her life had led her to him. To him and Elsie and Lily's House. Would she trade them for a father she didn't know? No. But that didn't mean she was happy about the lies.

Naomi directed Oliver to a street in the outer part of Nampa, where a blue car sat attached to a small, enclosed moving trailer. There, she fished a key from her bra and opened the car door and put her purse inside.

Oliver stared at the car doubtfully. "Are you sure this car can pull the trailer? It's a small one, but depending on how much stuff you have in it, it might not be strong enough."

"It is," Naomi said. "I bought the car yesterday and made the sales person drive with me to the trailer rental to be sure."

"Yesterday?" Halla asked. Had Naomi been going to leave even before Halla arrived?

"My next-door neighbor told me she'd seen you. So I planned to leave as soon as we talked." She looked ready to say more but shut her mouth. "I'm not sure how heavy it will be after I load it, but I'll drive slowly."

"You haven't loaded it?" Halla was instantly worried. The murderous expression on Reuben's face made going to their house a terrible idea. "You can't go back there."

"Oh, I won't," Naomi said hurriedly. "I've been moving

stuff for a while. I have a storage unit one street over."
She waved behind her. "I'll fill up the trailer and go to a
motel in Boise tonight. Tomorrow I'll visit my attorney,
and then I'll disappear."

So many questions Halla wanted to ask: if Naomi had
enough money, if she knew anyone she could stay with
in Phoenix until she got settled, if she was sure Reuben
couldn't find her. But all the words clogged in her throat.

"We'll help you load it up," Oliver volunteered. "And
I can recommend a good motel in Boise."

"Oh, it's okay. I'm sure you have better things to do.
Though I'd appreciate the hotel recommendation. I might
have to stay a few days before everything is ready."

Oliver cast a glance at Halla, and his gaze freed her
tongue. "We'd like to help you," she insisted. "Can you get
into your storage today?"

"Yeah. If you're sure it's not a problem, I'd love the
help."

"Let's go then," Halla said.

"You think she's going to be okay?" Elsie asked as they
parted ways with Naomi and hurried back to the truck.
"What happened between you two anyway?"

It took only three minutes for Naomi to drive to her
storage unit, and by then Halla had filled her friends in on
the basic facts: her mother was really her grandmother and
she had a biological father somewhere who didn't know
she existed. Both Oliver and Elsie looked as stunned as
Halla still felt.

"I can't imagine what she's been through," Elsie said.
"Or rather, I can all too well. Poor thing."

"Well, we can at least help her pack up." Oliver

brought the truck to a stop behind Naomi's trailer. "Hard to believe she kept all that from you, though."

Halla gave him a tremulous smile. "I don't know if I should hate her or feel bad for her. I'm furious one minute and then full of pity the next."

"That's okay," Elsie said. "I felt that way for a long time about my mother. I know I've said it before, but Naomi could have left you like my mother did. Fear makes you do strange things."

Like jump out of a window and roll down a rooftop. Like run from a hospital when all she'd really had to do was open her mouth and tell someone about the abuse.

She pushed the thoughts away and joined Naomi as she opened her tiny unit. Inside were different kinds of saws, two drills, six plastic tool boxes of varying sizes, several cardboard boxes filled with cut wood, stacks of half-finished quilts in clear bags, two suitcases, two tote boxes, and three duffel bags. No furniture besides a rocking chair, but leaving Reuben obviously wasn't a spur of the moment decision.

Naomi directed them to place the heavy items toward the front of the trailer, and the lighter objects further back. She'd changed from a frightened, abused wife to a poised, competent person. Did she really use these tools? When Elsie exclaimed over some partially finished bookends, Naomi's thin face came alive as she described how she made them. The bagged quilts were even more beautiful, and Halla balanced them with care as she took them to the trailer.

All the belongings fit with plenty of room to spare, though Halla wouldn't have guessed if possible. A few of the tools were heavy, and Halla wondered how Naomi would have handled loading the trailer without them. She would have had to call a friend or beg help from a stranger passing through the storage units.

All too soon, they were finished, but Halla felt uncertain at letting Naomi go. This glimpse of the confident Naomi made her want to know more. To hear about Naomi's childhood. To learn more of Becka.

"Oh, wait, I almost forgot something." Naomi went to the back seat of her car and began rummaging through the only duffel bag she'd placed inside the vehicle rather than in the trailer. She returned with a small box covered in black velvet and handed it to Halla. "Go ahead. Open it."

Halla flipped up the lid to find a gold locket inside. She touched the fancy swirls and the engraved *I love you,* wondering what it meant. She didn't recognize the piece of jewelry. She started to give it back, but Naomi shook her head

"My mother gave it to me when I was sixteen," she said. "With pictures of her and me in it. I gave it to Becka on her sixteenth birthday. I placed a photo of her over the one of my mother. They're both still there, though. Your photo was to have gone on top of mine."

Halla opened the locket and saw her mother's face for the first time—or the first time that she remembered. Becka's nose and eyes were Halla's, but the shape of her face was narrow like Naomi's and her hair was darker.

"She's beautiful," Elsie said, leaning her head in front of Halla to study the picture. "I can see the family resemblance."

"I have more photos of her." Naomi gestured to the trailer. "I kept them all. I can make copies for you."

"I'd like that." Halla drew out the locket and put it around her neck. Her fingers were trembling, so Oliver had to help her fasten it. The metal felt warm against her skin.

Naomi smiled. "It looks good on you." She brushed her hands onto her black skirt. "Well, I guess I'd better get going. I'm sure you have plans, and the longer we stay out here . . . I don't know if Reuben can trace me."

"Are you sure you're going to be okay?" Halla asked. Maybe she should offer to have Naomi follow her to Phoenix.

"I'll be fine. There are some things I need to take care of. But call me, okay? Please. And not just for the pictures."

"Do you still have that pen?" Halla asked her.

Naomi took it from her purse and handed it to her. Taking the paper where Naomi had written her number, Halla wrote her own phone number carefully beneath. She ripped the paper in two and handed the portion with her number to Naomi.

"Call me if you need help. If you're really planning on going to Phoenix, I can ask around about apartments. My foster mother has connections. I know we have a lot to work through, but I would like to see you again."

Naomi stared at her for a full three seconds before she started to cry. Her shoulders shook and great sobs wrenched in her chest. She looked so forlorn and lost that Halla hugged her. Naomi clung to her.

"Thank you," she said in Halla's ear. "Thank you. I love you so much."

"I love you too, Mom."

For a long time, they held on to each other, until Naomi's shaking stopped. When they finally separated, Naomi squared her shoulders. "I'll call," she said. Extending a hand to first Elsie and then Oliver, she said goodbye.

Halla watched her drive away, leaning against Oliver, grateful for his strength.

"She's going to be okay," Elsie said. "It's good for her to do this on her own. She needs it."

Halla's guilt subsided a little at the words. Maybe Elsie was right. In a way, her mother was tumbling down the rooftop right now like Halla had, hoping she'd find a soft place to land.

"Let's go home."

"Home, home?" Oliver asked. "Or the camper?"

Somehow Halla found a grin. "The camper for now."

"You sure? It's probably hot. We could go to my sister's."

"Not your mother's?"

He grimaced. "I think we'll give her a little more time to come around. Besides, she thinks I left to drive home this morning."

"Let's go to the camper," Halla decided. She was itching to get out of her skirt, and she didn't want to share Oliver even with his sister's family. "Do you know anything about air conditioners?"

By the time Oliver pulled up near the camper, it was past two in the afternoon. The inside of the camper was stifling hot, but after twenty minutes and a call to Lily, Halla and Oliver figured out the air conditioner, which might not have been strong enough for the heat of Phoenix but was ample for Nampa. That taken care of, they played a board game Lily kept stored in one of the camper's cupboards.

When Payden called, Elsie left them at the table and went to her bed to chat.

"Should we play again?" Oliver asked Halla. "Maybe I can beat you without Elsie around."

"Maybe I'll beat you." She began setting up the board again.

Oliver's phone buzzed, and he glanced at it, his expression changing to one of surprise.

Halla struggled against a sense of foreboding. "What is it?"

"An alert from the office. I get those through texts." He opened up his phone and started reading. When his brow furrowed, Halla knew it wasn't good news. "There's been a fire," he said quietly. "Not in my area, but close. No surprise with how dry it's been. They need all hands on deck. Which means my boss wants me back as soon as possible."

"No!" Just when she'd been thinking about asking him exactly how late he could stay on Monday.

"I have to be there."

She nodded. "I know." Not for the first time she was grateful he was a forester and not a firefighter with the US Forest Service. That meant he wouldn't be on the front lines, even though he'd spent years at the beginning of his career on a hotshot firefighting crew. That didn't mean he'd be completely out of danger. He'd still be in the woods, looking for ways to minimize the spread of the fire.

"I do have to be there," he said, looking thoughtful, "but Coeur d'Alene is less than seven hours away, and it's an hour earlier there. I won't be expected until eight Monday morning, so I have a few hours before I have to leave."

"You'll need sleep," she protested.

"Not as much as I need you. And there's always coffee. I'll be okay." He took her hand and looked at her hopefully. "Or you could come with me."

For a moment, Halla was tempted, but sitting in Lily's camper while he was out in the forest wasn't exactly her idea of spending time with him. "How long will you be out?"

His face fell. "Even if they get the fire under control, I'll be out a week with my controlled burn. Bad suggestion. Sorry."

"We'll make it work." She leaned into him, and he put his arm around her. "As soon as you're back at your place, we'll talk," she said. "I have a lot of things to catch up on too."

He kissed her then, as if he couldn't resist, which was better than good.

Elsie finished her call, and everyone was hungry, so they made dinner, played another game, and downloaded a movie to watch on Halla's laptop. All too soon it was close to one in the morning and time for Oliver to go.

Halla walked him out to his truck, where Oliver pulled

her close under the starry sky. He trailed kisses from her ear to her eyes and down to her lips. Her mouth opened under his pressure and for a long moment all she knew was him—his touch, his taste, his smell. So much better than in her dreams. All her senses tingled. She had never felt so alive.

"I wish this moment would never end," he said against her mouth. The huskiness in his voice made her shiver with desire.

"Me too."

He drew away and studied her face. Moonlight shone down on them, as if it were a spotlight—as if they were the only people in the entire world. One of his strong fingers traced her bottom lip, and she sucked in his finger, biting it playfully. With a little groan, his lips met hers again, his tongue stroking hers. His fingers played in her hair, pulling her closer.

Her heart was both soaring and breaking at the same time. How could she let him go and return to seeing his face only on the screen?

"Halla," he said, pulling back slightly. "I've been wanting to say this to you for a long time." He stopped.

"What?"

He was probably as worried as she was about the upcoming separation. They'd weathered a year of friendship—no, far more than friendship, she could admit that now.

"I love you," he said.

Her mouth opened in a silent gasp. Of all the words she'd expected, those weren't on the list.

He gave a self-deprecating laugh. "I have known how

I feel for months now, but I didn't think you'd appreciate hearing it until we met in person, and maybe even now is too soon, but I can't let you go without knowing how I feel. You are my best friend, the first one I think of when something happens in my life, good or bad. The first one I think of when I wake up in the morning and before I go to sleep at night. Yes, I tried dating girls in Coeur d'Alene, but I couldn't find a single one I looked forward to talking to like I do you. And having you here, seeing you like this, only confirms what I already know to be true. I love you, Halla."

The stars overhead seemed to sparkle more brightly. Oliver had described her feelings exactly, both with the dating and how eagerly she looked forward to sharing her day with him.

"I love you too," she said.

His eyes widened and then his mouth was on hers again, the touch igniting a passion she didn't think possible through a simple kiss. Halla was dizzy and exulted.

When the kiss ended, Oliver placed his forehead against hers. "Let's think about options because I don't want to spend one more day away from you than I have to. We'll talk about them as soon as I finish with work, okay?"

"Okay," she agreed.

With reluctance, he opened the truck door, but he didn't make it far before they were kissing again. But eventually, Halla found enough courage to let him go, and he found enough strength to leave.

Kendall finished the dishes with her Bluetooth headset in her ear while talking to Elsie and Halla, who were heading back to Phoenix, her call coming over the speaker on Elsie's phone. Between working the weekend and her two dates with Wylen, Kendall had left a mess in the sink, and she knew how serious Elsie was about the kitchen. Kendall wanted it to be perfect for her. Besides, Wylen would be here soon for their river rafting date, and if he needed to fill a water bottle for their excursion today, she didn't want him thinking the place normally looked like a bomb had gone off.

"So, how did your date go last night?" Elsie asked after a few minutes of conversation.

Kendall turned off the water and sat on a chair at the table. "Great," she said dreamily.

"I can't believe you went from turning him down to two dates in two days."

Three dates after today, but Kendall decided not to bring that up.

"Was the party with his friends fun?" Elsie pressed.

"It was really low-key. Everyone brought something to share, and the hosts had the most delicious homemade barbecued chicken wings I've ever tasted. We played games while we ate. It was a lot of fun seeing Wylen around other people outside work. I learned he has a bit of a competitive streak."

"And both his friends had dates?"

"Well, they're married, but it was okay." There had been no jibes or hints about them still being single, and though the friends and their wives were closer to Wylen's age than hers, Kendall hadn't felt out of place. "One of the women did mention that it was high time he brought someone to their monthly get-togethers."

Elsie squealed. "Wow. You know what that means, right?"

Kendall did, but she didn't want to jinx it. "I really like him. It's like everything I ever thought I felt for Joel, except Wylen's not a selfish idiot, which makes it even more scary. He's responsible, hardworking, and he treats me like a princess. You should see the sweet texts he's sent me after each date—and at work yesterday."

"That's a good thing. Not something to be scared about," Halla interjected.

Kendall snorted. "Yeah, but maybe I like him too much."

"How can you like a guy too much?" Elsie asked.

Kendall chewed on her lip, checking her watch. Still over an hour before Wylen arrived, plenty of time for her to unload her emotions so she didn't drown in them. "Because sooner or later I'm going to have to tell him about Teisha. I'm not her mom on a daily basis, but she's still a permanent part of my life, and I need whoever I fall in love with to be okay with that."

There was a moment of silence before Elsie said, "Maybe you should worry about that when you're really sure about him. About where you're heading."

"Or maybe I should tell him now, and make sure he's okay with it before I fall in love." Before she fell any further, she meant. Right now if he walked away, she could still pick up the pieces. But in a month or two or three . . . Kendall didn't want to think about it. Sure, they might be going nowhere, but her heart didn't feel that way. This was real. Or could be.

"I don't know," Elsie said. "You've only been dating a few days. What if it's too soon?"

"What if I tell him in two months, and he feels like I've been lying to him?"

Elsie sighed. "There is that."

"Well, at least give it today," Halla added. "He may be a total wimp on the boat, and you might have second thoughts anyway."

Kendall laughed. "I don't know. He handled the motor boat pretty competently on Saturday. But you're right. I can give it another day or two, at least."

"Good, then it's decided." Kendall couldn't tell which of her roommates said this, but she thought it might be Elsie.

Another call buzzed in Kendall's ear, and she grabbed the phone to check the caller ID. She'd hoped it was Wylen, but it was Susan's number on the screen. "Hey, I have to go," Kendall said. "Susan's calling me, and she usually doesn't this time of day. It might be about Teisha."

"Goodbye, then! Text me about it later," Elsie said.

"Bye!" Halla echoed.

"See you soon. Bye." Kendall punched to accept Susan's call. "Hello?"

"Hey, it's Susan," came a breathless voice through Kendall's headset. "I know it's your day off, and I hope I didn't wake you, but I need your help."

"Sure, what is it?" Kendall came to her feet and began to pace nervously. Was something wrong with Teisha? Susan had never called her like this before. "Is Teisha all right?"

"Oh, yes. Sorry. She's fine. I'm calling about Jasper."

Kendall breathed a silent sigh of relief. "What happened?"

"He had a sudden sharp pain about an hour ago before he left for work, and he was feverish, so I took him to the emergency room. The doctors are with him now, but I'm not sure how long this is going to take."

"I'm so sorry. Do you need me at your house for the preschool?" Not exactly how Kendall wanted to spend her day, but Susan had done a lot for her.

"No, my assistant has that under control, and Lily sent one of her girls who isn't in school over to help. But I do need help with Teisha. She was okay the first half hour here, but she's really cranky, and I don't want to leave Jasper until I know what's going on. Could you watch her?"

"Of course. Absolutely! What hospital are you at?"

"The one where you work, actually."

"Okay, then you're in good hands. I'll be right there."

"Thank you so much. You and my sister and Lily are the only ones I feel comfortable leaving Teisha with, and

Lily's already got her hands full with the new girl she picked up last week—and apparently another one arrived yesterday. My sister's so busy with her two boys and the new baby that I worried it would be too much."

"It's no problem. You know I love spending time with Teisha."

"Yeah, so that's why I'm calling."

"I'll be there in less than twenty minutes."

Kendall hung up, finding herself in her small living room, where she'd paced mindlessly during the conversation. She ran back to the kitchen to grab her phone and to her room for a bag, and finally to the kitchen again for a few snacks. There was no telling how long she'd have Teisha with her or what she might need.

To say that she forgot about her date with Wylen couldn't be farther from the truth. She worried about it all the way to the hospital. What was the likelihood that Susan would be finished within an hour? It could happen, but more than likely, Kendall would have to cancel their river run. She had an extra hour as a buffer for them to arrive, but she knew how long emergency room visits took, and Teisha wasn't old enough to take on a rafting trip. Still, Kendall would wait until she was at the hospital to call Wylen, just in case.

She found a frazzled Susan in a crowded emergency room, walking and bouncing a red-faced Teisha. "Hey, sweetie, I have snacks," Kendall said to the toddler. "You hungry?" Teisha came to her willingly.

"Oh, thank you!" Susan flopped down on a chair. "I didn't bring anything for her. We just ran out the door. I'm lucky she's not still in her pajamas."

Kendall sat next to Susan, Teisha on her lap, and brought out the graham crackers Elsie always kept around for pie shells. She also had pieces of cheese, raisins, granola bars, and boxes of apple juice that were left over from a picnic at the beginning of summer. It was enough to keep any toddler satisfied. For now.

Kendall couldn't help sticking her nose in Teisha's scant hair and breathing in her scent. "Any word?" she asked.

Susan shook her head. "They gave him something for the pain when I was in there with him, so he was feeling better. But they took him for tests, and I came out here to wait for you. I was thinking you could take her to your apartment. I'll come and get her as soon as I know."

"Whatever you need. And I can help tomorrow if you need me."

Susan's face crumpled. "Thank you. I'm just so worried. Jasper's never sick, and to see him like this . . ."

Kendall put an arm around her. "I know. But I'm sure he'll be okay. As soon as Teisha's finished eating, if we don't know any more, I'll go ask around. Then I'll take her home, okay?"

"That would be fantastic." Susan jumped up from the chair. "I left my purse in Jasper's room. I'll be right back, okay?"

"Sure."

Susan leaned over and cupped her daughter's cheek. "I love you, sweetie."

"Wuv you," Teisha said through her crackers, giving Susan a happy grin.

While Teisha was eating, Kendall took the opportunity

to text her brother-in-law's cousin, to let him know she wouldn't be able to make it to the river. Then, knowing she couldn't put it off any longer, she called Wylen. He picked up on the first ring.

"Can't wait to be with me, eh?" he joked. "Or are you making sure I'll be on time? Don't worry. I'll be early. I'm on my way over now."

"Actually, I'm really sorry, but I have to cancel. I've had a little emergency."

"Are you okay?" Worry seeped into his voice. "What happened? You know I'm a doctor, right?"

Kendall laughed. "It's not me. Susan, a friend of mine, took her husband to the emergency with stomach pain this morning. They still don't know what's wrong, and I've only gotten here myself, so I haven't been able to ask around."

"Does it sound serious?"

"I don't know anything at this point, except that he also has a fever. And they have a little two-year-old who is not happy about staying here while Mommy freaks out, if you know what I mean, so Susan asked me to take her home. I'm not sure how long I'll be here, but I want to stay long enough to make sure Susan's okay."

"I can't say I'm not disappointed," Wylen said, "but you need to be there for your friend. So you're at our hospital?"

"Yeah, in the ER."

"Then your friend's husband is in good hands."

"That's what I told her." Kendall couldn't help grinning.

"Okay, so if we can't do the river rafting today, let's do it tomorrow."

"I'd love to," Kendall said. "But I might still be on babysitting duty. Depending on what this is." A tendril of fear wound through her. What if it was serious and Jasper died? He was a big part of why Kendall had chosen the couple for the adoption in the first place.

Wylen laughed, unaware of her inner turmoil. "Then we'll have to play it by ear."

They chatted a few more minutes, long enough for Teisha to decide she was finished with her food and ask to go potty. "Hey, I've got to take this little cutie to the restroom," Kendall said to Wylen, "or I'm going to have a wet lap."

"By all means, hurry. I'll talk to you later. Let me know if anything changes."

Kendall texted Susan to tell her about the bathroom. "Be a big girl, okay?" Kendall said to Teisha. "Don't go in your pants."

"I'm a big girl," Teisha agreed with a smile.

"You certainly are." How long had the sweetheart been talking in full sentences? It seemed like only yesterday she'd had only one-word answers. Having a preschool teacher as a mom had definite advantages.

In the bathroom, Teisha needed help, but Kendall had been at Lily's house when Lily's daughter was that age, so she knew what to do. Afterward, Teisha wanted to wash her hands and the counter and then dry everything. She also tried out the air dryer and explained, very seriously, to another child how to use it.

"I was beginning to think you fell in," Susan said to Teisha as they dropped into a chair beside her.

"Teisha doesn't like to leave water on the counter," Kendall said.

Susan nodded. "We talked about cleaning up after ourselves and others in preschool last week. They'll all be careful for another day or two, I'm guessing."

"Did you find out what's wrong?"

Susan shook her head. "No one seems to know anything."

"I'll go see what I can find out. I mean, they probably just don't know. It looks rather busy here this morning." Kendall was about to pass Teisha back to Susan when she spotted Wylen striding toward them across the room, his grin a little too wide. He looked amazing in olive-green sport pants and a white T-shirt, his dark hair slightly spiked as it never was at work. Her arms tightened around Teisha and the little girl took that as a sign to hug her.

"Someone you know?" Susan asked, following her gaze.

"A doctor who works here." It was all the explanation Kendall could give before he'd waded through the crowd and stood in front of them.

"Hi," he said, winking at her and nodding at Susan.

"What are you doing here?" Kendall managed to respond, as they stood to greet him.

"Well, if you can hang out here on your day off, so can I. Besides, this really hot nurse I was going out with today canceled our date, so I'd thought I'd come and meet your friend and this little cutie here." He bent to look into Teisha's face. "Hi, there!"

"Hi," Teisha said quickly before burying her face in Kendall's neck.

"This is Teisha," Kendall said. "And her mom, Susan."

"Nice to meet you, Susan." He shook her hand. "I'm Wylen Gibson. Sorry to hear about your husband."

"Thank you," Susan murmured, looking back and forth between Kendall and Wylen.

"I was about to go see if I could learn anything about Susan's husband."

Wylen took his phone from his pocket. "Why don't you give me his name, and I'll go check? You look like you have your hands full."

"Okay. Sure." Kendall had been working here longer, but Wylen was a doctor and could pull strings she couldn't. Besides, she didn't want to leave Susan without support for Teisha.

After Susan recounted all the particulars, Wylen waved at Teisha, who had unburied her head to stare at him, and disappeared into the crowd.

She and Susan resettled and Teisha kicked to get down. Kendall offered her another graham cracker, but Teisha wanted to play an ABC app on Susan's phone instead.

"I made you cancel a date," Susan said.

Kendall shrugged. "It's okay. We'll do it another time."

"Are you sure?"

"Yeah." But was she really that confident? Kendall was surprised to find the answer was yes. There was something between them, and it might be real. At least if he could accept her past, which was still an unknown.

"He's really cute," Susan added.

"Yeah, I noticed."

Teisha was already beginning to grow bored when Wylen finally returned. They stood up again to meet him, this time with Teisha in Susan's arms. "Well?" Kendall asked.

Wylen gave her a smoldering look that sent her heartbeat into overtime. "He's going to be okay." Susan gave a big sigh as he continued, "However, he's got appendicitis, and it's severe, but it hasn't burst, which is a good thing. They'll need to get him into surgery right away. I told his doctor I'd let you know. He'll be here in about ten minutes to explain more, but the prepping and surgery and everything should only take an hour or so. Your husband will have to stay in the hospital for a few days."

Susan's face had gone pale at the mention of surgery, but when she spoke, she sounded relieved. "Thank you so much." She turned to Kendall. "Looks like I'll be here for a while. I'll walk you down to get the car seat from my car, okay?"

"You should get some food on the way back," Wylen told her. "I hear we have an awesome cafeteria." He shot a teasing glance at Kendall. "Not that I've had time to visit it yet."

They parted ways with Susan in the parking garage. Kendall took Teisha while Wylen carried the car seat. Before they reached Kendall's Audi, Teisha began to slump in her arms, a sure sign she was falling asleep. She went into the car seat without protest, and Kendall emptied her snack bag and used it to prop up the child's head.

"So what now?" Wylen's voice was sexy as she leaned against the Audi to talk to him.

"Home maybe until she wakes, a playground after, then maybe to Lily's House to see the horses. She really likes those." He was close enough to smell his aftershave.

He put his hand on the car, one on either side of her. He leaned in for a slow, exploring kiss. "Can I come with you? I have my picnic blanket in my car. We can stop and buy lunch for the playground."

She kissed him back, her arms going around his neck. "Yes."

"And I thought I'd have to do more convincing." He kissed her again, and for a long while Kendall forgot everything else.

They finally drove to the park, and Teisha awoke too early from her short nap, a little grumpy, but eager to play. They went up slides and down them. They took turns pushing Teisha on the swing. Finally, they played tag until Teisha said she was hungry. She fell asleep two bites into the ham and cheese sandwich they'd put on ice.

"You're an awfully good sport," she said to Wylen. "I seriously couldn't picture you at a playground."

"Really? I could picture you here perfectly." He laughed. "Anyway, I like kids."

"Good to know."

Kendall and Wylen stretched out sideways on the blanket, each with one elbow propping up their heads as they faced one another, Teisha sleeping between them. Kendall felt a momentary sadness that if she hadn't made certain choices, maybe this could be her real life.

Or maybe if she'd kept Teisha, Wylen would have come into their lives anyway.

Almost immediately, she pushed the thoughts aside. If she hadn't placed Teisha with Susan and Jasper, she wouldn't have been able to fast track her RN degree. She'd be working overtime at a minimum wage job to support them, and Teisha would be with a sitter all day. There would be pressure, tears, and probably resentment. As it was, Kendall would be paying on school loans for a long time to come, and only in the last six months had she even begun to feel confident about paying her bills. Meanwhile, Teisha had a loving, full-time mother and a father who adored her. Kendall knew she'd made the best choice for her baby.

Wylen reached out and stroked her cheek. "What's up?"

Kendall met his eyes. Those dark eyes that seemed to peer inside her. Suddenly, she wanted him to know. She didn't want to hide this part of her. If he was to ever fall in love with her, it had to be honestly, knowing every part of her life.

"There's something I want to tell you," she said. "But I'm not sure how you'll take it."

He appeared to consider that a moment. "I'm game to try if you are."

"Then don't react right away, okay? Maybe think about it for a while, and we can talk about it later."

"Okay." His gaze didn't leave hers. What was she doing? She almost wanted to pull back the words.

"Teisha's adopted." Kendall's eyes left him to stroke

the toddler's cheek. "Susan and Jasper are pretty much the best adoptive parents ever, and I believe Teisha belongs with them. They've given her a two-parent home and stability she wouldn't otherwise have." A long pause where he didn't say anything, and she didn't dare look at him. Surely he'd already guessed the rest.

She rushed onward. "I'm Teisha's birth mother."

21

Kendall let a few seconds more pass before she looked up at Wylen. He was watching her, his eyes wide with surprise. "That's big," he said, his voice a little gravelly.

She nodded. "I wanted you to know. We have an open adoption, so I get to see her. Usually once a week for a few hours. Sometimes I watch her on her parents' anniversary, or when they need to get away. But that could change when she gets older. She might not want to spend time with me, or she might want to hang out more. Susan and I plan to listen to what she wants and needs. The important thing is that Teisha knows she wasn't abandoned."

Wylen took a deep breath. "I guess that explains why you were so good with Sage. I wondered why they switched you to her."

"They switched me because I've taken classes on caring for unwed mothers, but yeah, that's really why I related with Sage so well. No one knows about it at work. Only my family, and my roommates. A few close friends. I'd appreciate if it stayed that way."

"Of course," he said.

She wanted to ask him what he thought in relation to their dating, but she'd been the one to beg him to wait before making a decision, and she was afraid to know the answer. "I won't have to support her financially," she said, "and I hope I'll have my own children one day, so they'll obviously take precedence, but Teisha will always be a part of my life."

His handsome face was impassive, and she had no idea what he was feeling. Probably shock. "So many people take the easy way out," he said after too long a pause. "As a doctor, I value the decision you made to give her life."

It didn't mean he still wanted to date her, but it was something. She stroked Teisha's hair, staring down into the innocent little face. "I always saw her as a person, right from the beginning. I never planned on adoption—I wanted to keep her. But my life was a mess, and the more she grew inside me, the more I wanted for her."

He nodded, and she felt he heard the meaning behind her words. But she could also sense the strain between them. Things were different between them now.

The talk moved on to safer topics: the river run, patients at the hospital, the games they had played with his friends. A drop of sweat snaked down her back. The day was warm, even under the trees and with a fresh breeze blowing through the playground. It would only get worse as the afternoon wore on, and there was no text yet from Susan.

Teisha stirred and her eyes opened. "Kendamom," she murmured, pulling herself up and rubbing her eyes with the back of her hands. "Can we see horseys?"

"Sure, honey. That's a great idea. I'll text Lily to let her know we're on our way." Kendall looked over at Wylen. "I can drop you off at the hospital for your car," she offered.

"And miss meeting the famous Lily I've heard so much about?"

His words lightened the mood. At least he wasn't taking the first chance at an exit. "I don't talk about her all that much, do I?"

"Well, it was enough to spark my curiosity." He jumped up and extended his hands to Teisha, who reached for him willingly enough. Kendall felt a rush of warmth, but she warned herself not to read too much into his actions.

At Lily's House, another surprise awaited them. "Is that Sage on the porch?" Wylen asked, squinting as she released Teisha from her car seat.

"I think so. What's she doing here?"

"Beats me."

Kendall hurried up the walk with Teisha on her hip. Sage watched them, lifting a hand in greeting. "Bet you didn't expect to see me here," the girl said.

"No, I didn't." Before Kendall could question her further, Lily poked her head out of the house, her blond hair up in its usual ponytail.

"Good. You're here. I told Sage you were coming, and she wanted to catch up with you." To Teisha, Lily added with barely a pause, "Cherie's out on the swing set waiting for you. Want to go play?" Teisha nodded vigorously and kicked to get down. There was only a year and four months between her and Lily's youngest, and they were already good friends.

"I'll take her back," Kendall said, holding onto Teisha. "Sage and I can sit on the deck until the girls are ready to visit the horses."

Lily nodded, her ponytail bouncing. "Go on through the house, then. It'll give you a chance to cool off a bit."

Kendall started up the steps and into the house, but Lily's eyes pinned Wylen in place. "You must be Kendall's friend from the hospital," she said. "I think today is my lucky day. We have a lot of people who volunteer here, but no doctor yet, so let me give you the grand tour while Sage and Kendall talk. Do you ever do probono work? You know what we do here, right?"

"Um," Wylen said, flashing a startled glance Kendall's way. She shrugged. Lily was a master at finding resources, and it was doubtful she'd let him go before she said her spiel. "Sure," he finished, seeing that she was no help.

The house seemed deserted, with most of the foster girls in school, but the kitchen smelled like fresh bread. "My mother brought this over," Sage told her as she paused to cut a few slices of a loaf sitting on the countertop.

"Smells delicious."

"It's really good." Sage handed her a plate. "I see you took my advice about the doctor."

"Advice?" Kendall wasn't hungry, but she took a piece of bread, buttered it, and gave half to Teisha, who stuffed the end in her mouth.

"Well, maybe not advice, but I told you he liked you."

"I guess you were right."

They took their plates to the back deck. Teisha ran off to play as Kendall unrolled the awning that would shade them from the sun, turning on the fan Lily kept there for the purpose and pointing it toward Sage, who had lowered herself onto a lounge chair.

"Thanks," the girl said.

"So how did you get here?" Kendall asked, pulling a chair near Sage.

"I drove." Sage gave her a smile. "After I left the hospital on Saturday, I looked up Lily's House on the Internet and read all about how Lily helps girls—runaways or those in the foster system. When I realized my problems started because I was anxious, I knew I had to get away. For myself and for the baby." She rubbed a hand over her stomach. "Yesterday, I drove over and knocked on the door. Lily helped me talk to my parents and the adoption agency and family services. Anyway, looks like I get to stay. I'm not sure if it's my parents or the agency or whoever is paying, but I get to stay until the baby's born. Maybe until I finish high school. I think it's good for all of us."

Kendall rubbed her face. "Oh, Sage. I hope nothing I said made you leave home."

"No. Don't think that. Well, maybe when you said I was doing the best for my baby. That might have been a little bit of what made me come. Because every day was so much pressure at home. And my mom was so sad, and my dad angry. This way we get a break, and they're still involved. I'm not a burden on Lily either, because we're paying. I don't even really count as one of her foster girls. She can only have so many apparently."

Kendall didn't tell her that Lily would have taken her for free. Lily was practical and always made good use of donations and wouldn't turn down a payment, but she also wouldn't turn any needy girl away.

"You'll like it here," Kendall said.

"I do already." Sage's eyes strayed to where the little girls were playing. "Lily showed me a picture of her original six foster girls, the ones who helped her refurbish this house. Your sister was one of them?"

Kendall nodded. "Saffron. She's been married now almost three years."

"Right before you had your baby?"

"Yeah."

Sage was quiet a moment. "Lily told me Saffron and her husband had a baby girl a few months ago. I wonder . . . why didn't she take your baby?"

Kendall watched Teisha and Cherie's crouch in the grass near the swing, their heads bent together, Cherie's long hair skimming the grass. "I did think about it, and she offered, but they had barely gotten married, and her husband, Vaughn, was commuting to work in California, and that was enough pressure for them. Plus . . . it was too close. I didn't want to endanger my relationship with my sister. I didn't trust myself to let my baby go if she kept her. It's better this way. I love being with Teisha, but it's hard, and I think it always will be a little. I don't have to feel that when I'm with my sister and her family."

Sage watched the girls for a moment before nodding. "I think I understand. It's like me with my mom and dad. It's too close, even if they wanted to adopt her. Besides, I want my baby to have something better than what I had. Not that they don't love me, but it's so mixed up at home right now. This wasn't their choice, and I don't want them or my baby feeling it was pushed on them."

"It gets better." Kendall met her eyes. "I promise."

Sage nodded. "If that sexy doctor is anywhere as near as nice to you as he was to me, I can see it gets better."

Kendall laughed, but her heart ached at the comment. Yesterday she would have agreed wholeheartedly. "We'll see."

"Does he know about Teisha?"

"He just found out."

Sage grimaced. "Oh, boy. Do you think it'll be okay between you guys?"

"I really don't know."

"Sorry. That sucks."

Kendall accepted that with a nod. Given the way she felt about Wylen, it worse than sucked, but she really had no room to complain. She'd made her choices and the consequences wouldn't change because she'd met Dr. Gorgeous.

The little girls were at the back fence now, gazing over at the two horses in the back lot. Officially, the animals belonged to Lily's sister next door, but all the foster girls at Lily's House took turns taking care of them. It was part of the therapy. Lily believed there could never be too many chores, and that included mucking out horse stalls.

"I want to meet your baby's mother," Sage said into the quiet. "Maybe she's right for me too."

Kendall turned her head to stare at Sage. "Is that what this is all about?"

"I don't know. Maybe." Sage shrugged. "I still have time. It wouldn't hurt to meet her, right?"

"I guess not, but you could try other couples too."

Kendall realized that maybe she should talk to Susan before Sage did.

"I know, but I just . . . I don't trust my decisions much anymore. I know the couples will all be putting on their best faces, and how can I know if they'll really love her? Or if they'll let me see her sometimes so I know she's okay?" She paused. "I'm scared."

Kendall knew the feeling only too well. "Then you should definitely meet Susan and Jasper."

The back door to the house swung open to reveal Lily with Wylen, who looked surprisingly in a good mood for having endured the grand tour. Lily also appeared content, and Kendall was sure he'd agreed to volunteer his services.

"Just in time," Kendall said. "I think the girls are ready to visit the horses."

After feeding the horses apples, Kendall dropped Wylen off at the hospital and drove home with Teisha, who was sleepy again. The apartment was too quiet, and Kendall found herself counting down the hours to when Elsie and Halla would walk in the door. She wished Wylen had suggested a movie or something, but maybe it was better this way.

After dinner, she and Teisha watched a kid movie on Netflix until the toddler drifted off. Kendall snuggled next to her on the couch and fell asleep herself, replaying the day in her head. Still no word from Wylen about his feelings, not even his usual text about how he'd enjoyed the day. So maybe he hadn't.

Or maybe he needed time. Whatever his feelings, she needed to stop obsessing about him.

Teisha had been sleeping for an hour when Susan arrived. "Thank you so much," she said. Her short dark hair was on the wild side and her mascara was smeared, but she looked better than she had that morning. "Jasper's resting peacefully, and he insisted that I go home. I'll take Teisha to see him tomorrow—he's missing his baby girl—but he's doing so much better already that they may let him go home in the morning. They were able to do laparoscopic surgery instead of opening him up all the way, so he'll heal faster."

"That's wonderful."

Susan hurried to the couch. "Oh, I missed her so much." She leaned over and kissed Teisha before sinking next to her on the carpet in front of the couch. "Thank you so much. It gave me peace of mind to know she was being taken care of."

"We went to the park and then saw the horses. It was a good thing my friend Wylen came with us to the park. She was tireless. I don't know how I could have done it alone."

Susan laughed. "She does love the playground." She paused before adding, "So what did you tell him? Does he know about you and Teisha?"

"I wish you hadn't asked." With a sigh, Kendall lowered herself to the carpet near Susan and pulled her knees to her chest. "I did tell him, and he was nice about it, but it was strained between us after that. Teisha's too important to keep a secret, though, so I'm glad I did. Before I got in too deep, you know?"

"You're probably right, but I'm still sorry. After all you've been through. After all you've sacrificed for Teisha, you deserve more."

Kendall shrugged. "I'd need to tell him eventually anyway."

"He's that important?"

"I'd hoped he was." She took a deep breath. "Now I don't know."

"Let a little time pass." Susan stood and gathered Teisha from the couch. "How can he not love her?"

"Right." Kendall's smile was real. If Wylen didn't have room in his heart for Teisha, then all the room in the world wasn't going to be enough for Kendall.

"There is something else," Kendall said as she walked Susan to the door.

Susan's brow creased. "About Teisha?"

"No, about the new girl that arrived at Lily's House yesterday. She was a patient of mine."

Kendall told her about Sage and her family and her interest in meeting Susan as a prospective adoptive parent for her little girl. "I know you and Jasper were planning on a boy, so I wanted to give you the heads up."

"Are you kidding?" Susan leaned forward eagerly, holding Teisha more tightly to her chest. "If there's any chance we could have a little sister for Teisha, we'd jump at the chance. We'd love any child, and that's exactly what we told our agency. We assumed it would probably be a little boy, but a girl would be every bit as wonderful. I don't know what I would do without my sister, and I've always wanted a sister for Teisha. Thank you so much for telling her about us." Tears glistened in Susan's eyes. "You've just changed the worst day ever into one of the best. I'll call Lily tonight and make arrangements to meet Sage."

Susan took Teisha home, and the apartment was suddenly too quiet. But before Kendall could feel sorry for herself, Elsie and Halla were home.

"Finally!" she said, hugging them. "Drop your stuff in your rooms and come sit down. I'll order a pizza for dinner."

"Not for me," Elsie hurried to the bathroom. "It's almost eight. I have to shower and get to Payden's." The door closed, and Kendall's gaze shifted to Halla, who gave her a smile.

"He's making dinner for her at his apartment," Halla told her. "I suspect it would have been for all of us, but she told him she'd had enough togetherness this weekend."

Kendall raised her brows. "Elsie said that? Doesn't sound like her."

"Nope, so I'm pretty sure she wants to be alone with him. It took some doing getting her to admit it, but apparently something Tara and Rylee said at the movies got her thinking about him romantically. She might have almost kissed him. She's not quite sure."

"Yes!" Kendall did a little happy dance. "I knew it would work."

"Well, that teacher she thinks he's interested in has made it more pressing. I hope things are going to change between them. And soon." Halla flopped onto the couch with a sigh.

"It's about time." Kendall glanced at the bathroom door. "But I hope she doesn't take another ten years to marry him. So what about you?" She sat down next to Halla. "You have to tell me all about Oliver and your mother—I mean your grandmother. Or whatever you're calling her." The texts and brief telephone conversations weren't the same thing as being there.

"Mother. I think that's what I've decided. But hurry up and order that pizza first. We didn't stop for lunch because Elsie was so eager to get home to Payden. Good thing we gained an hour crossing time zones or she might not have let us stop for potty breaks." She sighed. "And after having to say goodbye to Oliver, I need plenty of carbs and gooey cheese to cheer me up."

Kendall pulled out her phone. "You know what? So do I."

Halla was immediately curious. "So what happened after you and Wylen took Teisha to the park? Your last text to Elsie didn't say."

"I told him I was her birth mother."

Halla's jaw dropped. "Make that double cheese and double peperoni. We both deserve it."

Elsie felt a little bad leaving Halla and Kendall moping on the couch, but they had each other, and she needed to see Payden. She wished they were meeting at his new house, but that deal wasn't closing for a few weeks and the current residents were still there. No matter. His apartment would work just as well.

He let her in as if he'd been waiting near the door, which he probably had since she'd texted him at the stoplight a block away. He looked tall and strong and was wearing her favorite navy and white polo shirt, the one she'd bought him for his last birthday. His beard scruff was freshly trimmed and his hair still slightly damp as if he too had come from the shower. Her own hair was a bit frizzy from the blow dryer, and she hoped he didn't notice.

"Hey," he said, hugging her. "You made good time."

"I hit all green lights." Her heart was beating like a thousand drums in her chest. Had his eyes always been so beautiful? Her gaze ran over his face. Yes, this was the same big, preppie, slightly baby-faced man she'd always known. The same but different. Was it because he was in love with the sweet-looking teacher?

A rush of panic filled her. She didn't want this to end. She didn't want to lose him.

"So, what's for dinner?" she forced herself to say, her nose catching a whiff of something delicious. They usually had pizza or tacos if he planned dinner. Neither were her favorite, but since she usually cooked or made him help her, it didn't bother her to have quick and easy some of the time. But the smell didn't scream pizza or tacos.

"It's something called spicy garlic lime chicken." He shrugged. "I thought you'd enjoy it after a long day of snack foods."

"That's sweet of you." He was always thinking about her like that. She stared at him for a long moment until she became aware that he was shifting uneasily. Was she acting weird, or was he? Maybe he had news he wasn't looking forward to telling her.

"Come on in." He stepped back and motioned for her to enter. "I thought we'd eat on the coffee table in case we decide to watch something later. Oh, and I made chocolate mousse." He laughed. "From a package, of course, so it's not like Ruth's, but it's still pretty good."

He had set the coffee table with everything except the plates, which were probably warming in the oven as she'd taught him. There were candles on it too, and a vase of flowers. That was new. Elsie stiffened. Maybe those were there to impress whoever he planned to date. Or was dating.

She swallowed hard and sat on the couch. She'd been

in this room so many times alone with him, but never had she imagined feeling so awkward. How on earth was she supposed to open the subject of what happened between them at the house? She was sure he'd felt something too, but maybe she was fooling herself.

"I'll go dish up and bring it in," he said.

She jumped up. "I'll help."

"No." His voice was amused. "Just relax. I know how exhausting traveling is."

She sat back down as he left the room, but the ensuing silence wore on her. Maybe she should put on some music. That was it. She'd set the mood with his favorite CD. Maybe after dinner she'd casually mention dancing, and he'd suggest they take a spin. She could nonchalantly close the space between them and look deeply into his eyes. Maybe that delicious urge to kiss would hit them at the same time.

At the thought, she rolled her eyes. Since when had they ever randomly started dancing in his apartment? Or anywhere for that matter? If they weren't at a wedding reception or at a karaoke bar listening to her foster sisters make fools of themselves, they'd never danced together.

Still, music wasn't a bad idea, and it would give her something to do. She popped up and went to the sound system that took up a good portion of his entertainment center. Payden liked technology, and his apartment clearly showed that love. He was even planning on running Internet and sound system wires throughout his new house before moving in.

She found one of his favorite CDs from an indie singer

name Charlotte Storm. That should be romantic enough without being too obvious. She lit the candles with the lighter on the coffee table and went to turn off the lights.

Too dark, she thought.

Back at the entertainment center, she tapped on some of the display lights in the shelves. There, that worked. She'd close her eyes and pretend she was resting to explain why she turned out the overhead light. "Can't let these beautiful candles go to waste," she'd say. "Where'd you get them anyway?"

She was about to return to the couch when she spotted it. The box. On another day she wouldn't have noticed, but it looked exactly like the plush jewelry box that held Halla's gold locket, only smaller. She swallowed hard, feeling the world spinning around her.

"Elsie?" Behind her two plates clunked on the coffee table.

She reached for the box.

With a hurried stride, Payden was at her side, his big hand closing over hers before she could open the box. He pocketed it, his expression unclear in the dim light cast by the entertainment center.

"Is that a ring?" Elsie asked. Her voice didn't sound like her—all high and breathy.

"Come on, let's eat. Our food is getting cold."

The words tugged at the chef inside her, but she thrust them away, staring up into his beloved face. "It is a ring, isn't it? You weren't kidding." Her voice cracked, and she struggled to hold back a sob. "But I don't want you to be with that teacher. I don't want you to move on without me."

"What?" He stared at her blankly. But after a few heartbeats, his expression changed to surprise. "Oh, it's not like that. You don't understand."

Elsie dared feel a little hope. Or did he mean that the woman he had his eye on wasn't a teacher? Was she too late? Had he already fallen in love? Had he been with this woman over the weekend while she'd been out of town?

In sudden embarrassment, Elsie wanted to flee. She wanted to run home to Halla and cry on her shoulder. But she remembered what Halla said about giving Payden a choice. They had a past together, and that was something this other woman didn't have with Payden. He'd wanted her once. Maybe the emotion could be revived.

Making the decision, Elsie launched herself into his arms, pushing herself up on her tiptoes and pulling his face down to hers. She put her lips on his. For a moment, he tensed, and she thought it was all over, but then his arms tightened around her, and he was kissing her back. Not a friendship kiss either, or like anything they'd ever shared before. The kiss was long and deep and passionate. She breathed him in, tasted the slight mint of his toothpaste that he'd probably used just before she arrived. She felt the heat of his mouth, the urgency between them. If a million fireworks had gone off in her head, she couldn't have felt more amazed.

Realization came in the next instant. She loved this man. Loved him. And she didn't ever want to let him go. She might not be experienced in matters of love, but nothing could equal this. Nothing even came close.

When she finally came up for air, Payden stared down

at her, his eyes fiery with desire. His arms didn't loosen but held her close against his body. Yet his expression was tinged with wariness.

"See?" Elsie said. "There is something between us. You felt it, right?" She dared to say it only because she knew he loved her at least as a friend. If it was only physical attraction, he'd let her down easy. "It doesn't matter if you did. I did, Payden, and I'm not letting you go that easily. I'm going to fight for you! Even if it takes me ten years."

A smile touched his lips, and Elsie's hope nosedived. He was going to let her down easily, maybe offer to set her up with one of his friends in exactly the same way she had offered so many times over the years. Why had she been such a blind fool? She should have kissed him back the first time he ever tried to kiss her. She should have seen beyond the friendship and set herself up with him.

"Elsie," he said, as she opened her mouth to say more to convince him. She choked back her words. Maybe if she shut up now, she could end this night with a little dignity.

He took her chin in his hand, rubbing his thumb across her skin. She pushed against the warmth of his touch, craving more. Wanting him to kiss her again. As if that would happen.

And then it did. With his eyes on hers, he brought his face closer. He watched her reaction as they kissed, his mouth angling over hers as if it had been made to fit there. It felt like heaven, and her own eyes shut with enjoyment. His arms had tightened around her again.

Was he only giving her what she wanted because they

were friends? Or did he feel more for her as she now knew she did for him?

The answer might be in his pants pocket. She reached out to fish for the little box, but he beat her to it, putting his hand inside the pocket. "Yes, it's a ring," he admitted.

Tears welled in her eyes before she could stop them.

"No," he said, giving her a quick kiss and wiping moisture from under her left eye with the tips of his fingers. "It's not for anyone. Well, not for anyone but you."

"Me?" Somehow she managed to get out the word.

He shrugged. "It's always been you. Since the day you walked into my life. I know you've looked at me more like a brother, but I always knew there was more—or could be."

"But I set you up with my friends."

He gave her a skewed expression, his brows arching. "Yeah, and I tried to make those work. I finally had to admit to myself that it never worked out because I was already in love with you."

"But . . . why didn't you . . .?"

"Say anything? Because you weren't ready. But I don't give up easily. I believed in you. In us. I knew the best was yet to come."

She reached for the ring box again, and this time he let her have it. Inside sat the ring she'd pointed out to him over two years ago when Ruth and her then-fiancé had finally picked out their own rings.

"It's beautiful," she breathed, itching to put it on.

"Look," he said, closing his hand over hers and shutting the box. "Did you mean what you said? We can take it slow, if you need to, but I want to be sure that you want this. Not just because we're friends."

She met his eyes, those beautiful blue eyes that seemed to hold eternity. She knew what she had to do. Payden needed to know exactly how she felt.

She took her hand from his, still clinging to the box, and knelt down on the carpet. "Payden Chambers, will you marry me?"

His eyes widened. "Elsie, you don't have to . . ."

"I don't need time," she insisted, offering him the box. "You're my best friend in the entire world, and apparently I'm crazy attracted to you, so why shouldn't we get married?"

He stared at her, a line of puzzlement on his brow. Then he reached down and pulled her to her feet. "No way, you aren't ruining this for me. I should be asking you."

"Too late. I already did it." Laughter filled her with light. "And it's a story we'll tell all of our friends and our kids."

A smile tugged on his lips. "So I'm never going to live this down?" He slipped the box from her hand. "At least let me put the ring on." He took it out of the box and went down on one knee. "Elsie, I've dreamed about this moment practically from the day we met. I've loved you for ten years. Through pimples, through high school, through boyfriends I wanted to kill, through college, and all the times in between. I love your laugh, your tenderness, your friendship, your mind, your body, and your kiss. I want you to live in my house and cook to your heart's content in the kitchen that I found for you. I want to make babies with you. Lots of them."

"Lots?"

He nodded. "I like kids."

"Okay." She did too, but he already knew that.

He wasn't done. "I love your family, your quirks, and how cranky you get at night when you're tired. I want to rub your back when you've had a hard day. I want to hold your hand at the movies. And I really, really want to kiss you again."

"Then hurry up already." She spread out her fingers so he could put on the ring.

"Elsie Reynolds, will you marry me?"

"Yes!" she nearly shouted. "I will." As he slid on the ring, it caught the light from the entertainment center and sparkled up at her. "But I still asked you first," she added saucily.

Laughing, he pulled her to him and kissed her again for a long, long time. And when they were finally able to pull apart, the dinner he'd worked so hard on was definitely cold. They ate it anyway, and it was the best meal Elsie had tasted in her life.

23

Kendall was glad her roommates were home and for the excitement of Elsie's surprise engagement. Between brainstorming wedding plans with Elsie and helping Halla search for her biological father when she wasn't pining over Oliver, there wasn't much time to dwell on her own dismal romance with Wylen.

Or non-romance, she should say. Because three entire days had passed, and he hadn't called or texted. He hadn't asked to reschedule their river run on their Tuesday off. She'd glimpsed him a few times at work on Wednesday and Thursday from a distance, and only once in a patient's room, where he'd smiled and made her stomach curl but hadn't initiated a private conversation.

By Friday morning, she was sure it was completely over between them. Her heart mourned more than she expected, and she had to remind herself that her relationship with Teisha wasn't something she should be ashamed of. Not now. She'd done the responsible thing at great cost to herself, and she'd paid the price for her mistakes—in some ways she'd be paying for the rest of her life. She was okay with that. She adored Teisha. If Wylen wasn't the man she'd hoped, then he didn't deserve either of them.

Easy to think, but seriously difficult to make her heart believe. There had been a connection between them. Something powerful. And now it was gone.

Before lunch, she checked in with all her patients, realizing she was having to force her smile. She hated that, so on her way to the break room where her lunch awaited in the refrigerator, she sent Susan a quick text: *How is Jasper today? I'd love a picture with him and Teisha, if you have time to send one.*

No one was in the breakroom except a couple at a corner table, who looked like they were ready to leave. She'd barely taken out her lunch and sat at the opposite end of the room near the door when a picture came through with Teisha snuggled up to her dad in bed as he read her a story.

This was last night, Susan said. *Teisha is loving having him home so much. He'll be home for another week, though, so she'll have plenty of snuggle time! They're taking a nap now. I'll snap a picture. Just don't tell Jasper, lol!*

Another picture came of Teisha sleeping with her dad, his arm under her back and her arms splayed on either side of her. One of her legs was over his stomach, and Kendall hoped she wouldn't kick him in his incision. Peace settled through her. She took a breath, turned off her phone, and reached for her lunch bag. As she looked up, she caught sight of someone standing near the door. It was Wylen.

She nodded and smiled as she pulled out her left-over smoked salmon from the night before. Elsie was experimenting with recipes for a small wedding dinner she and Payden planned to have for family, and even though both Kendall and Halla had reminded her that she couldn't cater her own wedding, she wasn't deterred. Meanwhile, Kendall was happy to benefit from the experiments.

She needed to microwave the fish, but Wylen was moving into the room. Better to start on the Tuscan salad and wait for him to run away so they wouldn't have to talk. She opened the salad container and dug in the bag for the fork.

When Wylen slipped into the chair next to her, she gripped the fork in her fist, her eyes lifting to his.

"Uh, you're not going to poke me with that, are you?" His smile made her stomach tighten.

She dropped the fork onto the table. "Sorry, you startled me."

He gestured to the phone. "You looked pretty busy with your phone earlier. I didn't want to interrupt."

Had he been watching her? Once, she would have teased him and said the words aloud. Now, she shrugged. "Just looking at a few pictures." She wanted to recall the words the moment they were out. What if he asked to see the pictures, and they put yet another wedge between them?

Wait, she wasn't trying to hide anything. "Want to see them?" she asked.

He chuckled. "If you want to show me."

Couldn't she just shut up? Teisha was the part of her life he obviously wasn't interested in and thus didn't deserve. "Not really."

His face sobered as he took in that bit of information. "Okay." He paused as the couple in the corner left together, passing close to Kendall's table. "How have you been?"

"Good," she lied. "It's been a bit chaotic at my apartment, though. Elsie proposed to Payden and he proposed right back and gave her the ring he'd already bought for her, so she's cooking up a storm and making us comb through bridal magazines, and Halla is turning the Internet upside down trying to find her birth father. I've been helping her." There, let him see she wasn't losing sleep over him.

He blinked. "Elsie proposed? I thought they were just friends."

"She was the only one who thought so." Kendall had told him about her roommates, of course. At least up until the moment of her fateful confession. Now the new developments in Elsie and Halla's lives gave her something casual to talk about. Something that didn't hurt.

"Right. Well, I'm glad they worked it out." The furrow between his eyes didn't seem glad to Kendall.

"Me too. I was going to be his next set-up. Although he is a really nice guy, so it would have been fun." Why didn't he leave? Her appetite was gone, but she had to eat, and she couldn't do that with him sitting there next to her without a lunch. She looked pointedly at her salad.

He moved his hand, putting it over hers where it sat near her fork. Startled, she looked up at him. "I did what you said," he began in a low voice. "I thought about it."

He meant Teisha and her confession, of course. Kendall wanted to tell him she'd already gotten his message loud and clear, but the words refused to pass her lips.

"You shared something very serious with me, and I understand that." His gaze held hers earnestly. "When I thought about it, I realized it mattered a lot to me, you having a child, and it took me a while to understand why I cared so much. Because frankly, with most women I've dated, I don't think I'd care. In med school, I even dated a woman who had a son. It puzzled me that you having a daughter bothered me so much."

Tears started in her eyes, though she hated herself for them—hated him for dropping this on her at work when she was tired and hungry. "It's okay," she said quickly. She tried to pull her hand out from under his.

His fingers tightened, and his eyes begged her to listen. "No, it's not okay. I finally figured out that the reason I cared was because I never had any lasting intention with any woman before. But I see something different in you. Something I've never seen before—maybe something I've glimpsed only between my parents—and I didn't know how your daughter would weigh into it all. Or change it all."

"She'll always be a part of my life," Kendall said, not daring to hope.

"I know that." He brought his other hand up to stroke away a tendril of hair that had escaped the twist she'd made to keep the locks from falling into any bandages. "And it would only be fair to you if I knew how I felt, and if it would make a difference to our relationship if it kept progressing."

Was he breaking up with her or what? It was hard to tell.

"For the past two days, I've been watching you," he

continued, "and I've realized that the one thing I want most in the world is to see where this is going between us. I'm not afraid of losing you to Teisha. I'm afraid of losing you because on Monday after you told me about her, I didn't do this." He leaned forward, his hand slipping around to the back of her neck, holding her gently as his lips met hers.

The tension rushed out of Kendall as she kissed him back, marveling at how much she'd missed him.

When someone came into the room, Wylen ignored them, finishing the kiss before drawing away and offering his hand. "I know you brought lunch today, but maybe it could wait until tomorrow. I'm really, really hungry, and I forgot my lunch, so I need you to finally show me where the cafeteria is. Let me buy you lunch there and tell you how much I've missed you."

"I think I can do that," she said. Feeling as if her feet only skimmed the floor, Kendall put her lunch back into the refrigerator and went with Wylen to the cafeteria.

Maybe she'd show him the photographs after all.

24

A week and a day had passed since Halla had said goodbye to Oliver in Idaho. Beyond that, she'd had only one brief call from him three days ago. A call that he'd made in a roomful of other workers with no option of privacy. That hadn't stopped him from saying he loved her.

He'd also promised to stay safe, and she'd believed him at the time, but the news reports had grown more impassioned, and the videos of the fire had her worried. So she'd thrown herself into work. She had two weeks of posts ready to go for her website and had finished her next post for her reporting job and was researching another.

She also might have found her father.

She had not been able to find a single Brock Watson in Colorado, and after calling all the Brock Watsons or B. Watsons she'd found in every other state with no luck, she'd finally reached out to Lily's friend Monica, who tracked down a Nampa high school yearbook with his picture in it. Halla had started researching and calling people in his year of school, particularly those who had been on the basketball team with him or who had been with him in the photos of the woods and metal-working classes. She also called a few of Brock's former teachers that Monica had managed to find.

Many of the people she reached remembered him, and slowly, a picture of her birth father had emerged. He hadn't been into computers or technology, but he'd been good with his hands, both in sports and with materials—especially metals. He'd been an average student who had a reputation for being kind. Women remembered him as helpful and fun in metal shop while the guys remembered him as someone who was guaranteed to make a basket or who could make cool things out of everyday objects. Teachers said Brock was always prompt with homework, willing to go the extra mile, and though he struggled with dyslexia, he'd kept reading. The dyslexia explain the average grades, despite his repeated efforts, and also why after finishing high school, he hadn't gone to college. Instead, he'd completed a welding certificate in twelve weeks and had gone to work locally.

Two female classmates and a former teammate recalled that he'd dated Becka, but only because he was on the basketball team and she'd stay after school sometimes to watch him play. Those who remembered Becka didn't say anything about her acting strangely, but one girl did mention that Becka always wore long sleeves, even on the most blistering days.

Halla appreciated learning about both her father and mother, but it wasn't until she talked to the shop teacher that she felt any real hope. Brock's single mother had died of cancer right after he graduated from high school, and the teacher had been the one to help him get into the welding program. Twelve years earlier, Brock had called to tell him thanks and that he was leaving Idaho for his dream job in Denver, Colorado. He'd remembered the company Brock was working with: Riverline Welding and Fabrication.

When Halla called the company, they wouldn't give out his number, but the fact that they took her message verified he still worked there. She told them her mother, Becka Jenkins, had been a friend of Brock's in high school and that she'd been born a few weeks before her death and was interested in learning more about her birth mother.

That would be enough for him to understand who Halla was. Maybe. In all likelihood, he wouldn't call her back. He might be married with a family of his own, and her appearance wouldn't be welcome. The thought of possible half-siblings was something else she hadn't considered before she left the message. If she had birth siblings, would they welcome her?

Hours ticked by as she tried to stay busy. She had several new texts from Naomi, who had finally arrived in Phoenix. Slowly, she and her mother were getting reacquainted, and instead of reminding Halla of the horrors she'd endured as a child, being with her mother reminded her of the happy moments they'd managed to steal together in Halla's youth. The memories were good, far better than the black hole she'd had of her childhood before.

They'd shared a nice though still somewhat awkward breakfast at the Eats and Treats this morning, the second since Naomi's arrival. Halla was pleased the pinched look in her mother's face was gone. Today, she was moving into an apartment she'd found, telling Halla only that it was "on the outskirts of Phoenix" and nothing more for her own safety, just in case. Despite the restraining order she'd been awarded against Reuben, she didn't want to take any chances.

After moving into her clandestine apartment, Naomi would look for a job, but in the meantime, she planned to make and sell crafts as she had secretly done for so long in Idaho. At breakfast Halla had joked that maybe her creative gene came from Naomi, and they'd both liked the idea. It gave Halla a strange sense of satisfaction to know that back in Idaho, Reuben no longer had anyone to control.

Pushing the thoughts aside, Halla went into the kitchen to get some strawberry ice cream. Elsie and Payden were supposedly cooking, but instead they were standing in the middle of the room, arms around each other, their lips locked. Making up for lost time, Elsie had told her.

They separated when Halla came into the kitchen. "You'll spoil your dinner," Elsie chided as Halla took out the ice cream.

"Since when have I ever turned down food? I can eat both my ice cream and your dinner. It smells delicious, by the way. What is it?" Halla popped off the lid to the ice cream and chiseled out a mouthful with her spoon.

"Steak using Oliver's brother-in-law's seasoning recipe," Elsie said. "Is it too costly for a wedding, do you think?"

Halla grinned. "Since we normally just have a few self-serve treat tables in Lily's back yard or in a rented hall if it's winter, yeah, it's definitely expensive."

Elsie frowned. "I want to impress his mom and stepdad. Especially his mom."

"Well, unless your mother has suddenly inherited money, you and Payden are paying for it yourselves, and whether it's seafood or steak, it's going to cost a ton. And you can't possibly cook it yourself anyway. Ruth might be able to, and we can help, but it's still going to cost too much. I think you should be upfront with his parents about what you can afford." Halla transferred her gaze to Payden as she added, "If they want something more, they can help. Otherwise, less hassle is better." She tapped Elsie's nose with her spoon. "You, my dear, are too stressed about this."

Elsie glanced at Payden for confirmation, and he nodded. "You are, a little. I'll talk to my mom and Dan. They're thrilled about us getting married, you know that, and they know our situation. With the house, we don't have a lot of spare income. Simple is probably best. Besides, my stepsister eloped, so whatever we decide, as long as it is a wedding they can attend, it's far better than what my mom got with her."

Elsie breathed a sigh of relief. "You know what? I think after tonight, I'm taking a break from cooking. I mean, outside the café."

"Good idea," Payden said.

Halla left them exploring each other's mouths and went to eat her ice cream in peace. She'd left her phone on the couch and checked it automatically to see that there had been a missed call. Her first thought was that it was Oliver, borrowing someone's satellite phone as he had the last time. She swallowed the ice cream, set the carton on the couch cushion next to her, and hit the button to call back. A man answered on the first ring. "Hello."

"Hi, I just got a call from this number?"

"Is this Halla Jenkins?" asked a deep voice. "I'm Brock Watson. I got a message to call you?"

Halla's heart jumped. Her father! What should she say? "Thanks for calling. Um, I'm not sure how to begin, so I'll plunge right in. I recently went to see my mother, Naomi Jenkins, in Nampa. Before that I hadn't been back in ten years. While I was there, I learned that she is actually my grandmother, and that her daughter, Becka, was my real mother."

"Are you sure?" This time his voice was gravelly.

"Yeah, I am. Becka never filed a birth certificate, or at least none was ever found, and when she died that night, we'd already been with my grandparents for a week, I guess."

He tried to clear his voice, but it was still hoarse when he said, "Did they raise you? Did you have to live with that man?"

"Until I was fifteen," Halla admitted. "Then I left. I was on the streets a couple weeks, but eventually I landed in a great place." Even though he'd left Idaho before she had, he'd probably read some of the articles about her, but she didn't need to bring up the details now. What she needed to know was if he believed he could be her father and wanted to meet her.

"Look," she said, "just so you know. I'm twenty-six, I have a good career as a blogger and reporter, a wonderful foster family with more sisters than I could ever want, and a great boyfriend who works as a forester. I'm not calling you for anything. I don't want anything. But Naomi, my grandmother, told me you are my father, and I wanted . . . I wanted to know if I could meet you." Halla stopped talking, and for a long moment he didn't say anything. Then she heard quiet sobs.

A woman's voice came on the line. "Give him a minute," she said. "I'm Vicky, by the way, Brock's wife. We've been married three years."

"I'm sorry," Halla said. "I'm not trying to cause any trouble. I barely learned this myself, and I had to call."

"It's no trouble. And believe me, he's happy you called. He half-suspected this once he got the message. He knew about you, but they told him you died."

"I know. It's not his fault. Look, does he use Hang-outs? We could video chat."

"Oh, goodness no." Vicky laughed. "Brock barely knows how to turn on the computer. He only uses it to go on my Facebook and see the grandkids. My grandkids, really, but they're ours now that we're married. They're both two. I have twin daughters, and they have one little girl each. We chat with them all the time on Facebook over their Messenger app. Want to try that? I think he's almost ready. He's got a tender heart."

That made Halla tear up. She'd braced herself for rejection, but this man had been so overcome with emotion, he couldn't even speak. What did that mean for them?

It took a few moments for them both to get on their computers, find each other's Facebook profiles and become friends. The pictures of Brock on Vicky's page immediately showed where Halla had gotten her very blond hair. Brock was pale blond, and his eyes were as blue as hers, so the eye color had come from both parents, and while Brock was obviously a fit man, his slightly rounded cheeks were also hers. No matter how thin she'd been in certain years, her face had never had Becka and Naomi's narrowness.

She wanted to scroll through the pictures of his life, but Vicky was already ringing for the video chat. Glancing in the mirror first and running a hand through her hair, Halla answered.

The man and woman in the photographs appeared on her screen in a dimly lit room, seated on a burgundy sofa. He wore dark jeans and a plaid shirt and gave the impression of strength, a man who worked with his hands. She could tell he needed a shave and that his beard stubble was as blond as the hair on his head. His thick lashes were also blond and sticking together with moisture. When he saw Halla, he started crying again.

Vicki put her arms around him consolingly. She was probably around forty, so she'd had her twins early to have grandchildren already. Her long blond hair hung straight on either side of her heart-shaped face. She looked round and soft and comfortable in her T-shirt and stretch pants.

"I should have known her old man was lying," Brock said as hoarsely as before.

"You were only nineteen," Halla reminded him.

He shook his head, more tears falling. "It was still my fault. I was working for my welding certificate, and I was all she had. I should have played it differently."

"Do you mind me asking what happened? How did you break up?"

"She left me." His jaw clenched and unclenched as if

even now the idea hurt. "We were living with a group of people, and they were doing drugs. I was afraid for her. I was hoping to get rid of them, so I called the police. But Becka found out about it and left. She said they had nowhere to go and that I was like her father." He rubbed the side of his finger over his eyes. "I'd never hurt Becka, not in a million years. I thought she'd come back, but she didn't. A few months later, one of her friends told me about the baby. I tried to find her. If I had, I think we could have been okay."

"She was going to tell you," Halla said. "She was on her way to find you the night she died. But she fought with her father, and he threw her against the wall. She was dizzy after their confrontation, and she shouldn't have been driving. But I guess with her father there, she didn't feel she had a choice." Halla pushed back her anger at Reuben.

Brock stilled at her explanation. "I appreciate you telling me. I never gave up hope that we'd get back together. Until she died, of course. It means a lot to know she still cared about me." He paused and added in a rush, "I'm so sorry you had to grow up with those people."

"It's okay now," Halla said.

"What I want to do is smash her old man's face in," Brock growled.

Next to him, Vicky put a hand on his arm. "Easy now," she said.

"My boyfriend"—the words still felt new and tender on Halla's tongue—"already did that. And my mother— grandmother, rather—she left him. It was tough for her all these years."

"Tell me about this boyfriend." Brock sounded so much like a real father that Halla had to smile.

Vicky punched him playfully on the arm. "If you want to tell us," she said.

For the next hour they talked. Halla told them about Oliver, Lily's House, and her two jobs—and introduced them to Elsie, Payden, and Kendall as they came in and out of the sitting room. They told her about Brock's brief first marriage, his job as a journeyman pipefitter, and his hobby of making miniature metal windmills. Then it was on to Vicky's job as a manager at Walmart and their most recent trip to Oregon to see Vicky's daughters.

"I'd like to visit you soon," Brock said. "If that's okay. We're on a major deadline right now, and I'm working fifty-hour weeks, so I can't get more than a day or two off at a time right now, but it'll calm down in a month or so."

"We'll both come," Vicky corrected. "All the overtime will pay for a nice little trip. We're so excited to meet you and your friends." With that, she excused herself so Brock could say goodbye privately.

"Thank you for calling," he said, starting with the tears again. "I never thought I'd be a dad. I'm so grateful to have the chance now." He paused and wiped at his face. "You should know . . . I want you to know . . . I love Vicky very much, and we have a great life together, but your mother was the love of my life. I never should have let her go."

Halla didn't point out that wishing wouldn't change anything. He obviously knew that too well.

"I'm glad to have a part of her back," he continued. "You have her nose, and her smile. And I recognize that necklace. She wore it all the time."

Halla's hand when to the locket on her neck. "I can't wait to hear more about her. And about you."

"Let's talk again tomorrow," he said. "I'll think of a few good stories."

"I'd love that."

After disconnecting, Halla spent the next several hours looking at pictures Vicky had posted of Brock. She wondered if her father was looking at her pictures, and if he and Vicky would follow the link to her blog and read about her life.

Elsie and Kendall were both in bed when Halla finally dressed in her Tweetie Bird night shirt—the soft, ratty one that everyone told her to stop using. What were a few tiny holes and a few stains compared to the comfort and security? Her gaze landed on her discarded carton of strawberry ice cream, which now contained only two inches of melted ice cream. Oops.

She took the carton to the kitchen and emptied out the liquid before throwing it away. She was tempted to start into another carton, but it was past nine, and maybe she should just go to bed. Maybe by tomorrow Oliver would be able to contact her.

Passing through the sitting room, she cast a longing glance at her computer. She desperately wanted to hear Oliver's voice, to see his face. Her body longed for his touch, even if it was only the brush of his hand.

They'd said they loved each other, and she believed in their relationship, but being apart was driving her insane. Having him in a danger zone only made it worse. She was tempted to look up the fire, to see if maybe there was news, or maybe text his sister, who'd sent her pictures of them at their family barbecue.

"Stop," she told herself.

She was brushing her teeth when her phone beeped out the unique ring she'd programmed in for Oliver. Spitting the paste into the sink, she grabbed the phone.

Oliver had barely walked in the door to his apartment when he fell onto his couch. He really needed a shower, but he craved hearing Halla's voice more.

She answered on the second ring. "Oliver!" her scream of delight thrilled him.

"Hi, beautiful." His voice came out hoarse from the fifteen-hour workdays he'd put in since his return to Coeur d'Alene.

"How are you? Is the fire out?"

"Not quite, but close." Weariness had set in, but he wasn't going to let her know how beat he was. "Probably by morning."

"Are you still in the field, or did you stumble over a place with reception?"

"I'm home. They cut me loose. I've worked a hundred and twenty hours in the last eight days because two guys were out with the flu. Now that they're back, my bosses would rather not pay me more overtime." For which he was infinitely grateful. Since he'd already put in forty-five hours in the past three days, he didn't have to be back at work until Monday at the earliest.

"I'm so glad you're safe. I was worried."

He turned on his side, stretching out his legs and pillowing his head with his arm. "I was directing crews more than anything else. There was concern about it spreading to one of the nearby cities, but we ended up only having to evacuate one small section of a town, so we were lucky. The homeowners will be returning tomorrow, I think." He heaved a sigh. "I'm glad to let the other guys finish up. I've missed you." The only thing he wanted at that moment was to see her face.

The timbre of her voice changed. "I've missed you too. And I've eaten way too much ice cream."

He laughed. "I could use some of that right now, but I'm too tired to move. My fingers work, though. Want to video chat? I'm a mess, but I need to see your face."

"Okay."

With a few clicks her face appeared on his phone. She was curled up sideways on her pillow, her short hair loose and a bit wild. "There you are," he said. "Is that Tweetie Bird original? I thought the girls banned him." She laughed. "I lock him up in my safe every night to make sure they don't kidnap him . . . again."

Not quite true, he knew, but he liked that she was attached to the shirt. Knowing what it meant to her, he wished he could hold her in it. "He's lucky to have you—and he's not the only one."

Many times in the past week, he'd caught himself wondering how he'd been so incredibly lucky to have found her. And his mind wouldn't stop worrying over how they could be together.

"What's been going on with you?" he said. "Have you heard from your Mom? What are you writing? Any news on your dad? And is Elsie really getting married?"

She chuckled. "Yes, to all of it. Elsie's been fattening us up by experimenting with food she might want to serve at her wedding, I had breakfast with my mother this morning, and I've finished all my deadlines. But even more exciting, I found Brock! I talked to him and his wife today. It went really well."

He listened in amazement as she told him about the conversation with Brock. When she got to the part about talking so long her ice cream melted, he stopped her.

"I can't believe it," he said. "Wow."

"I know, right?" Her eyes were alight with happiness. "He could have been married to someone who would be jealous or upset. He could have a ton of other kids and not want to see me. This just seems, well, lucky."

They were back to that again. Luck.

"I meant the ice cream," Oliver said with fake seriousness. "You actually let it melt? This guy must really be something." He cracked a smile with the last sentence.

Halla laughed. "Oh, he is. I think. You should have seen him crying. It was . . . I don't know. Embarrassing and endearing all at once. He was really glad you hit my da—Reuben. I'm never calling that monster dad again." She paused before hurrying on. "And Brock wants to see me. He's got some big project he's working on, but he said he and Vicky would come for a visit when it was finished. Until then, we'll make do with video chatting."

"I'm really happy for you," Oliver said. "That's a great

way to become acquainted. We should know." But another idea came to his mind, an idea so perfect, he couldn't wait to start the ball rolling. "Unless . . ."

"Unless what?"

"We could go see him instead. I mean, you drove all the way to Nampa, and Denver is probably less time, or about the same. I could fly down, we could jump in your car, and go together. You get to meet your dad, and I get to be with you. I'll pay for a hotel, if they don't have space for us."

When one hand went up to her eye to wipe away a tear, he knew he'd hit the jackpot. This strong woman, his Halla, needed this. And maybe it would make up for dragging her to Idaho and forcing her to face her past.

"You can't do that," she protested finally.

"Sure, I can. It'd be a drop in the bucket after all the overtime. Plus, I don't have to be at work until next Monday, and I can stretch that until Tuesday, if I need to. My boss owes me that much. And you told me you're ahead with your blogs, so it's perfect timing. We can surprise him."

"I don't know." She hesitated before adding, "They did mention they have guest rooms for Vicky's daughters when they visit."

"See? And it'll save them money in the long run. I want to come see you anyway. No, I *need* to see you." Could she detect the hunger in his voice? "Besides, I owe you big time after what happened in Nampa."

"If it weren't for you, I wouldn't have found Brock at all. I wouldn't know about my mother." Tears were leaking from her eyes in earnest now, and Oliver desperately wanted to be next to her wiping them away.

"If you'd rather, I can come and hang out in Phoenix instead." He laughed. "Maybe Lily would lend me her camper. What do you say?"

She hesitated only a second more. "Let's go visit Brock. But maybe not surprise him. It's all too new."

"Whatever you feel is best." He sat up, his tiredness all but vanished. "I'm hanging up now. I need to book a flight. The earlier, the better." He also needed a shower, but what she couldn't smell, he wasn't owning up to.

"Go, then." She gave him a smile that tugged at his heart—and the rest of his body. He couldn't wait to wrap his arms around her.

"G'night, beautiful," he said.

25

On Wednesday morning, Halla was at the airport to pick up Oliver, who arrived before eleven-thirty. "Oliver!" She waved a hand so he'd see her as he passed the security check point. He waved back and hurried across the space between them, dropping his carry-on to sweep her into his arms. The breath whooshed right out of her with the intensity of his greeting. Now it was them lip-locking, but she didn't care who saw.

He looked good—no, great—in his jeans and T-shirt. But though he'd texted that he'd slept during the three-hour plane ride, a hint of exhaustion lurked beneath his excited smile. She'd have to do something about that.

"You ready for our road trip?" he asked, pulling away, only to tug her back and kiss her breathless again. He smelled of cologne and tasted even better.

Finally, he let go long enough for her to answer. "I sent Vicky a message on Facebook last night about the possibility of us going to see them, and she answered back with a million exclamation points and volunteered their guest rooms and to pay gas. Brock is taking off work tomorrow, or if they won't let him do that, he'll at least go in late. So I think they're okay with us coming. I turned down the offer of gas, by the way, but I said okay to staying with them. We can always leave early if it's awkward."

He picked up his bag, and they began walking to her car. "I'm fine with whatever, but I'm paying gas at least. This is my date idea, after all."

She laughed. "Is that what this is. A date?"

"You bet." His grin widened. "Next time, it's Hawaii or Paris."

"You'd better mean France and not Paris, Idaho," she said. "Anyway, Denver is a thirteen-hour drive, and we'll lose an hour because they're in an earlier time zone." That would get them there at two in the morning.

"We'll need snacks. Let's head to the store before we take off. You have a cooler, right?"

"Yeah, but I already have the food under control—or Elsie does. She took my cooler into her café so she could pack a few things for us."

"Good, I've wanted to see the Eats and Treats, and try some of Ruth's pastries you've been telling me so much about."

Halla felt satisfied as his hand reached out to take hers. Love surged inside her, vying with the hovering dread of soon having to say goodbye to him again. They'd had a long-distance relationship for over a year, but she didn't want that anymore. She wanted him in person.

At the café, Elsie had everything ready. She hugged Halla as Oliver insisted on buying more pastries from Ruth at the counter.

"Good luck," Elsie whispered in Halla's ear, "and stop

worrying already. You and Oliver will figure it out. Things can change in an instant. Look at me and Payden." Elsie's gaze went to the ring on her finger.

"But in actual dating time, we've only been together a few days. I shouldn't feel this strongly about him."

"Now that you've met, the year of being friends counts," Elsie insisted.

Oliver came toward them with a smile, sack of pastries in his hand. "These are the best road trip snacks ever. Ready?" He set the sack on top of the cooler and lifted both of them.

Halla rescued the pastries before they could slide off. "Let's go."

They took turns driving, stopping every three or four hours to stretch their legs. The road was smooth and uncrowded, and for every four hours of driving, they were able to shave off twenty or thirty minutes from their original estimate.

Oliver drifted off to sleep during Halla's second turn at the wheel, and she let him sleep, notching down the volume on the CD so it wouldn't disturb him. She didn't wake him when it was his turn to drive. She was tempted to pull over to the side of the road and sleep herself, but she knew Brock and Vicky were waiting for them in Denver. She'd wanted to spend as much time as possible with them, but now she wished she'd planned a stop at a hotel halfway through.

Oliver awoke an hour outside Denver. He looked so

confused for a moment as he gazed around at the darkness that she laughed. "Pull over," he said, stifling a yawn. "My turn to drive."

She eased to the side of the road. "You needed the sleep. Can't have you drifting off as we drive."

"I won't drift off if we're doing this." His arms wrapped around her, and their lips met. Halla would have been content cuddling up in his arms right there forever, but all too soon, they exchanged places and Oliver steered back onto the road.

Halla couldn't sleep. She kept checking the GPS on her phone. By the time they pulled up at a modest ranch-style house, her heart was banging against the inside of her chest. Maybe she should have dressed up. Most girls probably didn't wear camouflage pants and a black T-shirt to meet their father for the first time.

Oliver hurried around the car and helped her out, taking her into his arms as if understanding her thoughts. "I'm right here," he said in her ear. "I'm always going to be right here. And they're gonna love you."

She blinked away the tears. "Thanks."

They grabbed their bags and went up the walk together. The door opened before they could knock, and out came Brock and Vicky, looking exactly as they had on her screen. Except he was much taller than she'd imagined. Halla's stature had definitely come from her mother's side of the family.

Without waiting for introductions, Brock lunged at Halla, grabbing her in the biggest bear hug she'd ever experienced. Then he was off and crying again, and so was she. Somehow she managed to introduce them to Oliver, then Vicky got them all inside with a good-natured comment about not wanting to wake the neighbors. In the living room, Halla and Oliver sat on a burgundy loveseat that was kitty corner from the matching couch where the older couple settled.

The ensuing silence was awkward, and as Halla searched for something to say, Oliver abruptly stood from his place next to Halla. "Sir," he said to Brock, "I need to clarify something about Halla and me."

Halla felt a little pride that he didn't overcorrect and say "Halla and I."

Brock's slow grin slid across his face. "Okay. Tell me."

"I'd like to hear it too." Halla wondered what kind of joke Oliver would come up with that would set them all at ease.

Oliver spared her a smile that made her insides smolder before turning back to look at Brock and Vicky. "Halla probably told you we've known each other for a year and that we recently started dating, but that's not the whole story." He paused, glanced at Halla again, and soldiered on. "The truth is, I'm in love with your daughter, and I've been in love with her for most of this past year. Now that we're here, I want your blessing to ask her to marry me."

Halla couldn't help the gasp that escape her lips. "But . . ." She trailed off when she simply didn't know what more to say.

Brock's eyes were wide with shock, and for a moment no one spoke. After an encouraging nudge from his wife, Brock said, "Well, I don't know if she needs my blessing. Or if you should be asking me because it's her permission you need, and she's done pretty well without me so far. I don't feel I can step in this late in the game and pretend like I know what's going on. I trust her to make her own decisions." His gaze went past Oliver to Halla. "But I do plan to be a part of your life now. I want to earn the right to answer questions like these."

Halla couldn't speak past the lump in her throat. She stared at the man she loved and the man she knew she would soon love and felt infinitely grateful.

"Okay, then." Oliver turned and went down on his knee in front of Halla. "Let's get married," he said. "I love you more than life itself, and I don't want to live one more moment without you beside me."

Halla thought of how awful the eight days had been without him, and she nodded. "Okay. Let's get married."

In the next instant, they were kissing, which made Brock and Vicky clap and hoot. Halla looked at the contented smiles on their faces and was grateful Oliver had included them. Brock had missed out on her entire life, but not this, thanks to Oliver.

"Wait," Vicky said. "Where's the ring?"

Oliver sat again next to Halla, taking her hand. "I've been working out in the woods fifteen hours or more a day to stop a fire, but Halla and I can go to the store tomorrow." To her, he added. "You can pick anything you want."

She wanted only him. Before her mother's locket, she'd barely worn any jewelry.

Vicky said something in Brock's ear, and he nodded. "I'll be right back."

Halla hoped they hadn't done something to offend

him, but Vicky was beaming. That was one woman who knew how to offer love and support. Halla felt the strangely protective urge to thank Vicky for looking after her father.

Brock returned shortly, carrying a wide gold band in gleaming gold. "This," he said, extending it to Halla, "was my mother's ring. I had it cleaned and shined up for when I proposed to my first wife, but she wasn't interested in only a band. She wanted a big rock, and once we divorced, I was glad she didn't have rights to this ring. I didn't make that mistake with Vicky." He grinned at his wife. "I know her better, so I bought her what she wanted. It ain't much, but it's yours now, if you want it. For a wedding ring, or just a family ring. And if you don't, that's okay too."

The band felt heavy in Halla's palm. It was curved on the edges and the engraving inside said *Love You Forever*. Halla loved it immediately. "Are you sure?" she asked, amazed that this near stranger would give her something that he obviously valued.

"I told you I was going to be there," he said. "Starting now."

"Thank you so much." She jumped up and hugged Brock and Vicky too. Then she turned and gave the ring to Oliver. "You okay with this?"

"If it's what you want." Love stared out from his eyes, thrilling Halla with its intensity. "Because if you'd rather have the moon, I'll get it for you."

She laughed. "I already have everything I want right here."

EPILOGUE

Halla stood near the grouping of Christmas trees at the reception center. Everyone she and Oliver loved had been at the church while they exchanged vows—even Elsie, who'd returned this morning from her honeymoon after the simple wedding her in-laws and Lily had helped organize a week earlier.

The day had been perfect, with both Brock and Lily's husband, Mario, giving Halla away. Oliver's family was in attendance, and Halla was amazed that the tension she'd still felt with Oliver's mother at the Thanksgiving celebration they'd shared with his family a few weeks ago had disappeared. Halla didn't even mind that Nanette's change of heart might have something to do with how impressed she was with Lily's House and the fact that she was more than a little smitten with Brock, despite his wife's very obvious and amused presence. As long as there was peace, Halla didn't really care about the reasons. Nanette wasn't likely going to be her best friend, but with Halla's mother back in her life and with Lily and Vicky, Halla didn't need her to be.

Brock had insisted on paying for the reception hall, and Halla's mother had bought her a wedding dress—one that she didn't hate, which in itself was amazing. Ruth had made the wedding cake and the refreshments, which were served by Lily's current foster girls, with Tara and Rylee in charge of the younger teens. Goblets filled with strawberry shakes were the crowning touch.

Halla sat at the bride's table now with Elsie and Kendall. Oliver stood a short distance away talking to her father, discussing places to see on their five-day honeymoon to Hawaii.

"I can't believe you're moving to Coeur d'Alene," Kendall said.

"I'll be back a lot," Halla responded quickly, though it was the one thing that tore at her heart. "Tickets aren't a lot of money if I buy ahead, and whenever he's out in the field for an extended time, I'll come stay with Elsie. I want to spend time with my mom too."

"Yeah, but with you two gone, it's going to be really different living at the apartment."

Elsie patted Kendall's hand in commiseration. "Any luck with the girls who've responded to our newspaper ad about the apartment?"

Kendall frowned. "Except for the chain smoker, who our landlord won't approve, and the drunken secretary, whose references claim she never pays, there's been nothing promising yet. I will probably end up not renewing the lease. Maybe I'll rent the extra room at my sister's after all until I find another place with roommates I'll get along with. I can't tell you how much I wish Tara and Rylee were finished with high school and ready to move out. But they're far from ready, that's for sure."

"Uh-oh, my ears are burning. Did someone mention my name?" Rylee appeared from somewhere behind Kendall, looking like a runway model, her blond hair streaming out behind her.

As usual, Tara was at her side, her dark hair twisted up into what looked like a very uncomfortable bun. "As long as they'll hide us from those guys, they can talk about us all day."

"What guys?" Halla surveyed the room in an attempt to understand Tara's comment.

"Those guys standing at the refreshment table, the ones with the cowboy hats." Tara gave a little shudder. "Ugh, those pointed boots and humongous belt buckles. It's all so fake and pretentious. If those boys fall over because of those top-heavy hats, they might cut someone with the sharp points of their boots."

"They're actually kind of cute," Rylee said. "Who are they anyway?"

Halla laughed. "Oliver's cousins from Idaho. They live on a ranch."

"I don't care who they are," Tara retorted. "Mark my words. I'll never, ever date a cowboy." She paused, her eyes going wide. "Oh, no! They're coming this way." The teen leapt to her feet and hurried away.

Rylee sighed in exasperation. "I'm going to dance with a cute cowboy. Let Tara know if she ever comes out of the bathroom."

Halla and Elsie laughed while Kendall rolled her eyes. "See? They are so not ready to leave Lily's House."

"Where's Dr. Gorgeous anyway?" Elsie asked.

Kendall's expression became dreamy as it always did when they mentioned Wylen. "He had to call the hospital to check on a patient. He's got someone covering for him, but he likes to keep a finger on what's going on." Pride laced her voice. She and Wylen had been inseparable for most of the past three and a half months.

"Aw, look who's coming over," Elsie cooed.

Halla and Kendall turned to see Teisha in her pink flower girl dress, looking like a perfect angel. She and Lily's daughter, Cheri, had each carried a basket of rose petals at the church, while Cheri's older brother, Jonny Jameson, had carried the rings. Now Teisha had JJ's ring bearer pillow in her hands, a folded sheet of blue stationery balanced on top.

Halla nudged Elsie, and the two shared a secret smile.

"For you, Kendamom." Teisha proffered the note to Kendall.

"Oh, thank you, sweetie." Kendall picked up the note, exposing underneath a huge solitaire engagement ring tied to the pillow with a white ribbon. Kendall's jaw dropped. She unfolded the note with shaking hands. "It's from Wylen," she said. "He's waiting for me in the bride's room."

"Guess that visit with his parents last month was as good as you thought," Elsie said.

Kendall looked ready to cry. "He included Teisha," she whispered. "Do you know what this means?"

Halla laughed. "It means you better hurry and go see him. I'll need the bride's room to change before I leave. No way am I going to Hawaii in any dress." In fact, besides her hiking shoes and flipflops for the beach, her going away clothing included camo, tank tops, T-shirts, a swimsuit, and, of course, Tweetie Bird.

"I'll show you." Teisha grabbed Kendall's hand.

"Oh, no you don't." Susan appeared out of nowhere to deviate Teisha.

Behind her loomed Jasper, with their newly adopted baby girl—Sage's baby—cradled lovingly in the crook of his arm. "This is one conversation I think Kendamom should have alone," he said. "Why don't you come dance with daddy?" He passed the baby to Susan as Teisha clapped her hands and reached for him.

"Does everyone know except me?" Kendall asked, throwing her hands up in mock disgust.

"Pretty much," Elsie agreed.

"That's okay." Kendall broke into a happy smile as she ran toward the door, navigating with her high heels in a way Halla could only envy.

Oliver appeared at Halla's side, pulling her up from the table into a hug. "You lost a few inches," he said, kissing her.

"I don't know why I let the girls talk me into high heels. I kicked them off, uh, somewhere. Right before I danced with JJ." Being only nine, Halla's foster brother had been only too happy for her to take them off. If only Halla remembered where she'd left them.

Oliver nibbled on her ear. "What do you say we get out of here? I want to take you somewhere private, if you know what I mean." He pulled away so she could see him and raised his eyebrows suggestively.

"I definitely do." Halla put her arms around his neck.

"But let's have one more dance. The changing room is occupied at the moment."

"Ah, right. I hope they hurry."

She laughed, and with a wave at Elsie and Susan, they twirled onto the dance floor.

"Well," Oliver said, staring down into her eyes. "Do you feel any different, Mrs. Montgomery?"

"Besides the fact that I'm now wearing two wedding bands?" Oliver had surprised her with a band of channel-set diamonds that matched the family ring Brock had given Halla months earlier.

He shrugged. "Can't blame a man for wanting to mark his turf. And they go perfectly together." He held her closer.

"I love them both." She snuggled into his chest.

They swayed to the music for a while, and when she looked up at him again, he said, "You sure you're okay with moving? You won't miss all of this?" His gaze scanned the entire room, but she knew he meant her sisters and Lily's House. And her mother.

Her chest tightened because she was going to miss it like crazy. Only her love for Oliver made it remotely bearable. "I can work anywhere," she said. "That's the important thing. We'll try it a few years. I'll be flying home a lot."

His smile was gentle. "What if we could stay?"

Halla couldn't help the flare of joy that surged in her heart. "But you love Coeur d'Alene."

"I love working in the forest. It doesn't matter which one, as long as I'm with you. Anyway, my real wedding gift to you is that I put in for a transfer with the Forest

Service after we got engaged, and I was offered a job last week in the Tonto National Forest. I'll still have to spend days at a time out in the woods, but we can live here."

Halla wanted to scream with joy. Instead, she hugged him. "Thank you. And I know just the apartment for us. At least for now."

"I thought you might."

The world fell away as they kissed on the dance floor. Somewhere, Halla heard a call to cut the cake, but that would have to wait.

Rachel Branton has worked in publishing for over twenty years. She loves writing women's fiction and traveling, and she hopes to write and travel a lot more. As a mother of seven, it's not easy to find time to write, but the semi-ordered chaos gives her a constant source of writing material. She's been known to wear pajamas all day when working on a deadline, and is often distracted enough to burn dinner. (Okay, pretty much 90% of the time.) A sign on her office door reads: Danger. Enter at Your Own Risk. Writer at Work. Under the name Rachel Branton, she writes romance, romantic suspense, and women's fiction. Rachel also writes urban fantasy, paranormal romance, and science fiction under the name Teyla Branton. For more information, a free ebook, or to sign up to hear about new releases, please visit www.RachelBranton.com.